MAINELY WICKED

Novels by Matt Cost
aka Matthew Langdon Cost

The Goff Langdon Mainely Mysteries

Mainely Power

Mainely Fear

Mainely Money

Mainely Angst

Mainely Wicked

The Clay Wolfe / Port Essex Mysteries

Wolfe Trap

Mind Trap

Mouse Trap

Cosmic Trap

The Brooklyn 8 Ballo Mysteries

Velma Gone Awry

Historical Fiction Novels

I Am Cuba: Fidel Castro and the Cuban Revolution

At Every Hazard: Joshua Chamberlain and the Civil War

Love in a Time of Hate

MAINELY WICKED

A Goff Langdon Mainely Mystery

MATT COST

Encircle Publications
Farmington, Maine, U.S.A.

MAINELY WICKED Copyright © 2023 Matt Cost

Paperback ISBN 13: 978-1-64599-460-2
Hardcover ISBN 13: 978-1-64599-461-9
E-book ISBN 13: 978-1-64599-462-6

Library of Congress Control Number: 2023938978

Encircle Editor: Cynthia Brackett-Vincent

Cover design and digital illustration by Deirdre Wait
Cover photographs © Getty Images

Published by:

Encircle Publications
PO Box 187
Farmington, ME 04938

info@encirclepub.com
http://encirclepub.com

Acknowledgments

If you are reading this for without readers, writers would be obsolete.

And thank you to the wonderful writing community that has welcomed me with open arms and made me feel at home. This includes so many fantastic people it would take an entire book to note, not just writers, but reviewers as well.

I am grateful to my mother, Penelope McAlevey, and father, Charles Cost, who have always been my first readers and critics.

Much appreciation to the various friends and relatives who have also read my work and given helpful advice.

I'd like to offer a big hand to my wife, Deborah Harper Cost, and children, Brittany, Pearson, Miranda, and Ryan, who have always had my back.

I'd like to tip my hat to my editor, Michael Sanders, who has worked with me on all my novels, and always makes my writing the best that it can be.

Thank you to Encircle Publications, and the amazing team of Cynthia Bracket-Vincent, Eddie Vincent, Chris Wait and Deirdre Wait, for giving me this opportunity to be published.

To the 600,000 people who go missing every year in the U.S.

Five Days Earlier

"You mind if I ride with you?" he asked through the driver's side window. "My wife dropped me here and went off to do some errands."

"Sure thing, but I don't know why we met here and not where the frickin' thing is," Liam said in apparent disgust.

"It's just around the corner but the address doesn't show up on GPS. Takes you to a boat landing for some strange reason. You ever see that *Office* episode where Michael and Dwight drive right into a lake?"

Liam guffawed. "Yessir. That there show is *some* funny. What frickin' idiots."

He laughed, a gentle sound, as he climbed into the truck. They were just off the highway at a deserted gas station that'd been closed down for some time now. The windows were boarded up, and weeds grew up through the cracks of the pavement.

"You want to go right out of here but then get over in the left lane," he said. "We're taking a left a couple of streetlights up."

Yesterday, on the phone, he'd known immediately that Liam was going to be perfect. When it was the right person, a certain tingle coursed up from his groin until his face flushed with the heat of it. He had a knack for recognizing the right one. It was a gift.

His instincts, as always, had proven to be correct. Liam lived in Machias by himself, his only family being a brother, and was willing to meet him. The bait was a used ATV priced at half what it was worth. There'd been four other callers who hadn't fit the bill, three men and a woman, whom he'd shooed away by admitting to many problems that the four-wheeler actually had.

Not Liam. He was perfect. He'd come all the way down from Machias. He was unlikely to mention to anybody where he was going. And if he did? At best, the person would know that Liam had gone to Brunswick to look at an ATV. Soon, he would 'burn' the burner phone, which was attached to a perfect stranger, and not him at all. It was seamless. And had been for some years now. The end was coming soon. Not a time to make mistakes.

And, of course, Liam was the chosen one.

"What'd you say your name was?" Liam asked.

"Bob," he lied. "Go left at this next light."

"You sure this thing runs smooth?" Liam took the turn with the green arrow. "You best be on the up and up. I done had a long drive to get here."

"You're going to love it," he said. "Runs like a charm."

"My brother says that it's too good to be true. That you're trying to scam me. Best not be. I know engines, and I'll be pissed if you wasted my time."

"Runs great," he said. "Bought it for my daughter, but she doesn't like how it messes up her hair and gets her all muddy."

Liam guffawed.

"You said you don't have any children?" he asked. "Lucky. Daughters are the bane of my existence."

"Nope. No brats at all. Never even been married."

"You close with your brother?"

Liam rolled down the window, snorted in through his nose, and spit a glob of saliva. "We see each other about once a month."

"You go riding with anybody?"

"Feck no," Liam said. "'Cept maybe my dog."

"You're going left up around the corner," he said.

"Thought you said it weren't far?"

"We're close now."

"I got a long, goddamn ride home."

"Turn here," he said. "You like apple pie? My wife makes a mean apple pie. She just made a fresh one this morning. Homemade whipped cream. Think you're going to like it."

"That don't sound all bad," Liam said. "After we get a look at this ATV."

"Coming up on the left," he said. "Dirt driveway at the bottom of the hill."

The driveway led a couple hundred yards through scrub woods to a farmhouse.

"Shit, you live in the middle of nowhere," Liam said.

"Pull around back." He pointed to the right side of the house. About fifty feet behind it was an old wooden barn. "It's right in there."

Liam parked the truck and trailer, and they got out. The barn door was open. They stepped into the spaces. There were stalls along the left side, empty of any livestock. In the back right corner sat a huge cauldron with four chairs ringing it.

"Where the hell's the four-wheeler?" Liam asked.

He pressed a stun gun into Liam's neck and depressed the button. Liam's eyes showed momentary surprise, and then the true shock coursed through his body.

The others emerged from the shadows as he secured Liam's hands and legs and taped his mouth.

Tonight, they'd sacrifice Liam. The ritual would start at midnight and conclude before first light. Then they'd bleed him out before putting him in the cauldron and cooking him. He'd discovered that ten hours was the appropriate length of time for human stew. Tomorrow night, for the Super Pink Moon, he would feast.

Chapter 1

"That one's wicked good," the man at the counter said, his heavy Maine accent dripping from every word.

Langdon was unpacking books from Encircle Publications. He looked at the book in his hand. It was *Death Through Destiny's Door* by C. M. Wendelboe. "We sell a lot of them," he said. Only Mainers would take a word meaning evil, he thought, and turn it into the opposite. Just to be contrary.

"Met him and the missus down to Bar Harbor this past October, it was," the man said. "Curt, said his name was, real good fellow."

"Must've been vacationing. Think he lives out west somewhere."

"Yup. That's what he said."

Langdon looked expectantly at the man. He looked to be about sixty with a bushy white beard drooping from the bottom of his chin. The tangled bristles matched his eyebrows. "Can I help you?" Langdon finally asked.

"Looking for a private investigator by the name of Langdon. Think I'm in the wrong place."

"That's me. You got the right place." Langdon held out his hand. "Goff Langdon. Folks call me just Langdon."

"This here's a bookshop." The man ignored the hand.

"My PI office is in the back. I own both places."

"That's a weird thing, now ain't it?"

Langdon chuckled. "Too hard to make a living off either one," he said. "But put them together, and I can get by."

"S'pose I got two jobs, one over to the fish hatchery, and the other fixin' engines." The man reached out and shook Langdon's hand. "Edouard Couture."

"How about we go back to my office," Langdon said, walking out from behind the counter. "Hey, Star, you got the counter," he said to a grizzled fellow who looked to be eighty years old but was actually just a very rough sixty.

"No problem, Boss." Jonathan Starling had once been an environmental lawyer before the bottom of a whiskey bottle embraced him in a loveless relationship. He'd been sober for over twenty years now, as well as an employee at the Coffee Dog Bookstore, the two things going hand in hand.

Langdon led Edouard Couture through the shelves to the back of the store. He noticed that the man, who didn't look like a reader, was scanning the titles as they walked back. Once again, Langdon thought with a wry smile, you can't always judge a book by its cover.

"Have a seat, Mr. Couture." Langdon pointed the man to a cushy armchair that he'd recently bought at the flea market in Fort Andross, the old mill building on the Androscoggin River.

"People call me Eddie. I reckon that'll do. Don't know no Mr. Couture, not since my father died, that is." The man slid his wiry frame into the plush cushions as if he were afraid of being swallowed whole.

Langdon went around his desk and sat in the black rolling chair. He tugged a pad of paper from a drawer and plopped it down. "So, what can I do for you, Eddie?"

"My brother's gone missing."

"How long's he been missing?"

"Five days."

Langdon paused, pen poised in air. "You sure he's not just taking some time to himself?"

"Ain't like him," Eddie said. "Not at all."

"Where he's live?"

"Up to Machias like me."

Langdon refrained from pausing again. "What brings you to Brunswick looking for him?"

"He came down this way to buy a four-wheeler."

"That place out to Topsham across from the mall?"

"Nah, it was somebody's home. He was buying it used. Was a real good price. *Too* good, if you asked me, but Liam always believed the best in people. S'pose you could say I'm the pessimistic one, mostly because the majority of folks I ever met is full of shit."

"When's the last time you saw him?"

"Stopped by my place the day he come down here." Eddie tugged at his matted beard. "In the morning it was. April 26th."

"He tell you where he was going?"

"Just said he was going down to Brunswick. Had a trailer hitched up to his truck so he could lug it back. Saw an advertisement for it in *Cousin Freddie's.*"

Like every Mainer, Langdon knew that *Cousin Freddie's* was a weekly booklet of classified ads for everything from hay to cars and car parts, lumber to apartment rentals that came out every Thursday. This Maine institution was a place to buy, sell, or swap items and had been for at least Langdon's lifetime. The basic deal was, you bought it for two bucks, and on the back was a form for a free ad you sent in by mail.

"And you've not seen him since?"

"Phone goes directly to voicemail. Stopped by his house two days later, and he weren't there. But his dog was."

"That certainly sounds suspicious," Langdon said. He couldn't imagine what his own dog—a chocolate lab named dog, small d— would do if not fed for two days. He'd probably start eating himself. "He's not the sort to leave his dog for a spell of time, I take it?"

"Seems a bit odd that he didn't bring Donny with him."

"Donny's the dog?"

"Ah-yup."

"You contact the police?"

"I reported him missing to the cops. They don't know nothing. Told me to wait a few days, he'd likely turn up. You ask me, they could care less. Some wealthy person goes missing, everybody's up in arms. Some ole feller who lives in a double-wide? Shit on a shingle is all you get."

"No sign of his truck and trailer?"

"Gone. You s'pose somebody hurt Liam and took his truck?"

"I've no idea, Eddie. Seems to me, the only lead we got is that the last time anybody saw him, he was coming down to Brunswick to buy a four-wheeler. Guess that would be a good place to start looking for him."

"Done told you that I don't know who he was coming to see."

Langdon figured it would be easy enough to look in *Cousin Freddie's* and see who was selling a four-wheeler in Brunswick. The question was, had he ever shown up, or had he gone missing prior to arrival? It was quite possible that he picked it up and left with it in tow, as well. Or option three. The sale had not gone as expected.

Langdon asked a few more questions, getting a description of Liam, and establishing the fact that he probably had the cash to buy the ATV on him, and what the man did for work. These were all things he'd follow up on. To the right person, a couple thousand in cash could be worth killing for, but generally not in Brunswick. Langdon got the man to fill out some paperwork and took a grand in advance to get started on the case. He walked Eddie to the door and watched him as he went down the hallway of the building to the street entrance. The man had to get back up to work, it being well over a three-hour drive. Said he worked the second shift. Langdon breathed deeply, turning around to appreciate his bookshop.

This year was the bookshop's 25th anniversary. The Coffee Dog Bookstore was located in a repurposed department store that now housed a variety of businesses and offices. Aunt Zelda leaving him $50,000 in her will sure had been a boon for him. Langdon had always been her favorite, perhaps because he'd raised his twin younger brothers after their dad left them all in the lurch. Over the years, the bookshop had grown into a place offering the finest collection of mysteries in Maine, and most likely all New England.

The shelves housed old-school authors such as Dashiell Hammett, Raymond Chandler, and Mickey Spillane. These legends were connected to contemporary authors by giants such as Robert Parker, Marcia Muller, and Sue Grafton. Current best-selling authors James Lee Burke, Michael Connelly, and Harlan Coben were mixed in with yet-unknown rising stars. Langdon was perhaps most fond of his Maine Writers shelf showcasing the likes of Gerry Boyle, Paul Doiron, Bruce Robert Coffin, Richard Cass, and Joseph Souza.

"Got yourself a new client?" Star asked from behind the counter.

Langdon took a glance around. The store was vacant of customers. One of his more recent professional goals was to not speak about his cases in front of the general public. It was one thing to do so with his friends, but quite another, he'd come to realize, in the bookstore, at the diner, or in the gym where there seemed too many a prying ear.

"His brother's gone missing."

"Had the look of being from Down East." Down East, Maine was actually the *north*eastern part of the state. Back in the 1700s, sailors coined the phrase as they traveled up the coast with the wind at their back, or downwind, as well as east following the jutting coastline of Maine that protruded far east into the ocean. From somewhere in the dim reaches of his brain came the memory of fifth-grade geography, where he'd learned that the easternmost part of the United States was in Down East, Eastport, to be exact.

"Machias." Langdon walked back into the store. "You still scouring *Cousin Freddie's* every week?" he asked.

"Sure thing. Just swapped out for four new tires for my truck last week. It's better than reading the funnies in the newspaper."

Langdon chuckled. He knew that Star was a voracious reader, even if he might dabble in the cartoons. "You got the one from a few weeks back?" He did a few mental calculations, knowing it was a Thursday publication. "April 22nd."

"Probably right out in the glove box. You want I should go fetch it?"

"That'd be great. Take dog with you. I'm sure he'd like to stretch his legs and pee in the bushes."

At the mention of his name, dog's ears perked up, and he jumped up from his bed behind the counter. He was always up for an adventure, even if it was just to the back parking lot.

While Star went out to his truck, a fellow Langdon knew as Stan came in looking for a book by David Gardner, a paranormal mystery, *The Journalist*. It'd just been published a few months back but was already gaining traction at the store. Langdon mentally put it on his 'to be read' list, which was already quite long. The downside to working with great books all day, every day, was a plethora of items in the TBR pile.

"I brought the week before and the week after, just in case." Star dropped three issues of *Cousin Freddie's* on the counter.

Langdon picked up the April 22nd copy. He checked the table of contents and skipped to the All-Terrain Vehicle section. There were three listed for Brunswick. Two, Langdon guessed, seemed on the expensive side for what Liam Couture might've wanted, but he didn't discount them, just zeroed in on the third.

> 1998 Polaris Magnum 452 2x4 automatic ATV. Runs real good. 4,000 miles. $2,000 or best offer. Brunswick.

There was a phone number attached. Langdon shrugged and dialed it. It immediately made that strange dinging noise followed by a disembodied voice saying the number was no longer in service. Of course, he mused, it was never that easy.

Chapter 2

"Picked up a case this morning," Langdon said to his wife as he joined her at an outdoor table at Sugar Magnolia's.

Dog had already nestled his muzzle onto her lap.

"That's what dog was just telling me," Chabal said.

"You going to be warm enough out here?"

"Sixty and sunny works for me," she said. "Not bad for the first of May."

"You paint this morning?"

"How'd you know?"

Langdon chuckled. "'Cause you got blue speckles on your forehead. Figured it was either paint or you had some strange disease." Chabal had been talking about painting the ceiling in the guest bathroom for some months now.

Chabal Langdon was just over five-feet tall with blonde hair cascading to her shoulders like a brook in the wilds. Her hazel eyes danced with a perpetual mystery and mischief above cheeks that bulged slightly. She also possessed a crackling, caustic wit usually aimed in her husband's direction.

"My, aren't you quite the perceptive PI," she said. "Kinda like Jack Reacher, just not as good-looking."

"The five-foot-nothing Tom Cruise version or the one you conjure in your mind from the pages of Lee Child?"

"Mm. More like a blend between the Rock and Mark Wahlberg."

The waitress came by. Her name was Sandy, and they knew her

well. So well, in fact, that she didn't even ask what they wanted. "Magnolia Cobb and BLT?" They nodded their assent, and she hustled off, it being busy today.

"You redden up the hair a bit, and you got me," Langdon said. At 6'4" tall, he figured he was about the height of the Rock.

"Reacher's got your blue eyes and goes by his last name same as you," Chabal said. "Maybe *you* are my Jack Reacher."

"Well, if I was Reacher, I'd be long gone by now," Langdon said. "He's a loner destined to walk the roads of the world alone. And you'd be pining for me."

Chabal snickered. "I pine for you every day, babe," she said. "Tell me about the case."

Langdon told her about Edouard Couture's visit and his missing brother, Liam. "Phone number in the classified was out of service," he finished up.

"That's a bit suspicious," Chabal said.

"It seems to me that the place to start would be the person who placed the ATV ad," Langdon said. "If I can find them."

"*Cousin Freddie's* should have a name and contact information," Chabal said. "At their offices."

"If they're willing to share it with me."

Sandy brought over their food and an extra plate. They put the salad between them, and each took half of the BLT. Dog rejoined them, having been off begging for food from the other tables. Langdon was not going to be sharing his bacon with him, but Chabal had been known to weaken in the face of dog's imploring gaze.

"You okay to work the store with Star this afternoon if I go fishing around?" Langdon asked.

"I might have to scrape a few blue speckles off my forehead first," Chabal said. "What's your plan?"

"Thought I'd start with Bart. See what the police know."

"You'd probably have more luck if you brought him a BLT."

"Good point."

Bart met Langdon at the town mall. He wasn't even sure why it was called a mall and not a park or a green or something more appropriate for an open, grassy area. It was just across the street from Sugar Magnolia's and was a divider between downtown and Bowdoin College. Bart was in the process of demolishing three hot dogs from Danny's sidewalk stand as Langdon sat down next to him on the bench. He didn't seem intimidated in the slightest at adding a BLT to his pile of food.

It'd only been last October that the Mall had become a battleground between anti-vaxxers, and groups opposed to them as Brunswick had become the center of the media world. Now, it was much quieter. A group of young children, perhaps from the elementary school, were playing games down by the gazebo, and a circle of Bowdoin students were playing with a hacky sack.

Bart was a huge bear of a man, five inches over six feet tall, and heading north of 350 pounds. He wore the blue uniform of Brunswick PD, having been demoted from detective to the uniform division for helping Langdon track down a missing boy with slightly unorthodox tactics. Sergeant Jeremiah Bartholomew and Langdon had been friends ever since the summer after Langdon's sophomore year of college. Bart, drunk, had come into the bar where Langdon was bouncing and picked a fight with four drug dealers. Langdon, jumping in to prevent Bart from being stabbed, had cemented a friendship between him and the ill-tempered and gruff policeman.

"Don't think about it," Bart said to dog, who was eyeballing his pile of food.

"Long time, no see," Langdon said.

"Figure you must need something," Bart growled.

Langdon chuckled. "Just been trying to survive mud season." This was an official season in Maine that ran from the end of March to as late as the middle of May.

"You ask around about the missing guy from Machias?" Langdon had called earlier and asked Bart to see what he could find out.

"Yeah. Gleason, that little dickwad, drew that one."

Langdon waited but Bart had moved onto the BLT. "He get anything on who placed the ad in *Cousin Freddie's*?"

Bart belched and wiped his mouth with the back of his hand. "Email address was invalid. Phone number was a burner. Gleason's working on getting the number it was attached to but hasn't heard back from the company yet. The ISP might be of some help, but probably not much. Still tracking down the credit card number that was used. If you ask me, it's going to come up being some grandmother's number out in East Bumfuck."

Langdon knew that you had to give the company a real phone number to use a burner, a number they didn't have to share… unless it was with the police, that is. Or the Feds. "What's the official position of Brunswick PD?"

Bart shrugged but his eyes flashed angrily. "Missing person. Not from here. Not our problem."

"Even though he was obviously lured here under false pretenses?"

Bart snorted. "Lured here under false pretenses? What are you, the head Nun?"

"No address? Just the email and phone number?" Langdon turned angrily to stare at his friend. "This thing stinks more than one of the sisters caught out in the courtyard smoking a cigarette. I can feel it."

"You got it. We'll run down the telephone number once we get it, but I'm not betting on it being anything but a dead end. Betting the credit card was stolen, too."

Dog took off giving valiant chase to a squirrel who disappeared up a tree. Langdon knew how he felt. At least he'd gotten a glimpse of the squirrel.

"No sign of the truck?"

Bart shook his head and shoved some BLT into his mouth.

"He have E-ZPASS?"

"Nope."

"You checking the cameras up to Gardiner to see if he came that way and whether or not he went back?" That was the only toll booth north of Brunswick in Maine, about half an hour up the road.

"Got his license plate coming south. Not going north."

"Sounds like he went missing in Brunswick, is what it sounds like," Langdon said.

"First of all, the only evidence that you have that he might've been coming to Brunswick is the word of his brother, who is known to hit the sauce pretty heavy and doesn't have much past a third-grade education."

"Who says Eddie hits the sauce pretty heavy?"

"Machias PD. Hauled him in on drunk and disorderly many a time."

"My guy Eddie might be smarter than you give him credit for," Langdon said.

"Doubt it."

"Well, you got proof that he came south of Gardiner, at least, suggesting that his brother knew what he was talking about."

"Second of all," Bart said with a glare at being interrupted. "If he did come to Brunswick, he could've just as easily headed back up Route 1."

"You got a photo of the guy?" Langdon asked. "His brother didn't have a single photo of his own brother. The guy doesn't seem to do social media. Nothing on the internet."

"My kinda guy," Bart said. "I emailed you one already. Gleason got it from the Machias PD. Seems Liam's gotten himself arrested a few times for drunk and disorderly, too."

"Thanks."

Bart stood up. "Got to get back to work." He whistled and dog came running as Bart tossed him a piece of bacon.

Langdon knew that, despite his bluster, Bart had a big heart. Whether it was sharing his food with dog or donating to charities, in his own quiet way, he tried to be a good person. As a matter of fact, Langdon might've been the only person who knew that Bart had a softer side that included writing poetry.

"Hey," Langdon said, "How about we have a barbecue Saturday? I think the weather looks good enough. We can have a fire and a few cocktails."

"You going to invite that hippie lawyer?"

Langdon tried to cover his grin. Bart had a love/hate relationship with Jimmy 4 by Four. "Most likely."

"I'll think about it." He waved his hand and went over to his cruiser on Park Row.

Langdon and dog walked back into town. Brunswick had the only true Maine Street in the country. It was two lanes either way with wide sidewalks fronting small shops, banks, restaurants, and various businesses. Up the hill behind him was First Parish Church marking the western edge of Bowdoin College's spacious campus. Down on the far side of downtown was Fort Andross on the Androscoggin River. In between was the town that Langdon had grown up in, lived in, had businesses in, and was comfortable in. It was his town.

Dog padded along at his heels, not due to superior training, but because Langdon knew enough to carry dog treats in his pocket. These he periodically shared, the understanding between them of food for good behavior. New apartments were being built above the Tontine shops, and just past that was the outdoor seating at Goldilocks Restaurant. A fair amount of people were scattered at the tables, as it was the first real warm day of the year. Langdon waved to a man he knew, continuing past and crossing the street to a favorite hangout, the Wretched Lobster.

He found his good friend and owner, Richam, downstairs in the barroom. The first-floor restaurant had lace tablecloths and was the kind of place where the music was muted soft rock, but the downstairs was much more comfortable. The bar itself was made of Brazilian cherry, polished to a fine sheen with plush padded stools and shelves crowded with every liquor imaginable. Postcards sent from patrons on vacation around the world were pinned, taped, and tacked to every inch of available wall space. Lanterns with brass bases bolstered dim, recessed lighting along the bar, smaller lanterns deployed on the seven or eight high tables scattered across the room. A dartboard took up one corner, while two pool tables sat on display, silent and inviting at this time of day.

Richam was a slim man with a military bearing even though he'd never served. He'd moved to Brunswick with his pregnant wife twenty-five years earlier from a South American island nation when the politics of the country overflowed into violence. He wore thick-framed black glasses, had a narrow mustache, and was always impeccably dressed. Even though the owner of the establishment, he preferred working as the bartender downstairs, a place where he'd gotten his start.

"Richam."

"Langdon."

"How you been?"

"What brings you in? On a Saturday?" Richam looked at the watch on his wrist. "At two in the afternoon?"

"Just thought I'd stop in to say hello."

"Can't be lunch, or you'd have brought Chabal. And it's odd for you to be without dog."

Langdon chuckled. "Oh, he stopped in upstairs to see if your staff needed any help with cleaning up from the lunch rush."

"You know that we can't have dogs wandering around upstairs. There're codes against that sort of thing."

There was a clattering on the stairs, and dog bounded into the room. The canine was nine now but hadn't slowed down a whit. Richam threw him a piece of carrot that bounced off his nose. He wasn't so good at catching.

"Must be slow upstairs," Langdon said.

"I might have to start closing down on Mondays," Richam said in his precise and clipped way. "Especially with summer coming and people taking advantage of the outdoors."

"You could probably use a day off."

"You want something to drink?"

"Nah."

"Is that why we haven't seen much of you?" Richam asked. "You laying off the booze?"

"Not quitting but easing back. It seems that at a certain point, drinking too much is no longer sustainable."

Richam nodded. "How's business?"

"Books have been hopping off the shelves," Langdon said. "Maybe people are finally getting tired of Amazon."

"Don't talk like that." Richam looked around warily. "They're probably listening in."

Langdon chuckled. "On the PI news, I picked up a missing person case today."

"Figured this wasn't just a social visit."

"If I send you the picture, can you print it up on photo stock and show it around? Ask if anybody's seen the guy?"

"Ha. You want me to do you a favor, and you're too cheap to print your own photo?"

"Bart just sent it to me, and I haven't been back to the shop yet. Didn't think you'd mind." Langdon had his phone out as he spoke and was forwarding the email from Bart.

"The bloke got a name?" Richam was looking at the picture on his phone.

"Liam Couture. Came down from Machias to buy an ATV. Never made it home."

"Lisa comes in to work the bar at three. I'll print it out and have her show it around then."

"Thanks. How 'bout you and Jewell come over Saturday for a barbecue?"

"Raven's coming up from Portland."

"Bring her along. It'd be good to see her."

"I'll check with Jewell and let you know."

Langdon waved his hand, and he and dog went back up the stairs.

The bookshop was just two blocks down the street, on the same side, and Langdon stopped in to print some more photos and get his Jeep.

Chabal was waiting on a customer at the counter, and Star was on the phone, so Langdon went straight back to the office to print up letter-sized glossies of Liam Couture to show around town. When he came back out, the store was empty, and Star was off the phone. He dropped one of the photos on the counter.

"This is the gent we're looking for," Langdon said.

"Ya thinkin' he might've come down from Machias to buy a book? You make one heckuva gumshoe, you know that?" Star asked. "I'll keep my eyes peeled."

"I think I've seen him before," Chabal said. "Where was that?"

"Seriously?" Langdon asked his wife.

"Ah, that's right, I was scrolling through Tinder and saw him. It just made my juices flow. If you know what I mean."

Langdon shook his head. "Hard to get good help these days. I'm going to get Danny T. on this, see what he can turn up." He turned and walked out the door with a wave of his hand.

Chapter 3

Annie Brown parked in the lot next to Sugar Magnolia's. There were only a few other cars there, which she found strange, as it was dinnertime. She checked herself in the rearview mirror. Not that she was wearing more than a trace of makeup, but it wouldn't do to have something terribly amiss. She'd waited until right before leaving to slip into the modest blue dress, not wanting the dogs to cover it in their hair before she left.

Six o'clock. Right on the dot. Annie took a deep breath and opened the car door. Well, it couldn't hurt, she figured, to at least give it a chance. Maybe Tom would be the one. He was witty on the phone. Was a doctor. Was good looking. Okay, Annie grinned, maybe she'd done a little bit of stalking. There wasn't much that you couldn't find out on the internet. She was fairly certain that Tom had done the same thing with her.

If he had, he might have surmised how dull her life was. She worked as a copywriter, a job that allowed her to be home with her dogs. But her true passion was painting. Landscapes. Houses. Animals. With the pandemic sweeping the land for the last year plus, there were days on end when Annie never even got out of her pajamas. The grocery store was about her only trip out. Once a week she got together with Maddie, usually at Annie's place, so she didn't even have to leave then, but did have to get out of her sleepwear.

The sign on the door said CLOSED. Annie blinked in confusion. She'd looked up Sugar Magnolia's on the website, and it didn't say it was closed on Sundays. One of those strange Covid occurrences, she reckoned, shrugging her shoulders and sighing. This was most certainly a sign that she was destined to be single for the rest of her life. At some point, she'd have to switch from dogs to cats and become the crazy old cat lady. There was no sign of anybody else, suggesting that she'd been stood up anyway.

Should she just leave? Annie looked around. Still nobody. She'd give it five minutes and then go, she reasoned, arguing with herself. No more than ten. Ten tops. But she wasn't going to stand outside of a closed restaurant as the sun descended in the west. She'd wait in her car. Annie went around the corner of the building to the parking lot. A sleek black BMW was parked next to her. Maybe this was Tom. It seemed to be a car that might belong to a doctor. The windows were tinted, so she couldn't see in, but the door opened as she went to walk past.

"Annie?" the man said.

She paused and looked at him. He looked a bit like Tom, but she couldn't quite tell in the shadows. He was dressed all in black.

"Annie Brown?"

"I'm sorry. Tom?"

The man stood up as if to greet her, taller than she'd realized. And there was something different about his face. He pressed something into her neck. A tingle raced through her body, and then it was as if all her muscles had frozen as he took her arm and guided her into his car just as her legs gave out, and she collapsed on the seat. He jabbed a needle into her arm and her world turned into a fuzziness and then nothing.

Annie woke with a mouth dry as a bone and a raging inferno inside her skull. She couldn't move her arms or legs. Licking her lips was like rubbing them with very coarse sandpaper. With an effort, she opened one eye. Very blurry. A second eye. Slowly, her focus came back.

The only light came from a fireplace in the corner, stones holding the embers. Annie's eyes followed the flames and smoke upward to the chimney. What she could see by the faint light led her to believe she was in a barn. There didn't appear to be any animals.

The man from the car stood in front of her dressed in a monk's robe, the cowl hiding his face in shadows.

Her tongue was like a bar of soap in her mouth. Why couldn't she move her arms or legs? Annie tilted her head to take stock of herself. Her first realization was that she was completely naked. She tried to protest, to ask, to attack—but all that came out was a cackle like a turkey leaving its roost. Annie then realized her arms and legs were bound to the circular table she was splayed out on.

"Why?" she croaked.

"Because we are carnal beasts," the man said. "And this is what we want to do."

"We?" Annie caught a flitting movement in the shadows of the barn and realized there were others out there, just out of sight, vague outlines in the dark recesses. "What do you want with me?"

"I wish to get to know you. To understand you."

"What? Why?"

"Because, my dear Pumpkin Pie, we are to be joined together for all of eternity. We will be one with each other."

"What are you talking about?"

"On the Blood Moon, you'll be sacrificed to the power of the natural world, the world where Satan rules, not God. I'll bleed you out, butcher you, cook you, and then eat you."

Chapter 4

Langdon found Danny T. sitting at the counter of the diner with a cup of coffee in front of him and what looked to be the crumbs from several donuts. The diner was an institution in Brunswick and a place Langdon had been frequenting since his early twenties. For many a year, he'd eaten breakfast here almost every single day. As of late, he'd taken to limiting it to once or twice a week. A fruit smoothie had replaced the greasy bacon, eggs, potato, and toast that his younger body had metabolized without repercussions to his waist. Sadly, this was no longer the case.

Danny T. was about five inches over five feet and must have weighed a minimum of 300 pounds. Despite his slovenly appearance, his greasy hair, and dirty clothes, Langdon was well aware that nobody had his finger on the pulse of the town of Brunswick like Danny T. He was a former fisherman, blackballed from the Gulf of Maine waterfront for having chosen to cut through a net full of herring to save a buddy's arm. The man had spent the last thirty years clerking at various establishments until his slovenly appearance and utter lack of personal hygiene invariably got him fired.

"Danny T.," Langdon said dropping into the stool next to him. "Where ya been? I've been looking for you for the past two days. Not like you to not be around. Not here. Not home."

The man looked sideways at him. "Was just thinking that that seventh donut might've been unnecessary."

Langdon chuckled. "You been off on vacation?"

Danny T. looked slyly out of the corner of his eye. "Met a woman."

Langdon almost fell off his stool. "You met a woman?"

Rosie came over with a chipped mug and poured a cup of coffee. "What're you doing in here past morning time?" she asked. Rosie was five inches shorter than Danny T. but every bit as wide. Her hair and cheeks fit her name and there was a perpetual sheen of perspiration on her brow.

"Dog was hungry. Figured he could clean up the scraps for you." Sure enough, dog was scurrying around the floor finding fallen morsels of food.

Rosie threw a piece of toast on the floor, and dog gobbled it up.

"Looking for a fellow," Langdon said. He set a photograph on the counter. "Name of Liam Couture."

Rosie looked at it, shook her head, and looked up. "Never seen him before. He from around here?"

"Nope. Machias. But he seems to have gotten lost in Brunswick." Langdon took a sip of the coffee and wondered about a jelly donut. Luckily for his diet, Rosie moved off down the counter to take a payment. "How about you, Danny T.? You seen this fellow around?"

Danny T. didn't even look at the photo. "I don't wanna get involved," he said.

"Involved? What are you talking about? I'm just asking if you've seen this fellow around."

"That's how it always starts. Next thing I know, I'm driving a car at a guy with a gun shooting at me. No thanks."

"What?" Langdon feigned astonishment. "You're going to bring that old thing up? That was like twenty years ago. Or more."

"How about last fall when that gang of crazy men attacked me and 4 by Four out to the Brew Pub?"

"As I recall," Langdon said. "You didn't get a scratch." Not quite true for 4 by Four, Langdon thought, the memory still heavy in his heart.

Danny T. sighed and looked over at the picture. "Nope, don't know him. Never seen him."

Langdon was usually able to get to Danny T. through his stomach, as he always appeared to be hungry, but the man had just professed to be stuffed to the gills with donuts. "You want to make some money?"

"Nope." Danny T. shook his head emphatically. "I'm flush."

Flush, Langdon wondered? He'd never known the man to have enough food in his belly nor money in his pocket. "Where you working now?"

"MacDonald's down the street," Danny T. said. "They're paying eighteen bucks an hour."

Langdon knew this was probably close to double what the man had ever made since getting blackballed from the fishing boat.

Rosie came back down the counter. "I'll share the picture around if you leave it here."

"Worth a hundred bucks to the person that leads me to him," Langdon said.

"Why's he missing?" Danny T. asked.

Langdon looked over at him. "Why, my friend, I suppose if I knew that, I'd have a better idea of where to find him."

"OK, well, is he a drug dealer? A Russian gangster? A government mercenary? A radical environmentalist? A crazy QAnon supporter?"

All fair enough questions, Langdon thought, given Danny's previous experience of the PI's cases. "No. He's a redneck who works in a fish hatchery and likes his toys."

Danny T. snuffled, almost like he was going to cry. "Even worse."

Rosie waddled her way back down the counter, and Langdon ordered a dozen donuts from her. He figured maybe he'd have one and bring the rest back to Chabal and Star.

"How 'bout I take the Tigers in tomorrow's game for a fin," Langdon said. Danny T. was not always the most intelligent person regarding money but did love to gamble. Sometimes, a simple wager for five bucks would tempt when the offer of a C-note was disregarded.

Rosie slid a box of donuts onto the counter in front of Langdon.

He took one out, noticed Danny T. eyeballing the box, and slid it over in front of him.

"You gotta give me two runs," Danny T. said. He took a chocolate-covered Long John donut, an inspiration from Rosie's niece on the west coast, and shoved half of it into his mouth.

Langdon bit his tongue. The Sox were his favorite team. They had twice the wins of the Tigers thus far in the early season. At the same time, he was getting help on the case for five dollars. But the principle of the matter rankled. "Okay." He pulled his phone out and sent the photo to Danny T.'s phone. "Just ask around and see if anybody's seen him, will ya?"

"You know the Tigers only got eight wins, don't you?" Danny T. chortled, a step up from snuffling, as he pulled a second donut from the box and went to work on it.

"Who's this mystery woman you met?" Langdon asked.

"She works at the recycle place down on Union. That's where I bring my bottles."

Langdon knew that Danny T. drank upwards of eight Dr. Peppers a day. No booze, juice, milk, or water. "Still didn't tell me where you've been the last two days."

"I was home," Danny T. said, a grin creasing his wide face. "Just didn't answer the door when you came by."

"Or your phone," Langdon said.

"I was busy." Danny T. shoved another donut into his mouth.

Langdon's phone buzzed with an email, and he clicked on it to see it was from Bart. Hopefully, the police report he'd asked for. He was going to read it at the counter and finish his coffee as Danny T. pulled a third donut from the box. Didn't the man just say he'd had too many before Langdon even arrived? He thought it best to get out with the few remaining donuts in the box while the getting was good.

"You need anything else?" Rosie asked, leaning her humongous forearms on the counter, a bead of sweat falling from her chin.

"Nope, gotta run," Langdon said. He dropped a twenty on the counter. "Ask around about the missing fellow, though, would you?"

Langdon had to go give dog a slight nudge to follow him out the door. The canine had rested his head on the booth table of a young couple and was imploring them with his sad eyes to feed the hungry. Langdon thought he looked much like Danny T.

Langdon pulled open the gate of the Jeep for dog to jump in and then slid into the front seat, pulling up the email from Bart on his phone.

He scanned through the missing person report. Liam Couture was five-foot-eight, 140 pounds, had brown hair and eyes, a slight scar on the back of his right hand, a tattoo of an eagle on his left bicep, and was seventy-one years old. His brother had said he was wearing jeans and a light tan jacket the morning he'd seen him going off to Brunswick. He lived alone, and there was no indication that he took any medication. It was believed that he might be a heavy drinker and possibly dabbled in harder drugs such as crystal meth or heroin. Eddie Couture was his only living relative. He was unmarried and had no children. Originally from California, he had moved to Maine almost fifty years ago.

Langdon scanned down to the information on his vehicle. A black, 2002 F-150 with over 200,000 miles on it towing a fifteen-year-old beater Haulmark trailer. Liam owned a rifle that was not at his house. It was quite possibly on the gunrack in the truck. It was a Winchester Model 70 Extreme Weather SS. Langdon made a mental note to ask Eddie if his brother had fishing gear or a dirt bike that might've been in the back of the truck. Or anything else of a personal nature, for that matter.

Langdon looked at the time. It was coming up to five. He figured he should probably go help Chabal close the bookshop. With that thought, his phone buzzed with a text from Bart.

Where are you?

On my way to the bookshop. He texted back.

Sending a woman to see you.

What about?

Busy right now. She'll tell you.

Langdon doubted that Bart was too busy to explain. He hated texting, maybe even more than talking on the phone, and saw no reason to waste his time. Things that came under the heading of squandering his life included telling Langdon what some woman was about to tell him anyway.

Maddie, short for Madison, Campagna, was a dark-haired woman of about forty years of age. She had green eyes that matched her olive complexion and a face that made Langdon think of Cleopatra as played by Elizabeth Taylor.

"What can I do for you, Maddie?" Langdon asked. She'd already instructed him that Mrs. Campagna was her mother.

"My friend is missing," she said with no drama and went straight to the point.

"And you reported this to the police?"

"They said I had to wait until she'd been gone for seventy-two hours."

Langdon knew that it was usually two days, one if there was reason to believe foul play, and three if the police truly believed the missing person would show up within that time of his or her own volition. "When did your friend go missing?"

"Last night," Maddie said, the words rushing out. "Well, she was going on a date, see, and she was going to call me after and let me know how it went, and when she didn't, I called her this morning. No answer. About noontime, I got worried and went over to her house, and she hadn't been home."

"How do you know she hadn't been home and just left again?"

Maddie brushed a stray lock of hair from her face that had sprung free from the half updo. "She has two dogs. They went ballistic when I walked in. You'd have thought they hadn't eaten in days."

Langdon looked over at dog. What would he do, Langdon wondered for the second time in two days, if he were to miss a meal? "Is it possible... that the date just went very well?" This, then, Langdon reasoned, was the reason for the police suggesting giving it seventy-two hours.

Maddie blushed, a flush that began in her cheeks and cascaded down to her neck. "Annie isn't like that. Not that she's a prude, mind you, but she's not going to sleep with a man on the first date. And she most definitely wouldn't forget about her dogs. They're her babies."

This was worse than awkward, Langdon thought, but the questions had to be asked. "Annie is single? No husband, fiancé, boyfriend, or—"

"Yes. Annie hasn't dated or been with anybody in close to two years now. I've tried to hook her up with friends of mine, but hey, what can you say? The good ones are married and those who aren't— aren't for a reason. So, she gave a go with a dating app. Took close to three months, but she finally connected with somebody she liked. They were meeting up for dinner last night right here. In Brunswick."

"Do you know where?"

"I think she said Sugar something or other, I've been searching my mind, but I can't quite recollect. I was going to do a Google search on restaurants in Brunswick with Sugar in the name, but I haven't gotten around to it."

Langdon had a feeling that the place was one of his and Chabal's favorites. And there was a problem with that. "Sugar Magnolia's?"

Maddie snapped her fingers. "Yes. That's the joint."

"Where you from, Maddie?"

Maddie's thin eyebrows scrunched in a perplexed manner at this question out of seemingly nowhere. "I live in Cape Elizabeth."

Langdon nodded. "What brought you to Maine?"

She looked confused. "This is where I grew up. I've always lived in Maine."

"And how long have you known Annie?"

"She's the first person I met when I moved to Cape."

Langdon tapped the desk with his fingers. He thought about asking where she'd lived before Cape Elizabeth, but then again, she wasn't the one missing. "Sugar Magnolia's is closed on Sundays."

"What? Then why…?"

Langdon wasn't sure if her response meant anything other than surprise. "Do you have the name of the… person that she was meeting?"

"No. Nothing. She said she'd tell me all about it afterward, that there was no sense sharing details if it didn't go well."

"Why'd you come here?"

"To hire you, I suppose, to find Annie." Maddie choked on the name. With an effort, she kept her composure. "Because she's missing. And that fat cop seemed to think you were good at your job. Finding people."

Chapter 5

Langdon sat at a small wooden table across from Mrs. Donna Reed. It was her credit card that had been used to pay for the *Cousin Freddie's* advertisement with the ATV for sale. He had an inkling that she was quite unaware that she'd done so. Bart had shared the information with Langdon, saying that the Berwick police department had been contacted but wouldn't be visiting with the woman for at least a few days.

Mrs. Reed was a heavy woman in her eighties and was smoking a cigarette as they talked. She had on heavy make-up that did little to hide the ravages of time. Her husband had been dead for some years now, she said.

Berwick was about an hour from Brunswick. It was a quaint small town that had once been built on selling lumber and worked closely with the mill town of Somersworth across the river in New Hampshire.

"As I said, I'm investigating a missing person," Langdon said. He'd declined the offer of tea.

"What does that have to do with me?" she asked.

"Liam Couture came to Brunswick looking to purchase an ATV. He did so after seeing an advertisement for an ATV for sale. In *Cousin Freddie's.*"

"Liam what?" Mrs. Reed had a loud and hoarse voice.

"You don't know a man by the name of Liam Couture?"

"I should say not."

"Have you heard of *Cousin Freddie's*?" Langdon asked. "It's a weekly booklet that people use to sell things."

"I know what goddamn *Cousin Freddie's* is. What's that got to do with me?"

"You see," Langdon said gently. "Your credit card was used to pay for the advertisement in *Cousin Freddie's*. Listing the ATV for sale that Liam Couture came to buy."

"I don't have no ATV." Mrs. Reed spread her arms wide. "Do I look like somebody who owns a goddamn ATV?"

"I'm concerned that somebody may've stolen your credit card and used it without your knowledge."

Mrs. Reed stood up and walked into the other room. She returned with a large fake-leather purse and pulled a ponderous wallet from within. From that, she plucked out a credit card with her thick fingers and displayed it triumphantly. "Nobody stole my card. It's right here."

"Do you have the ability to check your credit card statement online?" Langdon asked.

"Online?"

"I believe that somebody may have stolen your number off your card and taken an advertisement out in *Cousin Freddie's* without your knowledge."

"My card's right here!" Mrs. Reed said belligerently.

Langdon already knew that her card had been used to make the payment. It'd do no good to persuade her to call and verify that. She'd most likely be quite upset when her statement came in the mail. "Do you know anybody in Brunswick?"

"That's where you said you was from. Is that where the feller went missing?"

Does anybody ever really know where a missing person is, Langdon thought, working to keep the words from his lip. "Yes. I think so."

"Got me a nephew over that way. Not Brunswick, mind you,

with all those expensive neighborhoods and overpriced homes, but Lisbon Falls. He works in Brunswick, though."

Langdon lived in one of those neighborhoods. He didn't think it was unusually spiffy, more middle-class than anything, but in comparison to the ramshackle double-wide that Donna Reed lived in, his colonial was the Taj Mahal, and the Meadowbrook development it was nestled in was like ancient Athens. "Your nephew got a name?"

"Course he does. Who the hell don't have a name?"

Langdon waited patiently. If nothing else, patience was a trait he had cultivated in both the bookstore and PI business.

"Gregory. Gregory Popa." Mrs. Reed lit another cigarette. "He's an accountant over there. Smart, he is. Know he didn't get that from his dumbass father."

"Do you have contact information? A phone number? An address?"

Mrs. Reed sighed and walked over to a drawer and pulled a dusty Rolodex from it. She leafed through, pulled a card from it, and set it in front of Langdon. He copied the information on Gregory Popa into the notes on his cellphone.

~ ~ ~ ~ ~

Gregory Popa was not quite what Langdon had expected of an accountant. He was surprised he'd never met the man as his accounting firm was on Bank Street, just across Maine Street and around the corner from the bookshop, in a yellow building that he most likely leased. A discrete sign over the door said, *Gregory Popa, CPA*. His own business, Langdon thought, and wondered why he'd never seen the man at any Chamber of Commerce functions or even just around town.

There was a receptionist who guided Langdon to a second-floor office. She was no-nonsense and merely waved him in and turned and walked off. Popa had brooding-dark eyes and possibly the longest face Langdon had ever seen on a human being. A thick-black beard made his countenance stretch even further. He wore a black shirt with a shocking red tie.

"Mr. Popa, thank you for seeing me." Langdon stepped into the office and sat down. "My name is Langdon. I own the bookshop across the street. The Coffee Dog Bookstore."

"You said you got my name from my Aunt Donna?" It was hard to tell if the man was smiling behind the bushy beard, or even if it was he who'd spoken.

"Yes. I'm surprised I haven't run into you before. How long have you been in business?"

"I'm a busy man, Mr. Langdon. What's this about?"

"I'm afraid that somebody has stolen your Aunt Donna's credit card."

The man's face had a mottled brown complexion, almost like he'd not washed it properly. "Excuse me, but can you tell me who you are again?"

Langdon smiled and held out his hand. Popa took it grudgingly. "As I said, I'm a local business owner, same as you. I'm also a PI, a private investigator."

"Are you saying that my Aunt Donna has hired you?" Popa leaned forward, resting his forearms on the desk, and searched Langdon's face with eyes that'd gone abruptly from dull to extremely interested. "I've not seen the old bat in quite some time."

"She mentioned that you stopped by over the holidays this past year. She's quite fond of you. Said you brought her a coffee cake and a handle of Allen's." Quite a combination, Langdon thought. She'd gone so far as to offer him a drink from a similar bottle. Unlike those who had made the coffee-flavored brandy Maine's most popular drink for years, he'd politely refused.

Popa flicked his hand in the air. "That's right, I did. It was just a short visit. I was in the area."

"Why the visit, after such a long time?"

"Like I said, I was in the area."

Without his having had to lie, Langdon thought, Popa seemed to have accepted that Donna Reed had hired him to investigate and seemed willing to answer questions. "That was nice of you."

"You said something about her credit card number being stolen?"

Actually, Langdon thought, he'd said 'credit card.' "Do you own an ATV, Mr. Popa?"

"An ATV?"

"Yeah, you know, an all-terrain vehicle, a four-wheeler. Do you own one?"

"What does that have to do with my Aunt Donna having her credit card number stolen?"

"Because somebody used it to place an ad selling an ATV, is why."

Popa guffawed. But it sounded dry and forced. "You're saying somebody stole her credit card number to place an advertisement? I'm sorry, Mr. Langdon, but you're wasting my time."

"And now a man who answered that advertisement has come up missing."

"What the fuck are you talking about?" Popa stood up and glared across the desk.

Langdon leaned back in his chair. "Your Aunt Donna's credit card number was used to place an advertisement in Uncle Freddie's. The person who answered that ad, hoping to buy an ATV, has disappeared. I don't believe that your Aunt has any knowledge of this. Thus, I am working under the premise that somebody stole her number. That's the long and short of it."

"I don't understand how that has anything to do with me."

"Just to be clear. You do not own an ATV?"

Popa sat back down and laughed. "You are persistent, aren't you? Sort of like a dog with a bone. You know, Mr. Langdon, that when you visit another in their lair, you should show them respect, or else you should not go there."

Lair was a strange word to use for an office, Langdon thought. He sat quietly.

"I suppose," Popa continued, "that if I had an ATV and then sold it, I would no longer have it. I think it's time for you to go, Mr. Langdon."

Langdon stood up. "I'm sorry to have bothered you." He stepped toward the door, paused, and turned back around. "Are you married, Mr. Popa?"

"You're an odd duck, Mr. Langdon. No, I'm not married, not that it's any of your business."

"And do you frequent dating sites?"

"Dating sites?"

"Yeah, you know, Tinder and things like that?"

"No, I do not."

"And do you know a young lady by the name of Annie Brown?" He took out his phone and went to the picture that Maddie had shared with him as he walked back over to the desk. It was the photo that Annie had used for the dating site, surprisingly a very accurate image of her.

"I know no such woman."

Langdon withdrew the phone and looked at the photo of Annie Brown. She was about as normal looking as one could be. Average height and weight, perhaps just a few extra pounds. Her hair was brownish blonde. Eyes blue. Just a trace of makeup. The only thing that caught Langdon's attention was a little lift to her lips that matched a glint in her eyes that bespoke some secret joke brewing inside of her.

~ ~ ~ ~ ~

The phone rang twice. There was no greeting. Just airspace.

"This is Gregory."

"What is it?"

"There was a private detective here. Name of Langdon. He was asking all sorts of questions."

"What sort of questions?"

"He knew that my Aunt Donna's credit card number was used to place the advertisement. You told me nobody would ever be able to connect this to me. You said that you just wanted the card number to buy some things that you didn't want in your name. You didn't tell me you were using it to get that fellow down here."

"Take a breath. What else did this Langdon have to say?"

"He knew about Liam Couture. And he's asking about Annie Brown."

"What did you say?"

"That I knew nothing, of course." Popa listened to the silence as if there might be a hidden message layered within.

"What do you know of this Langdon?"

"He owns the bookstore in town. The Coffee Dog or something like that."

"The place right on Maine Street?"

"Yes. And he's the one who was involved in that missing boy case last fall, around Halloween. You remember that from the news, I trust? That was him."

"Did he seem suspicious of you?"

Popa hesitated. "No. They just tracked the card number to my Aunt Donna. He suspects nothing."

"I'll take care of it. You keep your mouth shut. You know nothing."

Chapter 6

If she were going to be spending this glorious Friday afternoon in the bookshop, Chabal figured it'd be a good idea to enjoy the outdoors for a bit. She had the latest Thea Kozak mystery by Kate Flora in hand and a hankering for a blueberry muffin with a frozen peanut butter coffee. As luck would have it, there was a table open on the sidewalk of the Lenin Stop Coffee Shop, and she draped her sweater over the back of a chair as she went in to gather her guilty pleasures.

When she came back out a woman was sitting at her table sipping a cup of hot coffee from a mug. She was tall, if thin, and had straight black hair that made it halfway down her back in a lustrous sheen. Dark glasses perched themselves on what was a very sharp nose. Her lipstick was bright red.

"Oh, I'm sorry, that must be your sweater," the woman said, standing up. "I'd thought maybe somebody had left it behind by mistake. I was going to run it inside after I drank my morning java."

Chabal waved her back down. "No worries. I'm by myself, so feel free to help yourself to the seat." She slid into the chair with her sweater on the back.

The woman hesitated. "Are you sure? I don't want to impose."

"I'd welcome the company," Chabal said. In reality, she was itching to dig into the book, but that could wait.

"I'm Jade." The woman settled tentatively back into the chair.

"Chabal Langdon. What a beautiful day."

"Supposed to be cold again next week," Jade said. "I suppose we should enjoy it while it lasts."

"You live in Brunswick?"

"Across the river in Topsham, actually. But I'm a teacher here in town."

"Really? What do you teach?"

"Science at the Junior High. 7th and 8th grade."

Chabal broke off a piece of blueberry muffin and nibbled at it. "That must be rough. I remember my kids when they were that age. I can't imagine a whole classroom of them."

Jade laughed, the sound like wind chimes on this gorgeous May day. "They're not so bad. They just need to be reined in, is all. And what do you do?"

Chabal pointed across the street. "My husband and I own and operate The Coffee Dog Bookstore."

"Oh, that's exciting. I've been meaning to come in, but times have been difficult. I have to confess that I've been giving much of my business to the evil empire."

"Luckily, people in Brunswick have been great about supporting us." Chabal blanched inside, not having intended that as a slight for Jade. "I mean, most of our regulars have kept up with us, even through the worst of Covid. Curbside and whatnot."

"I just moved back to town last summer when I got the job at the Junior High," Jade said. "But I promise to get in."

"Oh, don't worry about that. Where'd you come from?"

"New York." Jade took a sip of coffee. "But I grew up here. Didn't care much for the big city and came on home."

Chabal decided to not press for specifics. "You glad to be back?"

"Oh, it's wonderful," Jade said. "Tough times to get out to meet people, though. And a long winter. Somehow I forgot how long they are."

Chabal snickered. "The winters are always long. You should feel lucky. We barely had any snow."

"Oh, I remember them well. Born and raised here, went to college in the city, and stayed for too many years."

"You must know people from back in the day?"

"Not really. Sometimes it feels like I only know teens and preteens. But I hope things open up more as the good weather comes. See, the first nice day in months, and I've already met an actual adult. Things are looking up." She laughed, the kaleidoscope of notes trickling from her parted lips.

"No school today?"

"Teacher workshop. My department head canceled a meeting, and I thought I'd get a coffee to keep me awake for the rest of the day."

"We should get together sometime," Chabal said. "Maybe have an adult beverage?"

Jade smiled, her teeth gleaming white against her skin. "I'd like that. What are you doing later?"

Chabal grinned. "Well, it *is* Friday, and my husband owes it to me to shut up the shop on his own. You know Goldilocks? Next block up behind me?"

"Sure. I've been there once or twice."

"How about we meet there at five?"

"I'd like that. I'd like that very much." Jade stood up. "It was very nice meeting you, Chabal Langdon."

~ ~ ~ ~ ~

Langdon pulled into the parking lot out behind Fort Andross. It was a huge old mill building from back when mills drove American industry, always on the water, in this case, the Androscoggin River, for it was the water that, originally, drove the machinery until most converted to electric power, itself generated by small hydro plants. It'd been converted into a wide range of businesses. There was a flea market with tables set up every Saturday, storage units, restaurants, and various businesses.

Jimmy 4 by Four's legal office was on the third floor overlooking the river. It'd been a tough choice picking between this and a view of the downtown, but the inner hippie who'd escaped the pressures of a corporate New York City law office won out, and he'd chosen the river cascading down over the dam for his daily perspective.

Langdon and 4 by Four had become friendly soon after Jimmy Angstrom, as he was known then, had broken down in a Vanagon on his way to central Maine, instead stopping and starting a life in the Brunswick area. They'd worked a case together where a mill was dumping chemicals into the river and poisoning the local water supply, an event that had cemented their friendship in complicity based on justice and not law.

The matronly receptionist was on the phone but just waved at Langdon to go on back into the interior office. 4 by Four had gone from thousand-dollar suits in New York City to being a hippy in Bowdoinham, and recently changing to what he was now—a fashionably dressed hipster with a longtime affinity for smoking weed. He wore skinny jeans cuffed at the bottom to show his bright socks, a Kurt Cobain T-shirt, and a sports jacket. It was not your normal lawyer attire, but Jimmy 4 by Four was not your normal barrister. His knowledge of the law was extensive, and he'd built a reputation that was top of the line. Not to mention that he would wear a dress shirt and tie if he had to go to court, which was seldom. Not many were willing to go in front of a judge with him in opposition.

"Langdon. Where've you been hiding out?"

"In plain sight, my friend," Langdon said. "Down the street in the bookshop."

"I keep thinking I might get around to reading a book for fun one of these days."

Langdon chuckled. "Or at least come in and buy a few as Christmas presents."

"Not a bad idea. I'm certain you owe me thousands of dollars in legal advice over the years. I could've done all my holiday shopping for free and then some." 4 by Four stepped over to a trolley holding several bottles and glasses. "You want a drink?"

Langdon looked at the grandfather clock in the corner of the room. If it was to be believed, it was noontime. "I'm good."

4 by Four looked at him, surprise jumping from his face. "You didn't go and quit drinking booze, did you?"

"Nope. Just not today."

4 by Four shrugged, dropped a couple of cubes in a glass, and poured a generous amount of Patrón. "What can I do for you?"

"Just thought I'd come by and ask if you'd be up for a barbecue tomorrow night? Come by around six and we'll eat around seven and then have a fire."

"Sure. Can I bring a date?"

"No problem. Who?"

4 by Four laughed. He'd always had a fondness for the ladies. Just not commitment. This 'playing the field' had not waned, even now as he hovered around sixty years old. "I don't know yet but that'll give me a project for this evening."

"Just so you know, Richam and Jewell will be there."

"Jewell doesn't always... appreciate... my dates, now, does she?" 4 by Four grinned broadly.

"You ever use any dating apps?"

"Ah, I sense a change in tension. Herein lies the real reason you didn't just text me to come over tomorrow night. There's a mysterious and hidden agenda to your visit."

Langdon chuckled. "You know I've always thought it best to leave things to the experts. I don't believe in trying to do my own electrical work, plumbing, carpentry, accounting, and so on. I sell books. I hire people to do those other things. They, in turn, buy books, and the economy goes around."

"And you come to me for legal counsel."

"That and dating trends in 2021."

4 by Four sniggered. "Try the whole twenty-first century, my friend. What, you and the Chabal been married for some twenty years now?"

"Something like that," Langdon said, trying to remember what year they'd gotten married. He remembered how long they'd been together. Twenty-three years. Marriage? That was just a date. A formality.

"You telling me there's trouble on the home front?" 4 by Four looked sideways at Langdon with a contrived sneer. "Are you singling Chabal up? I think she's always liked me."

"She likes you fine with a ten-foot pole," Langdon said.

"You know where that expression comes from, don't you?" 4 by Four asked. "Down New Orleans way they have to bury their corpses above ground because of the high-water table forcing coffins to the surface, and that, coupled with space problems, means they bury their dead in tombs that have to be reused. The tombs in the subtropical climate become like ovens, and soon all that is left is bone and ash. One day and a year after putting a casket in the tomb, the bones and ashes are swept off the back with a ten-foot pole, creating space for the next potential zombie."

"My point exactly. Chabal would be willing to go out with you as long as she was able to sweep your ashes into the depths of the earth." Langdon thought that the tequila on the bar trolley seemed to be calling to him, but he ignored it.

"Whatever you want to believe," 4 by Four said. "What do you want to know about dating apps?"

"What do you know about a dating site called *Patience*? They got a tagline something like, 'for middle-aged men and women wanting love without all the hurry.'"

4 by Four sniggered. "I love that site. And that slogan is a joke. My experience is that it's filled with forty-something women desperate for love before that particular bus passes them by and stops running."

Langdon thought of suggesting that it was also likely populated by women in their fifties as well, but knew that his playboy friend thought that was a bit old for him. Not for the first time, Langdon asked himself why he continued to consort with the lawyer. "If you wanted to pose on there under an alias and abduct a woman, how hard would it be?'

"Whoa, this just got serious real fast." 4 by Four finished his glass of tequila. "What do you got going on this time?"

Langdon told him about the visit from Maddie Campagna regarding her missing friend, Annie Brown. This led him to explain the missing Liam Couture, and the thought that these two missing persons might be connected.

"Do you know anything about Gregory Popa?" Langdon asked as he concluded with a description of his meeting a couple days earlier with the local accountant.

"No, I can't say that I do, but I'll look into it. He sounds suspicious as hell."

"Thanks." Langdon stood up. "I got to get back to the bookshop. Chabal is meeting a new friend for cocktails later."

"Female?" 4 by Four asked.

Langdon chuckled. "Hope so."

"All the dating apps work hard to protect the identity of the people using them," 4 by Four said. "But they have your records. I'm sure that Bart can squirrel out the identity of anybody that this woman—What'd you say? Annie?—who she was connecting with."

"Yes. I called him about it. They didn't declare her officially a missing person until yesterday, and they're working on obtaining the files from the *Patience* people. He thinks they should have something soon, but they're putting up some resistance. I guess keeping identities secret is part of the modern dating world."

~ ~ ~ ~ ~

Langdon spent the rest of the afternoon at the bookshop, closed it down at six, and took dog for a long walk back behind their house in the Town Commons. This, and driving distances, was the perfect time for deeper reflection. There were no distractions, not even dog occasionally careening across his path intent on some smell that was more exciting than a Bruce Springsteen concert.

Chabal got home at seven with the promised loaded pizza and Caesar Salad from Goldilocks. The evening had cooled, and they settled onto the couch with the pizza, salad, and *Peaky Blinders* on Netflix. They'd avoided watching this so far because the characters' heavy Northern England brogue was so hard for their aging ears to comprehend. Langdon was fairly certain he wouldn't have understood much of it even when younger. Fortunately, they realized that they could put the English subtitles on and read what they couldn't understand.

As they started the second episode of the night, Chabal lay sideways, draping her feet over dog, who'd taken up his position in the middle of the couch. Langdon slid her sock off and began to knead her right foot. Then the left. Two episodes seemed to do the trick for the night, and Langdon switched back to ABC for the morning and turned the television off.

"How was drinks with your new friend?" he asked.

"Fabulous," she said. "Keep rubbing."

"What'd you say her name was?"

"Jade. She's a teacher at the Junior High." Chabal pulled back her foot and presented the other one for Langdon to work on. "She just moved back to town from New York City. Doesn't know anybody outside of a few teachers."

"Moved back?"

"Yeah, said she grew up here. Then went off to college in New York, Columbia she said, and stayed there until the city life got to be too much."

"She doesn't know anybody from when she lived here?"

"Said she only had a few friends, and they've all moved out of state."

"How old is she?"

"Why?"

Langdon trailed his fingers up her calf. "4 by Four might need a date for tomorrow's barbecue."

Chabal kicked his leg with her free foot. "She's about thirty-five I'd say. Too young, too pretty, and too smart for that old goat."

Langdon smiled. Jimmy 4 by Four was a hopeless philanderer, but he never lied, and, as a matter of fact, was always straight-up with women that he didn't want any sort of serious relationship. There seemed to be a certain segment of the female population that was okay with that, either because they liked a no-strings-attached fling, or they were hoping to 'fix' him, it was hard to tell. And, both Langdon and Chabal knew that they could trust the man with their lives, and in fact, had.

"Hmm, my wife hanging out with young single women in bars," he said, one hand massaging a foot, the other caressing a leg, calf to thigh underneath the loose Capris.

Chabal shifted and dog, disgusted, got up and went off to the bedroom to go to sleep. "We were the center of attention for one table of four men," she said. "Although, I think 'we' is not the optimal word, but rather, Jade was the focus of many an eye."

"You, my dear, are the focus of the only two eyes that matter," Langdon said.

"Mm. You got that right." Chabal shifted her foot into his crotch and slowly rubbed it back and forth.

"4 by Four did ask to bring a date tomorrow, a woman not yet designated, probably not yet known."

"I hope he does. I invited Jade to come by, and I'd hate to have to kick his ass for drooling over my new friend."

Langdon leaned over and unbuttoned her pants, his hand trailing across her belly, his fingers sliding lower and lower. "I'll tell him that Jade is in search of a husband. That should do the trick."

Chabal swung her legs to the floor, stood up, and pulled her Capris and panties down to her ankles, stepping out of them as stepped forward, unbuttoning his pants and sliding them down, before straddling him on the couch. They spoke no more and rocked gently together like waves on a placid shore. Then, the tide shifted, and the moon began urgently tugging the water to land, and their bodies filled with white caps until they came together in a shuddering climax.

Chapter 7

The dreams had lessened over time but had never quite gone away. It was from the period that Annie called the Dark Age. It was as close to truly remembering that time as she'd ever gotten. The first eight years of her life seemed no more than flittering shadows glimpsed when she slept. There was a threatening figure whom she could never quite make out. This person was always creeping up on her, crawling just out of her sight, behind the bookcase so she couldn't make him out, under the bed.

When Annie was not yet ten, she started calling this person of her nightmares the Overlord. She supposed that the name had come from a cartoon or horror movie she'd seen, but wherever it came from, it was apt. What the Overlord wanted to do to her was so horrible, so abhorrent, so disgustingly appalling, that she'd never been able to explain in words or images what it was. It was not some one thing. It was everything. It invaded every pore of her soul.

As the terror became too great, Annie woke. She didn't open her eyes, though. This was something she'd started in her early teens, a coping mechanism that she'd devised, *she*—not her siblings, not her parents, and certainly not the countless therapists. She slowly deconstructed the sickening nightmare and replaced it, first with Mama Brown, and then with the addition of Papa Brown. Her real parents.

Not those monsters who abused her. The best thing that could've happened in her life was when their meth lab out back of their single wide exploded, killing them with it, and in turn, handing Annie over to the state.

Many children struggled to navigate the difficult journey of foster care and adoption. Not Annie. She struck pure gold. Meg and Harold Brown had adopted her when she was eight and showered her with love, medical attention, both physical and mental. They'd fallen asleep in her bed, comforted her, held her hand, and made her feel loved. It was their faces, their bodies, their souls, and their goodness that she used to banish the Overlord from her thoughts.

She knew that he was there. She built her defenses with the images of her parents before opening her eyes. Annie had tried to outwait him before. Outlast him. He was nothing if not patient. A tiny, wry, smile creased her cracked lips. Of course, he was, as she'd met him on a dating website named Patience.

"What are you thinking, Pumpkin Pie?"

The voice was smooth, making Annie think of Barry White. Some of her first memories were of her Mama singing the lyrics to "Never, Never Gonna Give Ya Up." At first, it was in the night when she had nightmares, later it was dancing around the kitchen.

"I was wishing I'd been more patient," she said. Annie knew it was not a good idea to ignore a direct question. She opened her eyes. "And then maybe I'd be home with my dogs instead of strapped to a tabletop."

"I'm going to undo your restraints, if you promise to be a good little Pumpkin Pie."

She nodded.

"Promise me that you'll be a good little Pumpkin Pie."

"I promise that I'll be good."

He rose from his seat and stepped forward to her naked body and tilted the round tabletop so that she was upright, kneeling and loosening first her legs and then her wrists from the leather straps that constrained her. He was standing very close. It repulsed Annie, his hand on her shoulder, steadying her.

"Here," he said, assisting her into a chair, much like he'd guided her into his BMW when he'd abducted her. Her legs just as shaky now as then.

"What is your name?" she asked. She knew he was not Tom. The picture from the dating site was similar, but the nose was all wrong, none of the hook from the picture. Instead, it was straight and fairly unremarkable. This had been a false name. But, as of yet, he'd resisted telling her his real name.

"Why, my dear Pumpkin Pie, would you need to know that?"

"I'd like to know what to call you."

He set a bowl in front of her with some sort of stew and a wooden spoon. "You may call me the Wendigo."

Annie nodded. She didn't believe this to be his real name. Or even a name at all. But she was a survivor. She had to find a crevice. Something to be exploited. A way to gain trust. A way to escape.

"Eat," he said. "I'm going to take you for a walk today. Give you a chance to stretch your legs."

She dutifully transferred a few spoonfuls of the food into her mouth. It tasted terrible, but she continued, her mind trying to untangle what taking a walk would entail. Was she to be killed? Tortured? Sacrificed?

"Do you wish to kill me?" he asked, startling her.

"Kill you? No. Why?"

"Don't lie to me."

"I'm not lying."

"Don't tell me that you really believe all that Christian bullshit about turning the other cheek. Man was meant for vengeance, not forgiveness. This is the true message of Satan. Be honest with yourself. If I gave you the chance, you'd kill me. And that is okay. That is your true nature. Not some sort of societal nonsense heaped upon you, upon us, to brainwash the real you."

"I'd do what I had to, to free myself," Annie said.

"That is better, Pumpkin Pie, but not quite fully honest. If you could carve my heart out with that spoon in your hand, you would." He handed her a robe. She realized it was a monk's robe, a cowl with a hood and a belt at the waist. It was black. Like his. "Put this on. There's a bit of a chill when you go outside and leave the warmth of the fire."

Annie rose to her feet and took the garment, pulling it on over her naked body, reveling in the comfort that it brought.

He stood up, grabbing an iron ring. This, he put around her neck, shutting the clasp with an ominous clink and putting a padlock through two smaller rings. There was a leather leash, about six feet long, attached to another ring at the back. He put two smaller clamps around her ankles and ran a leather cord through them and up to the leash.

"There, that should do it," he said. "Although you promise to be good, Satan is strong within you, as he should be, and I mean to take no chances with our most important sacrifice of the year."

"Sacrifice for what?" she asked.

"Walk with me." He led her to the door and outside.

There was the rear of a house in front of them, but he turned to the side and led her back around the barn. The sun was almost down, barely visible through the heavy forest. There was a path, wide enough for a vehicle but seldom used, grass growing up, with the faint impression of tire tracks still visible.

"Are you a Christian, Annie?"

"I suppose so. I don't go to church, but I guess I believe in God."

"So, tell me, Annie, are you not proud? Do you not feel satisfaction when you accomplish a task, a euphoria of exaltation in yourself?"

"I guess I've been proud of things I've done."

"Isn't pride the number one sin among Christians?

"I, uh, know that you—"

"Pride is what befell the angel Lucifer, pride and ambition." He stopped, turning to stare Annie in the eyes. "But you have raised yourself up from the pits of despair and become a stunningly successful and beautiful woman. Should you not be proud of all that you have accomplished?"

"I guess so." How, Annie wondered, did this monster have any knowledge of the pits of her despair?

"Haughty eyes and a proud heart—the unplowed field of the wicked—produce sin." He laughed loudly, the noise echoing strangely, she thought. "Let me speak to you the real truth. To be proud is *not* the unplowed field of the wicked. It is a normal human trait that should not be repressed."

He resumed walking, tugging on her leash, leading her, she saw, to the edge of a quarry that suddenly gaped open below them in the deepening gloom of the lengthening dusk. "This is where you will end up, Pumpkin Pie. At least your bones will. I hope that you've relished your years spent on Earth. Not in fear. Not in repression of all that excites you. But alive and embracing that which you enjoy."

Annie stared into the abyss below. It took a few seconds for her eyes to adjust and for her to realize that about fifty feet down from the rocky ledge they stood on was dark water. The quarry was not large, perhaps a hundred yards across, almost a perfect circle, once the site of a sandstone mine, now deserted for the past hundred years and forgotten.

"Come." He pulled on the leash, tearing her from her reverie.

The path circled the quarry, the dark water pulling at her like a magnet as they wended their way around it. "Why are you doing this?" she asked.

"Because I want to."

Chapter 8

Langdon usually left his cell phone plugged in but out in the living room while he slept at night. He figured that most things could be left until morning. Not so with Chabal, who worried about her kids, as well as a host of other things, and so kept her phone handy bedside.

It was this ringing that pulled them from sleep at 4:00 a.m. As well, dog, who leaped up like it was the starter pistol shot for the Kentucky Derby.

Chabal answered the phone, handed it to Langdon, and put her head under a pillow.

"Hello?"

"You awake?" Bart asked.

"Sure, I'm always up at this time making donuts," Langdon said. He swung his feet to the floor and eased his way out of the bedroom with dog prancing along behind him, certain that, dark or not, this must mean it was breakfast time.

"Hmm. Donuts. Is Frosty's open yet? I'll bring some over."

"Why are you calling—wait, did you say on your way over?" Langdon shook his head, trying to clear the cobwebs.

"I got some people who want to meet you."

"Yeah? Who would that be?"

"Harold and Meg Brown. Annie Brown's parents."

Twenty minutes later, dog happily fed, Langdon halfway through a cup of coffee, Bart's cruiser pulled in the driveway with a Subaru Outback following behind it. Langdon didn't bother going to the door, knowing that Bart would let himself in, and that dog would greet them.

"They got jelly in their glazed twists, now," Bart said, dropping two-dozen donuts on the dining room table in front of Langdon. "Harold and Meg Brown. This is Langdon."

Harold was thin and angular with bushy eyebrows while Meg was a bit plump with rosy cheeks. They both looked exhausted.

Langdon stood and shook their hands, gesturing them to sit down. "Coffee?"

"That'd be great," Harold said.

"I'm fine," Meg said.

Langdon filled a cup and brought it over. He figured Bart could fend for himself. "What can I do for you?" he asked, sitting down across from them, next to Bart, who was busy on his second donut since arriving.

"You know that our daughter is missing," Harold said. It wasn't a question.

"Yes. Maddie Campagna has retained my services to look for her." Langdon had tried to contact the Browns several times over the course of the week to no avail.

"We're sorry that we didn't return your calls," Meg said.

Chabal came down the hallway from the bedroom in jeans and a T-shirt, her hair mildly put together. She grabbed a cup of coffee and sat down at the head of the table.

"This is my wife and partner, Chabal."

Harold and Meg nodded at her.

"Why didn't you return my phone calls?" Langdon asked.

"We thought it best to let the police handle the matter," Harold said. "Once we convinced them that it was, indeed, a suspicious missing person case."

"And what has changed your mind?"

"She's been missing for five days, and there's been nothing," Meg said. Her red eyes leaked slightly at the corners, and she wiped them with a tissue that had become a permanent part of her hand.

"And Sergeant Bartholomew told us that you were good people," Meg said. "That you were good at your job and could be trusted. That you were like a hound dog on the scent, and we should place our faith in you."

"He did, did he?" Langdon looked at Bart and raised an eyebrow. Bart shrugged.

"Has there been any progress in getting the records at that dating site?" Langdon asked. "Patience."

"No. They are claiming client privilege," Harold said. "Protecting some son of a sea cook piece of—"

"Harold!" Meg grabbed his arm. "No need for profanity."

"Bart?" Langdon asked.

Bart spoke around half of a glazed chocolate donut. "Not looking good anytime soon. If you ask me, their legal department is farting around about it."

"What do you want from me?" Langdon asked, turning back to the Browns.

"We want to hire you," Harold said.

"To find our daughter," Megan added.

"I've already been hired to find your daughter by Miss Campagna."

"Maddie is a dear," Meg said. "We'll talk to her. I'm sure she won't mind sharing you with us."

"We will, of course, be picking up the tab," Harold said. "We just want to be kept informed of any progress."

"Tell me about Annie," Langdon said.

"Tell you what?" Harold asked.

Langdon shrugged. "Who is she? What makes her tick? Every bit helps."

Meg cleared her throat. Looked at Harold, who nodded. "We

adopted Annie when she was ten. Her parents died in a fire when she was eight."

"That's horrible," Chabal said.

"If anybody deserved to burn to death, it was her parents," Harold said. Meg cast him a reproving look. "Her father, he, uh, had been molesting her, most likely with the knowledge of her mother. They were not good people."

"Human beings can truly be monsters," Langdon said, a tight edge to his voice.

"The point is, she survived them," Meg said. "She had terrible nightmares for years. She endured terrible abuse, but after, she was able to put those monsters in the rearview mirror and move on with her life. She developed a visualization process that she begins every single day with. She was an honor student in school. Went to college. Was an artist. Had an idyllic marriage."

"What happened to her husband?" Langdon had read in his research of Annie Brown that she'd been married to a man named George.

"Boating accident," Harold said. "Terrible."

"But she picked herself up and put herself back together. Again." Meg said. "And moved on with her life. She's tough, Annie is."

Langdon looked at the older couple sitting at his dining table and realized they were about to fall asleep with their eyes open. Their faces were grey and etched with wrinkles.

"Maybe you two should get some rest," he said. "Perhaps when you wake up later today you can write down anything and everything you can think of about Annie that might be of help."

"Please tell us that you have some sort of lead finding Annie," Meg said.

Langdon already knew that there were no cameras outside of Sugar Magnolia's, and thus far, there'd been nobody who'd seen Annie Brown in Brunswick. If she had ever made it this far. "We need to get access from Patience. Their records should show who your daughter was meeting. That is about the only lead that we might have."

"Thought that pretty boy lawyer friend of yours might help out in that regard," Bart said. He had chocolate and sugar glaze coating his face.

Langdon hid his smile. Bart and 4 by Four were the best of friends but hid this affection behind a running animosity that had been going on ever since the lawyer had led a group of hired killers into their midst back during the nuclear power scandal some twenty-five years earlier.

"Please, anything that you can do to help," Meg said. "My daughter is missing."

"I'll speak with the lawyer Bart's referring to. He's very good."

"Can you do that now?" Harold asked.

Langdon looked over at the time on the stove. "There is little chance of waking, or even finding him, at this hour. He should answer his phone by nine."

"Are you staying locally?" Chabal asked.

"We live just down in Scarborough," Harold said.

"Have you slept?"

"We spent the day waiting at the police station for news," Meg said.

"They refused to leave," Bart added.

"Sergeant Bartholomew recommended that we speak with you about an hour ago," Harold said. "And of course, we'd had several phone calls from you and have spoken with Maddie every day about it, so it seemed like the thing to do."

"We have plenty of room," Chabal said. "All the kids are gone. We'll put you up for a few hours so you can get some sleep, and as soon as we can get ahold of 4 by… the lawyer, we'll all go pay him a visit."

There was nominal resistance, but the Browns were clearly exhausted and allowed themselves to be led to an upstairs bedroom.

~ ~ ~ ~ ~

Langdon had spoken with 4 by Four about getting access to the

Patience client files before the Browns came down the stairs at just past nine in the morning. The lawyer agreed to get right on it as soon as he had his morning tea with his avocado toast. He started to tell Langdon about the woman he'd met the night before, but Langdon had broken off the call, saying that the clients were still there. And, in fact, they were upstairs sleeping.

Bart had agreed to bring the specifics by and drop them off with the lawyer. The gruff cop was often impatient with the machinations of the police department. It rarely worked at the speed that he desired. It was this sluggishness of process that often led Bart to work with Langdon, off the record. It was this relationship that had landed Bart in hot water with the top brass more than once. He didn't care, and the PD was loath to fire him as his clearance rate was the highest in the department.

The Browns agreed to go home and sit by the phone, promising to speak with Maddie about Langdon representing both of them. Langdon tried to offer them breakfast, but they declined and hurried out. Meg looked to be close to breaking down, and Harold wasn't far behind her.

Chabal went off to open the bookstore and man it until noontime when Star came in to replace her. A couple of part-timers would round out the staffing for the day, something that was new in their twenty-plus years of running the business. This was giving them a bit more free time, something cherished over the holidays and enjoyed in the winter months as they took the opportunity for naps during the day, watching movies, and reading books. As of late, they'd grown a bit antsy at so much free time, not quite enough freedom to go away, and mud season in Maine was not the most conducive to outside activities. But, now, with this volatile new case enveloping them, the time was much welcomed.

His phone buzzed with a text from Danny T. Got a guy here at the diner who says he saw your missing man and would tell you about it for the price of breakfast.

On my way.

Langdon had just been contemplating stopping down there for a bit of food and gossip, as this was the center of scuttlebutt in town. He didn't have to call for dog as the canine was already at the front door as if he knew they were on their way to Rosie's. Not that the destination mattered much to dog, Langdon thought, but it was the journey he most enjoyed. The old fellow—he was approaching the decade mark in life—was always up for any adventure. He even loved going to the vet for shots, right up to that point when he was taken into the backroom, and then something kicked in, and he'd try to dig in his heels too late.

It was an easy five-minute drive, down through the center of Brunswick and out to Pleasant Street to the diner. Soon, he'd have to take the back way across, as the summer crowd would come streaming in with their assortment of license plates clogging the roads, their summer-chic bodies filling the stores and the restaurants. Not that Langdon was complaining. It was their custom that carried the bookshop and many other businesses through the rest of the year. But he would utter a sigh of relief when they headed south in September.

Danny T. sat at the counter next to a man with tousled white hair, a sandy-colored and tangled beard, bookending a bright red nose. He had on a parka with tufts of feathers sprouting from it like a field of cotton in bloom.

"Morning, Rosie," Langdon said, sliding into the stool next to the man with Danny T. on the far side. "Can I get the Lumberjack Special and whatever these gentlemen are having?"

"You got it," Rosie said, grabbing a mug and spilling coffee into it. She took breakfast orders from Danny T. and the other men at the counter and stuck the receipt to a board in the doorway to the kitchen.

"Hey, Danny T.," Langdon said across the man in between them.

"You owe me a fin," Danny T. said. "The Sox wiped up the Tigers."

Langdon was expecting that. In the world of Danny T., bets were never forgotten and must be paid up immediately, before anything else could continue. He slid the five-dollar bill across the counter to him.

"This is Graham," Danny T. said. "He's got something to tell you."

"Hello," Langdon said. "I'm Langdon." He held out his hand. The man reached up and took it cautiously.

"Seems to me that what I got to tell you might be more important than just some food," Graham said.

"If what you got helps me out, I'll take care of you," Langdon said. "Have you seen this man?" He laid a full-page glossy of Liam Couture on the counter.

"I seen him."

"Where'd you see him?"

"Down the road toward the highway. Out front of the old-deserted gas station."

"What were you doing there?" Langdon asked.

There was an uncomfortable silence.

"He ain't the police and don't pass judgment," Danny T. said.

"I, uh, bed down back behind it, down the ravine in a little hollow. I was just coming up for the day to go collecting bottles, and a truck with a trailer pulled up, so I hung back in the bushes. You know, sometimes people call the police when they see somebody come out like that, and I didn't want to be rousted from my home, so I just lay low."

Langdon noticed that their food was up, but that Rosie was holding off delivering it while Graham spoke. It was not her first rodeo with Langdon. "What kind of truck was it?"

"Gray. Had a dirt bike in the back. Pulling an empty metal trailer."

Langdon laid a picture of a gray Ford F-150 on the counter. It was not Couture's, as he had no actual picture of the man's truck, but was the same make, model, year, and color. "This the truck?"

"That right enough looks like it."

"You didn't happen to see the license plate, did you?" Langdon asked.

"Had no reason to."

"Did you see the man driving it?"

"It was this feller," Graham said, pressing his finger down on the photograph of Liam Couture.

"You sure?"

Graham snuffled, coughed, and drank some water. "Sure enough."

"Tell him the rest," Danny T. said.

"Is that our food?" Graham asked, pointing at the plates on the kitchen shelf.

Rosie looked at Langdon, who nodded, and she grabbed them and brought them over to sit in front of them. The next ten minutes were spent devouring food with little chance of conversation. Graham's hands were a bit unsteady, leading to some spillage, so he became dog's new best friend as the canine valiantly attempted to catch the bits of food before they even hit the floor.

"What's the rest?" Langdon finally asked as the plates were wiped clean. He'd done his own part in demolishing his breakfast, but there'd been no overflow to benefit dog, who'd made out like a bandit already. "What else did you see?"

"I didn't see him at first," Graham said. "On account of he was sitting so still and hidden on the side of the station. Then I caught a gander of him, and I chilled right to the bone, I did. I'm glad he didn't see me."

There was a lot there to dissect, Langdon thought. He figured the last part to be a good starting point. "Why're you glad he didn't see you?"

Graham shuddered. "There was something real bad coming off him, almost like a smell, but not a smell. You know what I mean?"

Langdon wasn't sure that he did. "Just a feeling, you mean?"

"Nah, worse than that. It was a stink that chilled my bones, it was."

"What'd he look like?"

Graham licked his lips, his eyes, cloaked in fear, drawn inward. "He looked over at where I was in the bushes, and I could swear he knew I was there. His eyes were black like a thunderstorm. I swear I heard screaming and cries, but his lips didn't move, only gave a bit of grin, like we was together in some sort of secret."

"What color was his hair?"

"Black. Like his eyes. He was tall. Real tall."

Langdon stood up. "Taller than me?"

Graham nodded. "Maybe a couple of inches."

"Can you tell me anything else about him?"

"He was dressed all in black. Everything about him was black."

"Then what happened?"

"He walked over to that truck, leaned in the window, and then got in, and they drove off."

"Which way they'd go?"

"Only one way you can go out of there. Towards town. They got over into the left lane right off."

"Anything else?"

"That's it. I figure that should be worth twenty bucks, now, don't you?"

Langdon looked at the man and his red nose and disheveled clothes. "Worth more than that," he said. "Rosie, put whatever Graham wants to eat for the rest of the week on my tab, please and thank you."

"Sure thing, Langdon," Rosie said.

"I'd rather have the cash."

"A week of good food will do you well," Langdon said.

Rosie was one of the good ones. A lot of restaurant owners would turn up their noses at having a homeless man coming in to eat every day. A man who was an eyesore and smelled a bit. But a man. She'd take care of him. And if any of her customers complained, it'd be them that got the boot. She was one of the good ones.

Chapter 9

Jade was the first to show up for the barbecue, bringing a bottle of red wine and a pasta salad that looked delicious. Chabal made the introductions, and Langdon opened the bottle of wine, pouring a glass for each. He figured this to be a good time to pour himself an ample amount of Glenlivet. He allowed himself one before eating and one after, with a glass of wine with the food. With that sort of limitation, it seemed fair enough to be generous with the pour.

Jade was a striking woman with mysterious eyes and hair that tumbled most of the way down her back. Langdon also discovered she was single. He was hoping that 4 by Four brought a date. Otherwise, he'd be fawning over her the entire night, and she'd be wiping drool off her black pants and white flowing blouse in the morning, just like Chabal had said last night.

Bart was the next one in the door, carrying a case of beer, which would be a nice addition for most parties, except for the fact that Bart would be drinking most of it. Langdon went out to start a fire in the pit in the backyard. The yard backed up on the Town Commons and was protected from neighbors on either side by trees. Bart brought a six-pack out and sat down to watch while dog joined in by taking the kindling Langdon piled into the pit and running off with it.

Richam, Jewell, and Raven had arrived and were in the kitchen when Langdon went back in to grab the burgers and dogs for the grill. Raven was Richam's long-lost daughter, with whom he'd recently reconnected and who was now living and working in

Portland. It was a little delicate as she'd been conceived back in the Dominican with an old girlfriend when Richam and Jewell had first gotten together. Everything seemed amicable, though, and Langdon crossed his fingers that it stayed that way.

Jimmy 4 by Four came through the door carrying strawberry shortcake and a bottle of Patrón. He kissed Chabal, fist-bumped Langdon, and poured himself a drink. "Richam, Jewell, long time no see, and I see you brought your ravishing love child."

Langdon went out the back sliding door to the grill and shut the door. That was who they were as a group. They bantered. They fought. No subject seemed to be untouchable, no secret allowed to remain hidden. When Starling arrived after having shut down the bookshop, they sat at the table in the backyard, nine of them crowded around it, and ate. Langdon managed two glasses of wine as they avoided talk of Covid, of politics, and just caught up with each other and what was going on in their lives.

After they ate, the group moved toward the fire as Langdon built up the flames to ward off the increasingly chilly night air. He poured himself a second generous Glenlivet. Raven and Jade seemed to be hitting it off, while 4 by Four had managed a seat on the far side of Raven and next to Jade. Bart and Jewell were engaged in conversation about immigrants, Jewell working for a nonprofit in Portland called CHERISH that helped new immigrants assimilate into Maine life.

As the brown liquor eased down his throat, Langdon felt all the anxieties, pressures, politics, hate, and dissension in the world melt away around him. All the sharp edges that poked and prodded were dulled. There was a warmth embracing him, his wife, and his friends against the chill night air. There was no danger. No missing people. Dog came over and lay his head on Langdon's lap so that he could have his head rubbed. It seemed a fair trade, love for rubs.

"Any luck finding those missing people, Boss?" Starling asked, sipping on a ginger ale. He'd not had a drink in twenty-five years but still looked every bit the alcoholic.

"People?" Richam asked. "You mean you got more than that one missing man?"

"There's a woman gone missing as well," Langdon said. "She came to meet a man in Brunswick for a date and hasn't been seen since."

"Odd stuff," Starling said. "Two people come to Brunswick from somewhere else and go missing within just about a week of each other."

"When did the first one go missing?" Jewell asked from across the fire. This brought other conversation to a standstill.

"A couple of weeks back," Langdon said.

"When exactly?" Jewell asked.

"His brother saw him the morning of April 26th," Langdon said. "He was on his way to Brunswick. That was the last person who saw him." He didn't want to complicate the conversation with the sighting by Graham, the homeless man, of Couture in the deserted gas station.

"The night of the supermoon," Jewell said.

"What?" 4 by Four asked. "I mean, what is a supermoon?"

"A full moon when it is at its closest point to Earth," Raven said. "April 26th was a Pink Moon *and* a supermoon."

"Why's it called a Pink Moon?" Bart asked.

"It was named by Native Americans," Jade said, "after a particular plant that would bloom pink in April, about the same time as the full moon in that month."

"Well, I'll be a monkey's uncle," Starling said. "Seems we got us a bunch of astrologists here."

"You're getting off-topic," Jewell said. "You're looking for a man who went missing the day of the Pink Supermoon, and now you got a woman missing as well?"

"That's about it," Langdon said.

"Because you got another supermoon coming this month," Jewell said. "And not just any old supermoon. This is going to be the Super Flower Blood Moon."

"Holy cow," 4 by Four said sarcastically. "Not the Flower Blood Supermoon?"

"The Super Flower Blood Moon," Jewell corrected, ignoring 4 by Four, "is a cosmic phenomenon when there is a lunar eclipse. Due to the positioning of earth between the sun and the moon, the rays from the sun are refracted and filtered through the atmosphere, giving the moon a red, or scarlet, glow."

"That sounds pretty cool," 4 by Four said.

"But what does it have to do with the missing people?" Langdon asked. He sensed there was a tangent here.

"This might be quite a stretch," Jewell said. She looked up in the sky like the answer might lie in the cosmos.

"What?" Langdon asked.

"You ever hear of the Church of Satan?" Jewell asked.

There was silence around the fire. The flames danced and flickered, casting shadows in the black May night. Langdon took the bottle from Richam and poured himself another glass of brown liquor, neat this time. No less generous. This vein of conversation deserved a third drink of the brown liquor.

After a bit, Jewell cleared her throat. "It was started back in 1966 by a guy named LaVey. They believe that Man's true nature is that of a carnal beast who lives in a cosmos that doesn't care about his—our—existence. They don't believe in God or Satan, but rather that Satan represents the true nature of who Man is. LaVey believed that Man cannot accept his own ego, so a group of people invented God to filter that rawness, and therefore, the worship of God is really the idolization of those creators of God."

"That's pretty messed up," Richam said. "Where'd you hear about all that stuff, honey?"

"You know I get into all those religious sects," Jewell said. "Voodoo, Hoodoo, Santeria—alternate religions and all."

"Some of those make sense," Richam said. "I'm not sure about worshiping Satan."

"To this church's worshippers, Satan is just a symbol of the true nature of Man," Jewell said. "But that's not the point. To spread their message in the 1970s, they started what they called a Grotto system. Like missionaries, men and women would go out and start offshoots of the Church of Satan. They'd develop cabals that would grow independently and follow their own paths. This became a problem, and this system was abolished, and all Grottos were disavowed."

"There was one of these in Brunswick?" Langdon asked.

"Durham, actually," Jewell said. Durham was a rural community next to Brunswick.

"I've never heard of them," Bart said. "You'd think the police would know if there was a local chapter of the Church of Satan in the area."

"It's not got anything to do with the Church of Satan," Jewell said. "They were like a radical offshoot, sort of like... well, Dennis Rader of the Christian community."

"Dennis Rader?" Chabal asked.

"The BTK serial killer," Bart said. "A good Christian, he claimed, who was possessed by demons causing him to bind, torture, and kill his victims."

"Basically, you're saying that this Grotto was too messed up even for the Church of Satan?" Langdon asked.

"Still doesn't explain why I haven't heard of 'em," Bart muttered. "Sounds more like an old wives' tale than anything real."

"Like I said, they supposedly disbanded in the 1970s," Jewell said. "But I've heard rumors that they continued. Their numbers dwindled, but those that stuck became even more extreme. They went beyond many of the tenets of the Church of Satan and melded their beliefs with some of the more extreme and radical beliefs of Voodoo. Not the real Voodoo, but the crazy-ass radicals that run around engaging in strange rituals while sacrificing cows and sheep and horses to their gods."

"Rumors from who?" Chabal asked.

"An elderly lady I work with at CHERISH told me most of it. Don't know where she heard it," Jewell said.

"Like I said," Bart said. "Old wives' tales."

"There's more to this world than you'll ever understand," Jewell said.

"And this has what to do with supermoons?" Langdon asked. This all seemed far-fetched, he thought, but his mind was engulfed with the darkness of the possibility.

"I heard once that this group had come to worship the supermoon as a symbol of the power of man," Jewell said in a muted voice. "It stands to reason that if they still exist, are batshit crazy, and worship Satan, well then, they might make sacrifices at the time of the supermoon."

"Human sacrifices," Raven said.

The dancing fire had grown cold. Langdon poured himself another tall glass of scotch. This didn't help in warming his bones or calming his soul. He looked up to see what sort of moon there was on this night and saw only blackness, with not a star to be seen. A wind had picked up, rustling through the woods of the Town Commons and assaulting the fire. Dog whined low in his throat. A coyote howled from the forest. Langdon let the blackness envelop him in its embrace, giving in to the darkness.

Chapter 10

Langdon and Chabal worked the bookshop on Sunday, and after the late-night barbecue on Saturday, returned home exhausted. They'd done little more than make a frozen pizza to eat, drink copious amounts of water, and tumble into bed early. Langdon had conscripted the two part-timers for more hours the next week, freeing up time for the case.

Thus, it was 5:00 a.m. when Langdon eased from bed and slid out the door. Dog had been banished to sleep in the living room as he often jumped up on their bed and wanted to wrestle periodically throughout the night. He was happy to greet Langdon with a butt-wagging, tail-shaking good morning. It turned out that dog was also down with eating his breakfast earlier than normal.

When Chabal found him at his desk a little after seven, Langdon was already knee-deep in research on the Church of Satan. He thought the whole thing was a bit far-fetched, but his mind wouldn't let it go. The more he dug into it, the more he wondered.

"Their principles aren't all that bad, for a place called the Church of Satan, anyway," he said.

Chabal sat down at her desk, next to his, in the living room. Since the kids had moved out, this certainly seemed the best place to work. If one of them wanted to watch television, the other put headphones on while they worked.

"Yeah," she said. "How so?"

"A list of adages that are common sense," Langdon said. "Such as, do not give opinions or advice unless you are asked."

"I wasn't about to," Chabal said.

"No, that was…" Langdon stopped himself as he saw the wicked gleam in his wife's eyes, suggesting she was messing with him. "That's number one on their Eleven Satanic Rules of the Earth."

"So they're the Mother Teresa for the Devil?"

Langdon snorted. "They're not much for turning the other cheek. If you have a guest in your house who annoys you, treat them harshly and without mercy."

"Sounds like they don't flinch from conflict. You know, when your brothers were here over Christmas, and they brought those two women back and were making noise until the sun rose? I certainly could've treated them a bit more harshly and without mercy." Chabal laughed, reveling in the thought.

Langdon chuckled. "Lord and Nicky are the salt of the earth, but I don't think they ever made it out of their teenage years." They were his younger twin brothers who, approaching fifty years old, lived together and partied like they were still nineteen.

"Of course, saving our lives on more than one occasion, I guess, gives them some leeway," Chabal said.

"Rule number eleven," Langdon said. "When walking in open territory, bother no one. If someone bothers you, ask him to stop. If he does not stop, destroy him."

Chabal logged into her computer. "Still, it doesn't sound like these tenets encourage you to lure unsuspecting strangers to your lair and then… what… kill them? Hold them hostage? Where do you suppose Liam Couture and Annie Brown are right now?"

"That's the million-dollar question."

"Did you see the Nine Satanic Sins?" Chabal asked, browsing through the site. "It sounds like the platform for our last president. Don't believe the media. Avoid herd mentality. It's kinda like that ideal of the only real truth coming from one mouth."

"Yeah, I read about that. But the fact is, it seems the Church of

Satan is against hurting others unless it is deemed necessary. They don't actually believe in Satan. The Devil is just symbolic of pride, individualism, and liberty. If anything, they worship themselves as supreme beings."

"Well, Jewell said that there was a Grotto back in the 1970s here in Durham that may've developed more radical beliefs. You find anything on them?"

"Not yet. Been poring over the original Church of Satan."

"I'll see what I can find."

"You hungry?" Langdon asked.

"What do you think?"

"Potatoes with leftover hamburger, hot dogs, onions, and cheese with eggs spilled over the top sound good to you?"

"I'll research Satan, and you make me happy," Chabal said.

"Might find some strange stuff if you search those two things together," Langdon said.

"Ha," Chabal said. "Go make me food."

In the kitchen, Langdon cut and tossed the potatoes in, slowly sprinkling in the leftovers and other ingredients as he finished his coffee. He wasn't sure that this whole Church of Satan sounded like such a bad deal. Don't bother others unless they bother you. And when bothered? Finish it. Made a lot of sense to him. A lot of modern religions labeled pleasurable activities as sins. Why? Heck, the Church of Satan was okay with homosexuality, whereas too much of Christianity wasn't.

Langdon texted Bart to see if he was free at some point for a confab, and then he carried two plates of potato surprise into the living room and set them down on their desks. This family moniker for the simple meal originated in the fact that there was often a leftover surprise lying within the concoction. Chabal was happy with her coffee, but he went back for an orange juice.

"Check this out," Chabal said. "I found a news report from 1972 in which the establishment of the Wendigo Grotto of the Church of

Satan was announced in Durham, and all were invited to join the brethren."

"Wendigo? I've heard that name before."

Dog started barking, followed by a knock on the door, and Starling stuck his head in the doorway. "Anybody home?"

"Come on in, Star. You want some breakfast or coffee?"

"No, I'm good." Starling bustled into the room, fending off dog, who thought he most certainly was playing some game that involved getting past the canine. "I got to thinking about the two missing people the other night when I got home. Jewell was talking about the supermoons, but then she veered off into that whole Church of Satan business. I got to thinking, what the heck does the moon have to do with anything?"

"Yeah, what do we have coming?" Langdon asked. "The Flower Barbie Moon or something like that?"

Chabal snickered. "That might be the scariest one of them all."

Star did not crack the smallest smile. "The Super Flower Blood Moon."

"That does sound pretty ominous," Langdon said.

"I got to thinking, you know, that the guy, Liam, disappears the day of the Pink Supermoon, and now, a few weeks before the second supermoon in as many months, the woman, Annie Brown, comes up missing. What if they weren't the first?"

"Whoa," Chabal said.

"So, I spent the night, all day yesterday, and most of last night digging into missing persons." Starling's red eyes attested to the fact that he had indeed hardly slept and had spent the time in front of a screen, or else, he might have come crashing off the wagon in terrible fashion. "And I have nine more."

"Nine more?" Langdon said.

"Nine more what?" Chabal said.

"Nine more people who have disappeared during months with supermoons who live within a six-hour drive of Brunswick. And that's only going back ten years."

"Thousands of people are reported missing every year," Langdon said.

"Hundreds of thousands," Starling said. "But most disappearances get resolved in the first year. Dead or found. But I'm talking about the unsolved ones. I found this site NamUs. The National Missing and Unidentified Person System. I cross-checked it with the register... Okay, never mind that. Don't forget I'm an old lawyer with a few tricks up my sleeves. Anyway, the nine I found all have some connection to Brunswick. Had a relative here. A boyfriend. One went to Bowdoin. And they all disappeared around the time of supermoons. Never to be seen or heard from again. And these people aren't the average run-of-the-mill missing persons. They're not homeless, addicted to drugs, depressed—I mean, they might be, but there were no outward signs of any of this."

"Nine unsolved missing person cases with ties to Brunswick," Langdon said slowly.

"That I've been able to find so far," Starling said.

"That occurred around the time of supermoons," Chabal said.

"What you're saying is that there is somebody in Brunswick luring people here routinely when the moon is full and at its closest point to Earth and then killing them for some reason."

"One would assume that they're killing them," Starling said. "But no bodies have ever been found. Maybe they're selling them into some sort of slavery thing."

"And it might be more than one killer," Chabal said. "If this thing about the Wendigo Grotto of the Church of Satan is still in existence."

"The Wendigo Grotto?" Starling asked.

Dog started barking, followed by Bart coming through the front door without knocking. "Whose truck is out there?" he asked. "I bashed into the back end and mashed it up pretty good."

Starling didn't rise to the bait. Bart often tried to get his goat regarding his pride and joy. He'd bought the 1966 Ford F-100 Ranger

Styleside a bit over ten years earlier and taken most of that time restoring it to near-mint condition right down to the "Twin I-Beam" emblem on the front fender.

Langdon and Chabal brought both of them up to speed on what they'd found out about the Church of Satan and its offshoot, the Wendigo Grotto.

"The Berwick police had a sit down with Donna Reed," Bart said. "Got her to confirm that her credit card was used to pay for the *Cousin Freddie's* advertisement."

"The nephew, Gregory Popa, seemed awful skittish when I was talking to him," Langdon said. "He seems to be our best lead."

"Yeah?" Chabal said. "Why the heck would he lift his aunt's credit card to lure somebody to abduct and possibly kill them? Is he that stupid?"

"Criminals generally aren't the brightest bulbs on the planet," Bart said. "To be honest, it's not very hard to get away with most crimes. Luckily, most of them are that stupid."

"That you know of, anyway," Langdon said. "It's sort of like the people who go around saying they never wore a seatbelt as a kid, and they're still alive."

"Duh," Chabal said. "Those that die have a hard time speaking up."

"But maybe Popa is one of the dumb ones. Or maybe he didn't know what it was going to be used for, eventually."

"He have any tattoos?" Chabal asked. "Say, something like a 666 on his forehead?"

Langdon chuckled. "No. Didn't see any horns or a tail either. But there was something off about him."

"I can stop by his office and see if I can shake him up," Bart said.

"When?" Langdon asked.

Bart shrugged. "His office is on Bank Street? I can go over there now."

"No chance at a tap on his phone?" Langdon asked, even though he knew the answer.

"Ha. Fat chance on that based only on the fact that his aunt's credit card was used to place an ad," Bart said. "Gonna need a little more than that."

"How about I come over and keep a watch on him," Langdon said. "Maybe if you rattle his cage a bit, he'll lead us to Liam."

"Or Annie," Chabal said.

"Not a bad idea," Bart said. "Though I wouldn't hold my breath that either one of them is alive."

Langdon's phone rang. He looked at the screen. "It's 4 by Four," he said, holding up a finger. "Good morning, counselor."

"Yes, it is. And about to get better. I got your name."

"From the Patience profile?" Langdon asked. "That was quick. What magic did you use?"

"I know how to bend an arm right to the breaking point," 4 by Four said, sounding very smug. "I even got myself a free trial profile."

Langdon chuckled. "Good for you. Thought you were already on it?"

"My membership had lapsed."

"Okay, let's have it, the name, not your personal listing."

"Tom Corbett. Lives out to Mere Point. Some kind of doctor at Mid Coast Hospital."

"A doctor, huh?" Langdon contemplated the irony of their potential killer being a doctor. "Send me the info. I owe you big time."

"How about you put a good word in for me with Chabal's new friend, Jade?"

Langdon stole a sideways glance at his wife. She wouldn't much like that. "I'll see what I can do. Send me what you got." He hung up.

"That man is a magician," Star said. "Hard to believe that he cracked the privacy policy of a dating site that quickly."

"Who's our Romeo?" Chabal asked.

"Doctor over at Mid Coast," Langdon said. "Tom Corbett."

"Two leads," Star said. "This thing is breaking wide open."

"I'll swing by there first," Bart said. "See what he has to say."

"No," Langdon said slowly. "Probably not the best of ideas. Officially, the police don't have his name. Anything comes of this, it could taint your case. How about I go have a chat with him? See what he's got to say."

"Who's going to stake out the Popa guy?" Chabal asked.

"I'm in at the bookstore from noon to close," Starling said.

They all looked at Chabal. "Great. I got nothing better to do than sit in the parking lot across from some accountant's office. Probably can't even drink coffee as it'll make me pee."

Chapter 11

"That's one strange dude," Bart said into the phone to Chabal.

She'd just watched him walk out of the accounting office of Gregory Popa. She was sitting in the all-day parking lot just off Maine Street and facing Bank Street. "Yeah, I saw a picture. He kinda looks like a vampire, doesn't he?" she said.

Bart guffawed. "That he does. And just as smooth."

Chabal wondered whether vampires were smooth or not. Not being much of a horror fan, her only real knowledge was from Count von Count on Sesame Street. That and the odd Anne Rice novel years back. She supposed he was pretty smooth. "He confess to abducting and killing a slew of people over the past so many years?"

"Not so much."

"You want to come take a seat and fill me in?"

"I don't want him to see me chatting with you," Bart said. "That'd kinda blow your cover, so I'm going to go around the corner to Federal Street."

Chabal watched as the patrol car drove off. "You don't need to hang around," she said into the phone. "I can keep an eye on him."

"I'll wait around a few minutes in case he goes right out," Bart said. "That'd be a red flag for sure."

"Whatever floats your boat," she said. "I take it he did *not* confess?"

"He was a little squirrelly, but that happens a lot when I pop in to see somebody unexpectedly. Especially when I'm wearing the blue." Bart had suffered his most recent demotion the fall before for pushing the boundaries of accepted procedure, putting him back in uniform.

"Okay," Chabal said. "I'll give you a call if he goes on the move."

"That sounds like a line right out of a movie."

"I'll be back," Chabal said in her deepest voice which was not very deep at all. "To you if he moves."

She hung up the phone and resumed the boring world of a stakeout. Luckily, this lasted only about an hour. At five minutes past noon, Gregory Popa came out and looked left and right before striding toward Maine Street in a loping gait.

Chabal had already scoped out his car, license plate supplied by Bart, in the next row over from where she was parked. She quickly slid out of her own vehicle and scurried after him. He'd crossed over Maine Street and was disappearing down Lincoln as she wended her way across that busy street of four lanes of traffic. Luckily, everybody stopped as she rushed across, it not yet being summer tourist season.

She'd at first thought that it most likely that Popa was merely going out for lunch, but as he crossed over Union Street and continued on, the choices of food grew almost nonexistent. And he was most definitely walking with purpose.

~ ~ ~ ~ ~

Tom Corbett was a long gangling fellow with black hair and a face flat as a skateboard. Langdon had looked him up, finding that he was also one of the premier plastic surgeons in all of New England. His office and practice were just off Cook's Corner, about a mile from the hospital. Langdon had called and gotten an appointment. He'd been told that the doctor could spare him twenty minutes, no more.

Corbett was associated with Mid Coast Hospital in that he was their go-to surgeon for breast reconstruction after cancer or accident. His real money maker, though, seemed to be what he called the 'Mommy Makeover,' which was a tummy tuck and breast augmentation all in one fell swoop for twelve to fifteen grand, depending on the size and type of boobs the woman wanted. These tucks and enhancements were done in one of his two on-site operating rooms.

As Langdon walked in, he made up his mind that if he saw anybody he knew, he'd just say that he was Christmas shopping for Chabal. He figured if he could do it with a straight face, that that would create quite the stir on the gossip highway of Brunswick. Unfortunately, or fortunately, he didn't see anybody he knew.

The receptionist was a young woman with a very serious expression who told him to have a seat and that Dr. Corbett would be with him as soon as he was free. Langdon wondered if he was tucking or augmenting. He smiled wryly to himself and thought that perhaps it was time to stop acting so juvenile.

After fifteen minutes of checking his social media accounts, a nurse in an actual white outfit beckoned him from a doorway leading to the back. He was shown into an office and not an operating room, where Corbett was seated at a computer. Langdon stood awkwardly for a minute until the man stood and turned, holding out his hand, a bony talon that felt brittle.

"Dr. Tom Corbett."

"Langdon."

The doctor eyed him strangely. He sat back down and motioned Langdon to do the same. "What can I do for you... Langdon?"

"I'm a PI in town here, and I've been hired to find a missing woman."

"What does that have to do... oh, is she one of my previous works?"

It was Langdon's turn to eye the doctor strangely. "By that, you mean a patient who you worked on?"

Corbett waved his hand impatiently. "I see each one as a piece of art that I've created."

"I see."

"Oh, my." Corbett put his skeletal hand over his mouth. "Has she died? Are you here to identify a body?"

"Has who died?" Langdon's ears perked up.

"One of my girls. Are you here because you have a body you can't identify but you have a lot and serial number?"

"A lot and serial number?"

"Every breast implant has two numbers on it, the lot number and the serial number, in order to more quickly identify a bad batch of implants, if the need were to arise. Not that it ever has, mind you."

"No, there is no dead body," Langdon said. "As I said, the woman is missing."

"What woman?"

"The woman who met you for dinner last Sunday night."

"A woman? Dinner? What the hell are you talking about?"

"Yes." Langdon watched the man's face intently. There'd been no sign of recognition, nothing but the confusion that matched his words. "Annie Brown."

"What the hell are you talking about? I'm a married man, and I sure as hell don't know any woman by the name of Annie Brown."

Langdon noted that he hadn't said happily married. He wasn't sure if the omission was more or less damning to his denial. "You met her on Patience."

"Patience? You are *testing* my patience. I have actual patients to see. I'll have to ask you to leave."

Langdon didn't budge. That was a pretty good line, he thought, almost like it'd been rehearsed. "Do you deny meeting Annie Brown on the dating site called Patience?"

Corbett stood up and Langdon noted again how tall the man was. Easily several inches taller than his own six-foot-four-inch height, but at the same time, probably weighed less. It was not that Langdon was overweight—okay, maybe a few pounds—but this man was rail thin.

"I told you that I was married. I do not, therefore, frequent dating sites."

Langdon stood as well with his phone facing Corbett. "Do you deny this is you?" He had a screenshot of Corbett's profile information.

The doctor took the phone, enlarged the screen with two fingers, and slowly his face went from anger to confusion. "No. This is me. What sort of game are you playing?"

"No game. I'm searching for a missing woman. Annie Brown. She was last seen right before coming to Brunswick to meet you at Sugar Magnolia's. After the two of you met on this dating site. Did you meet her for dinner or not, Mr. Corbett?" Langdon deliberately didn't refer to the man as 'doctor' to see if that raised his ire.

"And I told you that I'm married."

"You wouldn't be the first man to have an affair." Langdon thought of the many cases where he'd been hired to find proof of a cheating spouse. This was the first time that the target of the cheating spouse's affections had come up missing, though.

"I didn't… I do not know this Annie Brown girl, I've never signed up for a dating site in my life, and I don't lie to my wife."

For the first time, Langdon noticed a tic in the corner of Corbett's eye, just a flicker, but enough to suggest that this last part might be a lie. "Yet, there you are, with all of your particulars, on their site. They have confirmed your identity, and your credit card was used."

"That's a lie," Corbett said. His face suddenly flashed to a smile and his voice turned triumphant. "What card did they say I used? I check my accounts every few days, and I can assure you that there was no charge for a dating site named Patience."

4 by Four had emailed Langdon the particulars, including the profile, as well as the payment information. He took his phone back from Corbett and navigated back to the email. "MasterCard ending in 6385," he said.

Corbett sat down and swiveled back to his computer, his fingers clawing at the keyboard. After just a few seconds, he turned back to Langdon. "As you can see, there are no charges at all for Patience."

He nodded at the screen where his recent purchases were listed.

Langdon stepped up to him, his eyes scrolling down the list. He pointed his finger midway down. "What is that charge for $29.99?"

"Lifestyle Moderation?" Corbett clicked on the link. "I'm not sure."

An address and phone number came up. "I believe that often these dating sites don't post their real name on the credit card statement," Langdon said. "In case your spouse sees it." He dialed the number and then handed the phone to Corbett.

The doctor's face turned ashen. "Patience Dating Service, doing business as Lifestyle Moderation," he said, handing the phone back to Langdon, who hung up.

"Is there something you want to tell me... Dr. Corbett?" Langdon asked.

"I didn't do this."

"Pretty black and white if you ask me. You have a profile on Patience. You meet Annie Brown for dinner. Something goes wrong. Maybe she finds out about your wife and threatens to tell her? Whatever, things go wrong. Did you kill her?"

Corbett looked up at Langdon, his long-lean face desperate. "I didn't... My card must've been hacked. I've got to cancel it."

"You're telling me that somebody hacked your card just to sign you up for a dating service," Langdon asked. "Seems pretty far-fetched to me." But it didn't, he thought grimly. First, Donna Reed had her card number stolen so someone could place an ad in *Cousin Freddie's*, and Liam Couture came up missing. And now, Tom Corbett may have had his card number borrowed to sign up for a dating service, and Annie Brown disappeared into thin air. It seemed much more like part of a pattern than a lie.

~ ~ ~ ~ ~

"That's where he went?" Langdon asked. He and Chabal were sitting in his Jeep on Swett Street, a short crook of road that housed a slew of rundown homes converted to apartments.

"Around back," Chabal said. "The house is broken up into eight units now. Four up, four down. Popa went in number 27, ground floor, left side. Bart says that the name of the renter is Dwayne Bates. Been arrested a few times for dealing heroin."

"You think he graduated from dealing drugs to abducting people?" Langdon asked.

Chabal shrugged. "Maybe Liam and Annie were clients. Maybe they got bad batches and OD'd. Maybe they tried to stiff him."

"What's Bart say?"

"He said it'd be no problem to run him into the station for questioning. Thought maybe we'd have better luck getting answers. To quote our friend Bart, 'that fucking lowlife ain't gonna say a thing to a cop.' Seems they're on a first-name basis with each other, sort of like the married couple who have hallway sex."

Langdon chuckled. The punch line of that particular joke was that, when the couple pass each other in the hallway, they say 'fuck you' to each other. "You think we should get our gats before we go in and brace the perp?" he asked in his best Sam Spade voice.

Chabal shook her head. "You know, I've been thinking. You might look more like what Dashiell Hammett envisioned for Spade than Bogart did, him being slight of frame and dark featured. But you can't do Bogie's voice worth a lick."

"Yeah, so all the ladies tell me. Better looking but don't sound a bit like him."

"I didn't say better looking."

"Maybe you're not one of 'all the ladies.'"

"I'm the one and *only* lady in *your* life."

"Are you saying you don't think we need pistols?"

"Probably safer without them."

Langdon chuckled again. "How about dog? Should we bring man's best friend to watch our backs?"

Chabal looked over her shoulder at dog happily sticking his head out the window, eyes intent upon a squirrel clambering around in a tree. "Best not. He doesn't much care for heroin dealers."

Langdon opened the door and got out. "He tell you that?"

"Yep. Said they smell funny."

"Fair enough." They crossed over the street to the white colonial now broken into eight residences.

"We have a plan here?" Chabal asked.

"Figured we'd go knock on the door and ask Dwayne Bates if he knows Liam Couture or Annie Brown."

Chabal snickered. "Brilliant. I can tell you went to PI school."

"More often than not, the simplest solution is the correct solution."

"They taught you about Occam's Razor at PI school as well? Will wonders never cease?"

There was trash littered across the backyard. A forlorn bicycle lay rusting against the house. There was a blue kiddie pool now filled with machine parts. A swing set backed up to a scattering of trees, chains hanging down with no swings. Cigarette butts littered the ground.

Langdon rang the bell of number 27. He didn't hear it ring, so he knocked. After a bit, he knocked again.

The door was jerked open by a bare-chested man with a scraggly beard and tattoos lining his torso. "What do you want?" he asked.

"Are you Dwayne Bates?" Langdon asked.

"Depends on who the fuck is asking."

"My name is Langdon. I'm looking for two people who I think you may know."

"I highly fucking doubt that, man. Get the fuck out of here."

Dwayne went to close the door, but Langdon stopped it with his foot and forearm. "It would be in your best interest to talk with us."

"Fuck you, man." Dwayne reached back into the waistband of his jeans and produced a pistol, a short and ugly piece of business.

Langdon didn't wait to see what his intentions were as he reacted by grabbing the man's wrist with his left hand and slamming him in the face with a short-right jab that still packed a good pop, enough to make Dwayne's eyes water and his nose to sprout crimson. This allowed Langdon to disengage his grip from the pistol and hand it to Chabal, who casually pointed it at the bleeding Dwayne Bates.

"Maybe we should talk inside?" Langdon said, pushing his way into the apartment.

"What the fuck, man?" Dwayne whined. "You busted my nose."

"Nah," Langdon said. "Still looks pretty straight to me."

The living room was surprisingly neat. Langdon had expected it to be a mess. Instead, there was an expensive leather couch, several plush-looking armchairs, and a huge screen television set amidst what was a very tidy room.

"Tell me about Liam Couture and Annie Brown?" Langdon said.

"Let me get a paper towel and ice for my nose, man, and then we can talk."

Langdon walked with him into the small kitchen and let him rinse his face, put pressure on his nose and tilt his head back, and then, finally, wrap some ice in a tea towel—yes, the man had tea towels—and cover his rapidly swelling schnoz.

"Who are you?" Dwayne asked once they were seated in the living room.

"Name is Langdon. This is my wife, Chabal."

"More like Bonnie and Clyde, if you ask me," Dwayne said.

"I like that," Chabal said.

"They were villains," Langdon said. "I'd have to say we're more like Nick and Nora Charles."

"Wasn't Nick supposed to be short and fat?" Chabal asked. "I mean, before the moving pictures came along and made him all handsome."

"I'm just saying they were a duo, you know, husband and wife team. He was a PI. She was a rich heiress."

"Mm. I like the thought of being a rich heiress," Chabal said. "But if I had money, why would I marry a short fat PI? I mean, if I—."

"What the fuck are you two blabbing about?" Dwayne asked. "You wanna tell me what you're doing here and why you busted up my face?"

Langdon looked back at the bare-chested, scraggly-faced man. "I told you. We're looking for two people. Liam Couture and Annie Brown. And I'm sorry about your face, but to be fair, you pulled a gun. It seemed prudent at the time."

Chabal snickered.

"I don't know nobody with those names," Dwayne said, a tinge of defiance returning to his voice.

Langdon stared hard at the man. "How about Gregory Popa."

Dwayne nervously licked his lips and scratched his ear. "Nope."

"Funny thing about that is that he was just here, not much more than an hour ago. That means you're lying to me." Langdon turned to Chabal. "Shoot him," he said.

"What the fuck, man! Don't be shooting anybody!"

Langdon chuckled. "I'm just messing with you. We're not going to shoot you." He paused, pursed his lips, his eyes on the ceiling as if considering something. "Not unless we have to, that is."

"I don't know no guy named Popa, okay?"

"You have a license for that pistol in my wife's hand?" Langdon asked. "Having a record and all, I doubt very much that you do. I'm also betting that you have illegal drugs here. What if I was to tell you that the police would be very interested in any excuse to come in and search your humble abode."

Dwayne squirmed in his chair. "You're talking about Greg. I don't know his last name, but he was here about an hour ago. What about him?"

"Ah, progress," Langdon said. "How do you know him? I mean, he comes to visit your home, and you don't even know his last name. What sort of relationship do you have?"

"Relationship?"

Langdon shrugged. "Yeah, tell me what he comes over for. Sex? Drugs? To dispose of dead bodies?"

"Sex?" Dwayne seemed most concerned that Langdon had suggested he was having sexual intercourse with Popa, more so than selling him drugs… or burying corpses.

Langdon decided to read the question the wrong way. "So, you say he comes over for sex. Chabal said he was only here for—how long was it?"

"About fifteen minutes," Chabal said.

"That's pretty quick. Boom-bang, pop goes the weasel. I'm impressed with—"

"I'm not some queer," Dwayne said. "He buys heroin from me, okay?"

"Oh, my," Langdon said. "That sounds quite illegal."

Dwayne stared at him sullenly.

"And you don't know anything about two missing people?" Chabal asked.

"No. I never heard those two names in my life. Honest Injun."

"What does that mean?" Langdon asked.

"Mean? What?"

"Honest Injun. Other than being offensive, are you saying you're telling the truth?"

"I don't know no two missing people, and I don't know who those people are, is all I'm saying."

"How often does Gregory buy heroin from you?" Chabal asked.

Dwayne rubbed his face in his hands. "Couple times a month. Just enough to shoot up. That's all. Like I said, I didn't even know his last name. Most of my business is everyday users. Bit strange to only shoot up a couple times a month. Not many people can control it that well. But he is a bit of an odd duck."

Langdon stood up. "We might need your help again, Dwayne. Don't tell Greg that we stopped by. You keep your mouth shut, and we'll do the same. You won't have to worry about the police descending on your little operation here, not as long as you play ball with us. Understand?"

Dwayne nodded his head. "Can I get my pistol back?"

Langdon shook his head. "Don't think that would be a good idea, considering the circumstances." He gestured for Chabal to precede him out the door. They walked outside with the eyes of Dwayne Bates following them intently.

"What do you think?" Chabal asked.

"I'd say he's a heroin dealer. And I don't think he knows squat about Liam or Annie."

"Or Popa, really," Chabal said. "You were pretty badass, though. I don't know that I've ever known you to come out on top in a fight."

"Oh, come on. How about with that fellow named Shakespeare?"

"The one who shot you in the head and put you in a coma?"

Chapter 12

There was little difference between sleep and wakefulness for Annie Brown. It was all a nightmare. In her dreams, the Dark Age ran rampant, the Overlord always threatening, lurking, growing closer, growling at the edges of her consciousness. Awake, she lived in fear of the same, but now it was the Wendigo, a sneaking terror filling her innards.

The only good moments were the few minutes before she opened her eyes, transferring from sleep to woke, a brief respite from nightmare to reality. She started with her replacement of the deeply horrific emotion that she seemed to revisit every time she fell asleep.

In place of the Overlord, she constructed the smiling and rosy face of Mama Brown. It was like loading an image on a computer that was temporarily fuzzy and gradually came into focus as she added pixel after pixel. In this instance, her mother was in the kitchen baking chocolate cookies while Annie waited to lick batter from the mixer. Jazz music played in the background, which Mama hummed along with, swaying to the notes as she baked.

Once Annie had licked the mixer clean, she moved on to Papa Brown. Today, she chose him taking her to ballet class, especially because he was one of the few parents who stayed and watched. Annie was at the barre, doing her warm-up exercises and stealing glances at Papa, who sat there smiling the entire time, never taking his eyes off her. It gave her such confidence and allowed her to dance like a butterfly. Whether she was up on her toes in Pointe, leaping in the Grande Jetée, or spinning in Pirouette, Annie could feel the warmth of his eyes and beaming smile enveloping her in love.

Today, Annie added a third memory, that of Melissa, her college sophomore roommate and her first lover. They'd both been shy and timid and found themselves rooming together, as they had few friends, a seemingly random choice that had blossomed into something more. It started with sharing their secrets, pulling them together, moved to flirtations, lingering looks, and touching. Eventually, they were sharing a bed. At the end of that year, Melissa transferred to another college, and Annie became aware that she was more attracted to men. Not that she didn't occasionally get a tingle down there when seeing a stunning female. She just hadn't acted on it since that one glorious year with Melissa. They stayed in contact for a few years, and then, that, too, had faded away.

"Why do you always smile when you wake up, Pumpkin Pie?" he asked.

Mama, Papa, and Melissa dissipated in an instant. Annie opened her eyes to see the man standing there. He was the Overlord of her nightmares. What had previously been an unrecognizable figure in her sleeping mind, one that she knew must've been her biological father, had been replaced with this man who'd taken her. The Overlord she now knew as the Wendigo.

And he was more evil than the Overlord by far. He'd shared in great detail the things that were going to happen to Annie. And it was not very pleasant. He reveled in watching her face as he laid out scene by explicit scene how she would die, and possibly worse, what would happen to her both before and after.

"Because I've experienced love in my life," Annie said.

The last few days, it was he who lurked in her nightmares, becoming bolder and bolder with each passing night. It was as if the Overlord and the Wendigo had merged into one being, or so Annie had concluded.

"That is Satan, you know," he said. "As he represents our vital existence instead of spiritual mumbo-jumbo."

"Have you ever loved anyone?"

His dark eyes flashed, and he grinned, showcasing wide, white teeth. "I love myself and am, in turn, loved." He unstrapped her from the round tabletop, handing her the monk's robe to cover her nudity, and stepped back.

Annie pulled the robe over her head and pulled the drawstring around her waist, which was already slimming under the ordeal. He put the collar attached to the leash around her neck. She judged she'd been here about a week. Each morning the Overlord came into the barn and released her from her shackled bedtime. She'd eat a bit of the oatmeal he brought, and then they'd go for the daily walk around the quarry.

Annie was surprised this morning by bacon, eggs, and potatoes. She looked up with a question on her face.

He gave her his wicked grin. "I've noticed that you've lost some weight. We'd like to keep you plump."

As his meaning sank in, she stepped toward him and clawed at his face, but before her nails reached him, he jerked the leash down, and she went crashing to the floor, her face slamming into the wide oak boards. Annie bit her tongue and tasted blood in her mouth. She spit a string of red onto the wooden floor and rolled over on her back.

"Why?" she asked.

"Why what, Pumpkin Pie?"

"Why don't you just kill me and then do what you will? Why must you taunt me?"

"I'm just being honest with you. You wondered why your meal had increased, I told you. How can we be friends if we're not honest with each other?"

"I don't want to be your goddamn friend," Annie said, trying her best to control her voice. "I'm not your friend. I hate you. You've abducted me, held me hostage, tortured me. You're going to kill me and then eat me. How the hell do you think we could ever be friends?"

"We must be friends if we're to spend all of eternity together."

Annie checked her angry reply. She had to be smart. If she could overcome the Overlord in her dreams, surely she could escape the Wendigo in waking; she just had to use her wits. A faint memory suggested that she'd experienced this same thought before, but then it was gone, like a fleeting shadow on a summer day.

"How is it that we will spend all of eternity together?" she asked evenly. "Just to be clear."

"Come." He yanked her to her feet, the collar cutting into her throat. She allowed herself to be seated at the small table that held her breakfast. For such a thin man, he was surprisingly strong.

"Tell me how we'll be one as I eat," she said.

"Good, you have decided to be smart. I like that." He grinned wickedly. "After I eat you, of course, we will be one, you and me. Your flesh will become part of my flesh. Our souls will meld. All that is strong within you will make me more powerful."

Annie wondered about her weaknesses. Would he just shit them out? She hid her wry smile with a bite of food, the food tasting like bile in her mouth, her repulsion so strong she feared that she'd vomit. "What of the others?" she asked around a piece of bacon and a swollen and scarred tongue.

"What do you mean?"

Annie swallowed with difficulty. "Won't I also be *part* of them?"

"No, of course not. I alone will eat you. They will merely participate in the ritual sacrifice before bearing witness to my increasing power." He took a piece of potato and gently put it into her mouth. "Eat."

Annie had to chew and swallow before poking further. "Why are you the only cannibal?"

"Such a vulgar word." He put a bit of scrambled egg on the spoon and held it up to her mouth.

There was no point in defying him, so she opened her mouth. He took a piece of bacon and pushed it in before she was done chewing.

"Why will you be the only one that will eat me?" she finally was able to ask.

"Why? Because I am the Wendigo."

"What, exactly, is a wendigo?"

"Ah, the Algonquin people spoke of the wendigo as a beast who consumed human flesh. Where they were wrong was that they claimed he could never satisfy his hunger, but in fact, grew hungrier with every being he ate. But that is not true. Every time I eat a person, I grow stronger, heartier, and come closer to my destiny."

"You are very thin," Annie said. "Perhaps the Algonquin people were right."

"Right?" the Wendigo said angrily. "They spoke from fear. They wanted to believe that the Wendigo was weakened by eating them, but how could that be?"

"Gluttony is a sin."

"Sin? According to who? The Beast tells us to take what we want. Eat what we want. Drink what we want. Fuck who we want."

"The Beast is the devil. You are the Wendigo. Did you ever stop and consider that you might just be crazy as a loon? Batshit bonkers?"

He slapped her hard across the mouth. "Be quiet, woman."

Annie managed to not fall from her chair. She turned her head to look him in the eye, holding his gaze. There was blood in her mouth. Her face stung. But she wouldn't give him the satisfaction of seeing her be weak.

"Cuckoo," she said. "Cuckoo."

Chapter 13

"What'd you get from Corbett?" Langdon asked Bart. It was two days since the altercation with the heroin dealer, and they were having a business lunch in the basement bar of the Wretched Lobster.

"Not much," Bart said. After Langdon had confronted the man, Bart had followed up with an official inquiry. "He swears that he didn't sign up for a Patience membership. Says that somebody must've stolen his card number somehow. Easy enough to get the rest of his info as well. Places are getting hacked all the time and the crooks are getting smarter."

"How about the email address attached to the site?"

"It was in Corbett's name as well. It's now defunct, of course, and he swears it isn't his."

"You believe him?"

"Don't know. He's pretty convincing, but that's what doctors are good at, isn't it?"

"What's that?" Langdon asked.

"Lying to your face. 'Just a little discomfort,' they say before something truly painful happens. And then convincing you that your health is in danger for one thing or another. Buncha bullshit, if you ask me."

Langdon imagined that Bart's doctor had been telling him to lose weight for some thirty years or more now. He was saved a reply as Richam came over to their hi-top table in the corner of the barroom. Today, his tie was bright green, accenting green tints in his suit jacket and pants. He had that body that clothes always looked good on. At just six feet tall, he carried his 180 pounds well, lean and compact and seemingly not having gained a pound as long as Langdon had known him.

"What brings you gentlemen into my fine establishment?" Richam asked as he approached their table.

"Getting some grub and beer," Bart said. "What else would we be doing here?"

"Looks like you already got some on your uniform, Officer Bart," Richam said with a wide smile, pointing his finger at food stains on the man's collar that looked to be egg yolk.

"Yeah, well, shut your pie hole and bring me three cheeseburgers and a Budweiser."

Richam took his black-rimmed glasses off and wiped them on the green handkerchief in his pocket. "You want fries or onion rings with that? Or you can upgrade to a side salad for a dollar." He smirked.

"Both would be good," Bart said. "And you can leave that rabbit food in the kitchen."

"Very well, good sir," Richam said, the smirk still lurking at the crease of his mouth. "And for you, my friend?" He turned to Langdon.

"Reuben with a side salad," Langdon said. "I'm good with the water."

Richam gave him a side look. "I hear the wives are going out tonight."

Langdon nodded. "Yeah, down to Portland. Some wine and paint thing."

"Bringing Chabal's new friend along, the schoolteacher," Richam said. "Not sure I like Jewell going out with a younger single lady to the hot spots of the Old Port."

Langdon chuckled. "I don't think there'll be a whole lot of men looking to pick up ladies at a wine and paint event."

"Ha," Bart said. "I'll bet that hippy lawyer with the ATV name attends those things all the time. Last year when the Chippendales were into the strip joint down that way, he was there front and center. Said it was the best place to meet horny women."

Richam laughed and walked off to put their order in.

"You bring that homeless fellow, Graham, in to do a police sketch?" Langdon asked.

"Yeah, just yesterday," Bart said. "Not going to do much good. According to that glue sniffer, the suspect is about seven feet tall, has talons and wings, and smells like dead bodies."

Langdon chuckled. "Should be easy enough to find him, then."

"Not too many dragon men walking around the streets," Bart agreed.

"Seems that Dr. Corbett and Gregory Popa are our best leads," Langdon said.

"And that punk drug dealer."

Langdon knew of Bart's hatred of drug dealers, dating back to when they first met. "I got Danny T. keeping an eye on Dwayne," Langdon said. "He lives right across the street from him. Said he'd keep watch out his window and see if anything out of the ordinary is going on."

"That's like having the wolf watch the sheep, isn't it?"

"I don't know if anybody would call Danny T. a wolf."

Bart guffawed. "You got that right. More like having Peter watch the wolf."

"Just as long as he calls us when the wolf shows up."

Richam brought their food over and two beers for Bart. He knew the man well.

"Maybe I should just go bust Dwayne Bates and rattle his cage," Bart said. "Maybe shake loose a few of his rotten teeth along the way."

Langdon shook his head. "He doesn't know anything about Popa other than that he buys junk from him a couple times a month. If you round him up, we won't be able to use him."

Bart took a bite of his first cheeseburger, half of it gone in one fell swoop. "Use him?" he asked around an array of beef, bread, pickle, tomato, lettuce, onion, and mayo.

Langdon was forced to look away to not lose his own appetite. "Popa might share something with Dwayne, especially if we suggest that Dwayne ask the right questions in the right way."

"Yeah? Such as?" Bart took a huge swig of beer.

"I don't know," Langdon said. "I'm working on that."

"I guess we could bust Popa buying horse from Dwayne. That'd be a reason for taking him in for questioning, and he might spill something."

"If it comes down to it," Langdon said. "Let's give it some time."

"Liam Couture's been missing seventeen days. Annie Brown's been gone for ten. Give it some fucking time?"

"I feel like we're only going to get one shot at this." Langdon took a bite of Reuben. "If we mess it up, poof, the bad guys get away and go somewhere else to continue killing people."

"You think they're both dead?" Bart began his second of three cheeseburgers.

"I don't know. But I don't think so. This whole Wendigo Grotto of the Church of Satan thing is pretty freaky. My gut tells me that Annie Brown is still alive. From what her parents say, she is a survivor."

"Not much to go on with that premise, partner," Bart said.

"Nope. But I do think she's alive."

"But not Liam?"

"No," Langdon said. "Not Liam."

"Why do you think Annie is still alive?"

"They're waiting for May 26th."

"To be sacrificed at the Blood Moon?"

"The Super Flower Blood Moon," Langdon said.

"Why?"

"More important is what I fear is going to happen to Annie."

"Other than being killed?"

"I did some research on what a wendigo is." Langdon finished his water. "The wendigo is a mythical creature from Native American lore that eats humans. Some say that people can become wendigos. It is seen as the embodiment of gluttony, greed, and excess: never satisfied after killing and consuming one person, they are constantly searching for new victims."

"To what purpose?"

"They have an insatiable appetite for human flesh."

"Holy fucking donut," Bart said. "You're saying that some sick fucker is planning on eating Annie Brown on the night of the Blood Supermoon?"

~ ~ ~ ~ ~

"What one are you going to choose?" Chabal asked Jade. They were sitting in a room with twelve other women and one man, sipping wine. Each of them had an easel in front of them with a blank canvas and was flipping through a catalog to choose something to paint.

"I'm going with the moon over Portland," Jade said.

"I thought about that one, but I think I'm going to go with the rainbow skating pond," Jewell said. The three women had driven down together.

"I'm going with the Tree of Life," Chabal said. "With the sunrise behind it."

"You said something about working with immigrants on the way down," Jade said across Chabal to Jewell. "What is it exactly that you do?"

"I work for a company called CHERISH to help immigrants assimilate to life in Maine."

"That must be hugely rewarding."

"Difficult and depressing mostly, but occasionally rewarding, which makes it all worthwhile," Jewell said. "Probably a lot like teaching."

Jade giggled. "We have our shining moments, but yes, difficult and depressing would be a good definition."

"Underpaid, overworked, serving government agencies that don't want to spend any money on those in need, but happy to overindulge in weapons for defense," Jewell said.

"Defense of what?" Jade asked. "We have a larger budget for defense than the next ten largest countries—combined."

"Exactly," Jewell said.

"At least you have the inner reward of making a difference in people's lives," Chabal said. "I sell books."

"Books make a difference," Jewell said. "Don't underestimate their power to change people for the better."

"Yeah, that's true," Chabal said. "But I don't get that warm tingly feeling you must when you help an immigrant get a job or find a place to live. Or when Jade has one of those aha moments with a student who suddenly has their world opened up for them."

"You're kind of a team with your husband in the PI business, aren't you?" Jade asked. "I mean, you must have times—wait, didn't you and Langdon save a little boy last year or something like that?"

"Yeah, sort of, but it didn't really turn out all that good for anybody." Chabal took a drink, eyeballing her developing painting of the Tree of Life. It was wild and crazy, limbs springing askew in every which direction. Perfect, she thought.

"That's the case for most of my victories," Jade said. "You work on bringing a child out of her shell all year, and finally, she stands in front of the class and gives a fucking helluva oral report, and you think, oh my goodness, I've done it. Two days later, she gets suspended for bullying on social media."

Chabal thought this sounded still raw, like maybe it'd just happened in the last week. "That sucks," she said.

"How about this thing you're working on now?" Jade asked. "The missing people?"

Chabal shook her head. "Doesn't look good," she said. "What's more, we suspect that it might be far more people than just the two who've disappeared."

"How many more?" Jade asked.

Chabal shrugged. "Ten, at least. Maybe dozens."

"What was that stuff you were talking about the other night at the fire, Jewell?" Jade asked. "Not about the supermoons and all, I know that stuff. I've always been drawn to the moon. But that other stuff about the Church of Satan and Grottos and whatnot. It gave me the shivers."

"It's been a hobby of mine since I was little to study religions," Jewell said. "It started when I realized that Voodoo is really just a mix of African gods and goddesses and of Christianity. I was twelve at the time. I don't know much more than I told you about the Church of Satan, though."

"Me and Langdon have been researching it a bit," Chabal said. "The group that appeared in Durham back in the early '70s was called the Wendigo Grotto. A wendigo is a mythical creature that has an insatiable appetite for human flesh. They got disavowed by the founder of the Church of Satan some thirty-five years ago but continued to meet for about five more years before vanishing entirely."

"How do you know they met for another five years?" Jewell asked.

"They put notices in the newspapers advertising their monthly meeting. All were welcome."

"Forget that," Jade said. "What's this about a creature that has a hunger for human flesh?"

"I doubt it's true, but the group did call themselves the Wendigo Grotto for some reason, did worship the moon, especially the supermoons, and were an offshoot of a satanic cult." Chabal dabbed a last splotch onto the canvas and leaned back. It was wild and colorful, just as she liked.

"But they disbanded, right?" Jade asked.

"Or went underground," Jewell said in a low voice.

The three women looked nervously at each other and then laughed.

"Do you have any leads on who may be responsible?" Jewell asked.

"There's a doctor by the name of Corbett whose profile was used to set up the date with the woman, Annie, but Langdon doesn't think it was actually him." Chabal added a dab to the tree branches.

"Don't those dating sites have strong privacy protections?" Jade asked.

Chabal snickered. "Remember that fellow you met at the barbecue the other night, you know, who couldn't take his eyes off you and had drool running down his chin most of the night?"

Jade screwed her face up tight. "Yes! What was his problem?"

Jewell laughed. "He's a lech, is what."

"But also a fantastic attorney," Chabal said. "I don't know what he did, but the place, Patience, spit the name and info out to him right quick."

"You think Corbett is innocent, though?" Jewell asked.

"Not sure," Chabal said.

"Any other leads?" Jade asked.

"Some homeless guy saw a man get into the truck driven by Liam Couture right before he disappeared." Chabal finished her wine, deciding that was enough for tonight. "Can't remember his name, but Danny T. dug him up. He did a sketch with the police, but it wasn't very good."

"You are fabulously talented as an artist," Jewell said, looking at Chabal's canvas. "I'd say you missed your calling with the whole bookselling and PI thing."

"I guess I married into that," Chabal said and laughed. "How'd yours turn out, Jade?"

Jade turned her canvas to face them. It was of the Portland Observatory, an eighty-six-foot tower on Munjoy Hill that used to signal the arrival of incoming ships into the harbor. Dominating the canvas was the full moon looming behind it. Where Chabal was a good artist, Jade was fantastic, and the moon seemed to envelop the whole room.

Jewell carefully turned her canvas away before commenting on how beautiful and powerful Jade's depiction of the Portland Observatory and the moon were.

Chapter 14

Langdon looked out the window. There was still enough light to take a walk. Chabal wasn't home from her paint-and-sip thing yet. He'd thrown a frozen pizza in the oven for dinner and ate half of it while reading a book by Kevin St. Jarre. He'd refrained from having a beer with it, instead having a glass of milk. Now dog was eyeballing him.

Okay, Langdon thought, might as well. He went to the back door, dog bursting excitedly past him, down off the deck, and into the woods. With a shake of his head and a chuckle, Langdon followed him, not into the heaviest brush, but choosing instead the path that led to the Town Commons trail. It was darker in the woods, shadows dancing in the dusk.

Tom Corbett had appeared to be telling the truth, as far as Langdon could tell. There'd been a slight tic when he claimed that he didn't lie to his wife, but if anything, that bolstered the fact that he hadn't set up an account with Patience, lured Annie Brown to a date, and then abducted her. If the man had tells, such as a tic when he lied, they'd most certainly have come up when Langdon had pushed him about more nefarious happenings.

There was a rustling in the bushes to his right, and dog came charging across his path, nose to the ground as he ran full speed, intent on some scent as he zigzagged through the trees. Langdon often wondered how he never ran into an obstacle with his head down like that, running full-out. Most likely a deer had crossed here, he thought, and hopefully nothing more dangerous, like a coyote or a bear.

Of course, Graham, the homeless fellow Danny T. had rousted out of the woodwork, had said the man who got in the truck with Liam Couture was tall, very tall, and Tom Corbett fit that description. Langdon made a note to find Graham and show him a picture of Corbett. If it wasn't the doctor, who then would've had access to the man's credit card? Family? Friends? Co-workers? Patients? Langdon smiled wryly at that, the possibility that a patient had stolen the doctor's card number to sign up for Patience.

Langdon looked up through the trees, wondering if he had time before dark to make the full loop. It'd be close, but what the heck, he hated to retrace his steps. Dog came running up, having decided he needed some sustenance to keep prowling the perimeter and driving predators away. Langdon flipped him a mini from his pocket, the snack bouncing off dog's nose. Dog was awful at catching but gamely tried every time.

Dog suddenly cocked his head, his ears alert, having heard something. Langdon asked him what it was, perhaps a squirrel? After a few seconds, dog determined that it was nothing and went nosing off into the woods to find something more entertaining as Langdon continued walking the loop, musing on the case.

Gregory Popa seemed a much more likely candidate for the role of confirmed sicko luring, abducting, and killing people. There was something dark about him, Langdon thought, not just his eyes and hair, but an evilness emanating from inside him. Of course, it could just be that he was addicted to heroin, although, as users went, he seemed to have it fairly well under control. Just one dose a couple times a month seemed to show that the man had a high level of self-control. He also didn't fit the description of the man who Graham saw with Liam Couture, as he was several inches under six feet and built sturdily.

Did that mean, Langdon wondered, that there was more than

one killer on the loose? That there was possibly still in existence a Wendigo Grotto of the Church of Satan practicing their twisted religious beliefs in the underbelly of Brunswick? And, if there were two members, what was to say there weren't more? That was a deeply unsettling thought. There had to be a way to use the Dwayne Bates drug dealing connection to find out more about Popa. Danny T. had agreed to keep eyes on Dwayne, but Langdon didn't believe the drug dealer was involved in anything other than selling a deadly drug. It might be best to let Bart arrest the man and get him off the street, even if it'd most likely be little more than a slap on the wrist with him soon to be back at it.

Dog was standing in the middle of the trail waiting for Langdon as he came around a bend and then settled into walking along in front of him, tail and ears down, hair on his back up, the mohawk look that he got when something wasn't right.

"What's up, buddy?" Langdon asked. "The squirrel a bit bigger than you thought?"

Dog didn't so much as wag his tail in reply.

Speaking of tails, Langdon thought it was probably time to put a tail on Popa. He winced, knowing that this would be his duty. He sometimes involved Starling or Chabal in his cases and had even been known to put other friends in danger. He thought of Peppermint Patti and Goldilocks, both innocents who'd been murdered by desperate men while helping out, and sighed. No, the tedious task of staking out Gregory Popa would be his duty. He couldn't risk anybody else in what could be a deadly game of cat and mouse. He also needed to have another conversation with Corbett, but he could probably set that up for when Popa was at work.

Dog whined low in his throat, jolting Langdon from his reverie.

"What is it, boy?"

Dog stopped in the path, crouching down low, his ears flat against his head, and whined again.

Langdon stepped up to him, leaned over, and scratched his butt.

"What's up? You okay?"

He looked around at the deepening darkness around them and wondered if there might be something more than a squirrel out there. He hoped it wasn't a fisher, a particularly large and nasty member of the weasel family.

They were past the halfway point, there being no sense to turn back, so Langdon urged dog onward. He wouldn't budge, so Langdon stepped past him and led the way. Not much of a guard dog, he thought and chuckled. Maybe a warning dog, but not much in the protection category. Langdon mentally kicked himself for his inner sarcasm. It'd been just last October that dog had saved him and Chabal from a very bad situation.

A stick cracked loudly off ahead to the right. Too loudly to be a falling branch, Langdon thought, pausing and staring over in that direction. Could it be a bear, he wondered?

Dog began barking. He wasn't usually much of a barker.

"Shh, dog, it's okay," Langdon said, patting the canine's head as they both looked in the direction of the noise.

After a few seconds of silence, they proceeded at a faster pace, the leisurely walk gone. The clouds above must've broken, for the path became more illuminated under the trees. Langdon looked up through the foliage to see the moon shining bright, about three-quarters full, helping light the way. He tripped on a root and almost fell, righting himself, and continued on, his eyes flickering between the path ahead and the woods around.

Something brushed against Langdon's leg, and then dog shot past him, his body vibrating, a keening coming from his mouth, and then he was gone into the bushes. Langdon called to him to stop, to come back, but the blackness enveloped him, and he was gone.

Langdon went to follow, and three things happened simultaneously. He tripped on a rock, dog wailed in pain, and something brushed the top of Langdon's head as he fell. On his knees, he put his hand to his head, and it came away bloody. He seemed to remember a faint thump as he fell and looked up to see an arrow embedded in the pine tree a few feet past him. He dropped flat to the earth and rolled.

Dog was snarling and barking and then howled again in pain. Langdon came to his feet in a crouch and ran toward the commotion, tripping and stumbling as branches clawed at his face. Some bastard was hurting his dog. He came into a little clearing, the moon lighting it up like a theater stage, to find dog standing there, growling into the darkness.

Langdon called to him, beckoning dog out of the clearing, out of the light. Dog turned, took a step, and almost fell before limping his way back into the shadows with Langdon. Whoever had been there was gone.

~ ~ ~ ~ ~

Jimmy 4 by Four looked around the bar. He was at the tavern of the Bernard Hotel in Freeport. It was comfortable, had good food and drinks, and, most importantly, its patrons were from away. When looking for a one-night stand, he'd discovered, a hotel bar was the best place to do so. Businesswomen, Bowdoin College mothers, and those who come to spend money at L.L.Bean and the other shops of Freeport were just a smattering of the available women frequenting the bar.

He'd eaten a Cobb salad and was sipping his second glass of wine, although he'd bought five other drinks for women. The one sitting next to him with a friend had cost him two drinks, after which they said goodbye and went up to their room. Two more for a pair sitting at a table behind him, but when he approached, they thanked him for the cocktails but said they were both married and that their husbands would soon be there.

There was a mousy woman at the end of the bar with the look of a librarian, who'd been his final attempt. She wasn't his top choice, but sometimes compromises had to be made, and he didn't want to go home alone tonight. It wasn't like he enjoyed being single, it was just that after a few weeks with a woman, they started to annoy him. 4 by Four knew that this was his issue and not theirs, but therapy hadn't really worked, and that, too, he'd abandoned after a few tries. He'd long since given up the notion that he'd ever find a woman to settle down with.

He looked down the bar at the mousy woman. She was on her phone, scrolling through something. Her drink was halfway gone. Just about the right time to make his move, sidle on down to her, introduce himself, and ask if she'd like another. She did look like a librarian with her round, brown glasses and hair pulled back in a bun. The excitement of the chase began to build inside him.

The bartender was in his thirties and had a man bun. He stepped over in front of 4 by Four. "She's in town for a conference. Divorced. Not interested in dating." While the patrons rarely knew 4 by Four, the staff knew him well, as he was a regular here, and he made it a point to tip well, very well.

"Sounds perfect," 4 by Four said.

"Is this seat taken?"

4 by Four looked to his left where a woman stood, her hand on the back of the stool, a question in her eyes, and a coy smile quirking her full lips. She had long brown hair and blue eyes, and a slender figure that he thought looked absolutely delicious.

"Please sit," 4 by Four said. "My name's Jim."

"Thank you." Her long dark eyelashes fluttered. "I'm Natasha." She pushed the stool a bit closer to him and settled into it like a bird perching on a branch.

"What brings you here?" he asked.

"To the bar?" she asked. "A drink, I suppose."

"Of course. Let me buy you one." She was about forty, he figured, twenty years younger than him, which he thought was just about perfect.

"I'll have a Cold River Blueberry Lemonade," she said to the bartender. "And thank you." She touched 4 by Four's elbow and squeezed lightly.

"I suppose I meant, what brings you to Freeport?" he asked.

"The shopping, of course, and then I had dinner in the restaurant here with a female friend, but she went home. I decided on a nightcap." The bartender placed the vodka drink in front of her, and she took a small sip. "Delicious," she said.

"Oh, so you're not staying here at the Bernard?"

"Actually, I am, just for the night, but I live in Pownal. And how about you?"

Her living local made it less likely that she'd jump into bed with him upon just meeting, 4 by Four thought, but she was stunningly attractive and would be well worth the long game if that were necessary. "I'm a lawyer in Brunswick."

"My, a lawyer. Smart as well as handsome." Natasha pushed a strand of her brown hair back over an ear. "What brings you to the tavern?"

"Dinner and a drink," he said.

They chatted about this and that and had one more drink each before Natasha said she had to go, her exact words being, "I must go before I turn into a pumpkin."

"I think it's merely your car that will transform into a pumpkin," 4 by Four said. "But you'll still be astoundingly beautiful, just no longer with the fancy clothes and jewelry."

Natasha put her hand on his chest and leaned in so that her lips brushed his ear. "If you give me ten minutes, can keep a secret, and come to room 206, I won't have anything on at all."

Who was 4 by Four to argue with that logic? He finished his drink, paid the tab, and followed the beautiful Natasha to her room. He took his time, knowing that fifteen minutes would be better, letting her wonder just a little if he was coming. Not that he imagined she got turned down very often.

He knocked on room 206, and she called for him to come in, the door slightly ajar, held open by the deadbolt. The room was dark, just the desk lamp on, but he could make out a figure on the bed, and he moved in that direction. He stopped to take his shoes off and heard a rustle from the bathroom, and then something jabbed into his neck.

4 by Four grabbed at the place where it stung, his hand stopping the syringe from being fully depressed as he ripped it loose. His legs wobbled under him, and the darkroom became fuzzy. He turned to face Natasha, who'd pulled a wicked-looking blade from somewhere and was thrusting it at him. He managed to knock her arm down, the knife sticking into his thigh. That was the final straw to legs that already felt like Jell-O, and he sank to his knees.

Natasha lost her grip on the knife, embedded as it was into the muscles of his leg. He grabbed at her legs with arms that were leaden. It was like trying to run underwater. She spun around, and suddenly 4 by Four felt her foot crashing into the side of his jaw, and he toppled to the floor, face down.

"Hey, what's going on here? Is everybody all right?" A man stood silhouetted in the doorway, the hallway light casting his shadow larger than life into the room.

"Help," 4 by Four managed to croak out.

Natasha took a step toward the man, jabbing him in the throat with the flat of her hand, and he stumbled back, gasping for breath. She ran down the hallway, past a tipsy couple working their way up the stairs, down through the backdoor, and out into the night.

She cut through the bushes into the lot next door where her car was parked. Once in the driver's seat, she removed the long brown wig to reveal bleached blonde hair buzzed almost to the scalp. Later she'd take out the blue contact lenses.

Once she was out of Freeport, she called him to let him know that she'd failed.

~ ~ ~ ~ ~

He swore under his breath as he climbed the exterior stairs. It was damn hard to find good help these days. First, the report had come in that Langdon was still alive, and now the lawyer with the funny name had also survived a carefully orchestrated attack. It was up to the Wendigo to send the message, then. It was up to him, as it always was, to protect the coven.

He knocked on the door of the ratty apartment on Swett Street, turning the knob as he did so. It wasn't locked. People were so stupid these days, he thought with a satisfied grin. He'd been afraid that he might have to cajole his way in or even force the door, both endeavors that increased the risk of exposure to prying eyes. So much better that the idiot hadn't bothered to lock his door. He ducked his head as he went through the door.

The fat man called Danny T. sat in a recliner, a bag of cheese puffs resting on his belly, his shirt covered in orange crumbs, as was his face. There was a baseball game on the television, which appeared to be the only item in the apartment not in need of replacement.

"Who the hell are you?" Danny T. asked.

"How're the Sox doing?" the Wendigo asked.

Danny T. put the cheese puffs onto the table next to him and made a motion to close the recliner and stand up.

The Wendigo took two long steps over to the fat man, put his hand on Danny T.'s forehead, and shoved him back. "I asked how the Sox were doing?" he said mildly.

Danny T. ran his tongue over his lips nervously. "Killing 'em," he said. "Both Dalbec and Bogarts got two-run dingers. First two innings."

The Wendigo grabbed a wooden chair and put it in front of Danny T., sliding into it with the easy grace of a predator. "You won't mind if I interrupt for a moment or two, then, will you?"

"Who are you?"

He shrugged and looked at the can of soda on the side table. "You can call me Dr Pepper."

"What do you want?"

"You're friends with that bloke by the name of Langdon, aren't you?"

Danny T.'s eyes flickered to the door and back to the man, who suddenly slapped him hard across the face.

His eyes blazed darkly but his face remained impassive. "Please answer me when I ask you a question."

"Yes." Danny T.'s voice quavered on the verge of sobbing.

"Very good. I think we might get along very well, me and you." He pulled a switchblade from his pocket, pressed the release, and the blade sprung forth. "Tell me about the case that Langdon is working on."

"What case?"

This time, he punched Danny T. in the nose with a short jab that rocked his head back.

Danny T. gasped, sobbed, but managed to say, "About the missing people?"

He smiled wickedly. "That's the one."

"Langdon asked me to keep an eye on the guy across the street and let him know if I see a guy by the name of Gregory Popa go over. I got his picture on my phone."

"I see. And why would this Popa go see the man across the street?"

"To buy heroin." Danny T. squirmed uncomfortably. "Look, man, I want you to get the heck out of my house."

He stuck the switchblade into Danny T.'s bicep, like the flick of a snake's tongue, in and out. "Pay attention, my friend," he said.

"What the—"

"Tell me about the homeless man."

"What homeless man?"

Again, like the flicker of a snake's tongue, this time into the fat man's belly, the blade went in and out. "I know everything. Don't test me. It will only cause you pain."

"Son of a gun." Danny T. began blubbering in earnest, blood drooling from his nose and sprouting from his arm and stomach.

"His name is Graham. Don't know his last name. He saw a tall fellow climb into the truck with that missing man." Danny T.'s eyes suddenly widened. "Tall fellow," he said. "With the stink of death on him." He put his hand over his mouth, as if aware he'd misspoken, and the consequences were likely to be dire.

"Where would I find this Graham?"

"Last I knew, he was bedding down behind that deserted gas station on Pleasant Street. Please don't hurt me no more."

He looked at the weeping fat man and felt regret. The man would make quite a meal. And he could feel his appetite growing with the moon. His hunger ached inside of him like a beast gnawing at his guts. "What else can you tell me?"

"That's all I know. Please. I told you everything."

"Yes, I believe you have," the Wendigo said and flicked the blade out once more and thrust it forward, this time into the jugular vein in the fat man's throat stepping quickly aside to avoid the blood arcing out as soon as he removed the knife.

Chapter 15

Langdon and dog limped their way back to the house. Chabal was in the living room watching some funny movie with a glass of wine in hand when they walked in.

"Oh my gosh, what happened?" she asked.

"Those woods aren't safe," Langdon said. "You want to take a look at my head and see if it needs stitches?"

Chabal led him to the dining room and sat him at the table so that she could see the top of his head. "What'd you do, fall down?"

"Somebody shot me with an arrow," he said. "And appears to have kicked dog or struck him with something."

"Shot you with an arrow?" Chabal went and got a washcloth and a bowl of warm water. "Like, a real arrow?"

Langdon told her about the ordeal in the woods while she cleaned his wound.

"Do we need to take dog to the vet?" Chabal asked.

"He seemed able to walk okay. Let's give him until tomorrow. See how he's doing then."

"Should we call the police?"

"I guess. If there's some maniac running around the woods with a bow and quiver full of arrows, they should be alerted."

"You think it has something to do with the missing people?"

"Most probably. I don't think I've pissed anybody else off lately. Not enough to try and kill me, anyway." Langdon plucked his phone from his pocket and called Bart. Luckily, he was on duty and agreed to stop by and get a statement.

Chabal walked off into the bedroom while Langdon, over the phone, gave the cop the bare bones of what happened. She went to the closet, took down the lock box, and unlocked it. She took the pistols and holsters from it, returning to the dining room to hand Langdon his Glock and shoulder holster.

"Looks like we best start carrying these," she said.

Langdon watched carefully as she removed her Baja, the Mexican thread hoodie, lifting it over her head, and then removing the T-shirt with a chocolate lab on the front.

"Might need to take your bra off to get that holster on," he said.

"You think so, do you?" she asked. She slid the holster over her head, pulling the bottom strap just below her breasts. She slid her slim SIG P365 into the holster on her side and put her T-shirt back on. "Maybe you'll get a chance to see those after Bart comes by and takes your statement."

"That would be the proper medicine for my injury," Langdon said.

"But we might need to start locking the door."

"I don't think we're under siege here," Langdon said. "This might be a bit of overkill." He pointed to his Glock, which he'd placed on the table.

"Somebody shot you with a fucking arrow," she said.

"I love it when you curse."

"Don't try to placate me."

An hour later, as Bart was getting ready to leave, having gotten the pertinent details, such as to have a BOLO put on for a person carrying a bow and arrow, his two-way radio cackled to life.

"Officer Bartholomew here," he barked into it. Bart pretty much barked everything he said.

"Bart, this is Judi down at the station. You're friends with that lawyer with the strange name, aren't you? James 4 by Four?"

"I wouldn't say friends," Bart said. "But yeah, I know him."

"Somebody tried to kill him down at the Bernard Hotel in Freeport. Thought you'd want to know."

"Upset husband?" Bart asked.

"I believe it was a woman."

"What'd she do? Slap him in the face for being rude?"

"Details are a bit sketchy still, but it sounds like she stuck him in the neck with some type of anesthetic agent and then tried to slash his throat with a knife."

"What? Where is he?" The flippancy was gone from Bart's voice.

"On his way to Mid Coast in an ambulance."

"Okay. Thanks, Judi."

Bart looked at Langdon and Chabal. "Somebody just tried to kill 4 by Four down at the Bernard in Freeport. Could've just been some broad he jilted," he said.

"Pretty big coincidence him getting attacked right about the same time as Langdon," Chabal said.

"Don't much believe in coincidences," Langdon said.

"Pretty well thought out attack for a spurned lover," Chabal said.

"You want to ride over to the hospital with me?" Bart asked.

"Best we have two cars there," Langdon said. "I should make a few phone calls, if you don't mind driving, Chabal?"

"You're thinking others are in danger?" Bart asked as they went out the door.

"I'm thinking I stirred the pot is why they tried to kill me, whoever they are, and yes, it does seem to be at least two people involved," Langdon said. "I don't know how they could've known it was 4 by Four who got Corbett's name from Patience."

"Maybe when they failed to put an arrow in your heart, they decided to send a warning to one of your friends," Chabal said.

Once in the car, Langdon called Starling. The man picked up after two rings. He was home reading a book. Langdon suggested he lock his doors, but when Langdon told him the reason, he said he was coming over to the hospital as well.

Richam didn't answer, so he texted him and then called Danny T., who also didn't answer.

"You think it's Corbett?" Chabal asked.

"He fits the description given by Graham," Langdon said. "Shit, that puts Graham on the list."

Langdon's phone buzzed with a text from Richam. Watching a movie with my wife. What's up?

Langdon pecked out a quick reply. Somebody tried to kill me and 4 by Four. He's going to Mid Coast. Not sure how bad he is.

Langdon's phone rang with a call from Richam, and he hurriedly filled him in on the little he knew. Richam said that he and Jewell were on their way to the hospital.

Langdon called Bart and asked that he have a cruiser swing by the empty gas station on Pleasant Street and see if Graham was bedded down there. Bart agreed that'd it be a good idea to take him in for the night, give him a cot and a meal for his own well-being.

"Oh, and can you send somebody over to check on Danny T.? He's not answering his phone, and he's in this as deep as anybody."

"Probably asleep," Bart said.

"Nope. The Red Sox are playing. He wouldn't miss a game."

"Okay. After they check for Graham, I'll have them swing by Danny T.'s. I think you're using up all our available units."

"Two?" Langdon asked.

"That's about it."

Bart was able to use his authority to get Langdon and him back to the room where 4 by Four was. The man was loopy from the drug, but luckily only a bit of it had been injected, or so the doctor said. A larger dose to the neck would've killed him. He'd also had a knife wound in his thigh and a badly bruised jaw. The doctor told them they could have five minutes and left the room.

"Who was it?" Langdon asked 4 by Four. "Who did this to you?"

"She was a... beautiful... woman I met at the bar." 4 by Four talked sleepily, yawning. "Told me to come to her room... and... she'd have nothing on. I'd've liked that." He smiled dreamily. "She was smoking hot. I wish she tried to kill me after making love to me. It'd have been worth it."

"She give you a name?" Bart asked.

"Natasha. Do you know Natasha, the muffin man, Natasha, Natasha, the one who lives on Drury Lane?"

Bart looked at Langdon, who put his hand on 4 by Four's arm. "Did Natasha have a last name?"

"Beautiful. She was simply ravishing."

"What'd she look like?"

"Long, brown hair, Rapunzel, let down your long, brown hair. And blue eyes. Shocking bright blue. Mm."

"Anything else?" Bart asked.

"I think he's asleep," Langdon said.

"Suppose we should go back to the waiting room," Bart said. The two of them walked to the door and out. "Spoke with the responding officer on the way over. A guest at the hotel was walking by in the hallway, heard a commotion, and opened the door. A woman with brown hair was standing over 4 by Four, but when the guy opened the door, she hit him in the throat and ran off."

"Who was the room under?"

"A guy named Bart Morris. He came walking in while they were wheeling 4 by Four out. He was attending a lecture at Bowdoin College. Said he had no idea about any of it."

"Did he happen to meet a stunningly beautiful woman with long brown hair and blue eyes? Possibly one that he mentioned he'd be gone to this lecture for the evening. And did he happen to lose his room key?"

"They'd just hauled him into the station in Freeport for questioning, last I knew. I'll make sure to find out."

Chabal had been joined in the waiting room by Starling, Richam, and Jewell. They updated them on 4 by Four's health and the little details they had.

"Serves him right," Jewell said. "Treating women like he does. Surprised this hasn't happened before."

"Oh, but it has," Bart said. "Remember when that Austin-Peters woman broke his jaw?"

There was a moment of silence, and then Chabal laughed, and they all joined in. "He had to leave town because we heckled him about that so bad, and his mouth was wired shut, and he couldn't defend himself."

"And it wasn't so long ago that he ended up here after trying to defend the honor of a woman being verbally assaulted by those QAnon people," Starling said.

"It's not like he ever lies to the women," Richam said. "He does have his own code of chivalry."

Jewell glared at her husband.

Bart's two-way radio cackled, and he stepped aside to speak into it.

"What have you gotten us into now?" Jewell asked Langdon. "Does this have to do with those missing people? Is it really that Grotto of the Church of Satan gone bad, if such a thing is even possible?"

"I don't know," Langdon said. "All I know is there are two missing people, perhaps many more, and now somebody tried to kill me and 4 by Four."

"And Danny T.," Bart said. He cleared his throat as all eyes swung to him. "Only they didn't just try. He's dead. He was just found in his apartment with multiple knife wounds, including one that slashed his throat."

Chapter 16

Langdon waited until a light came on in the house before pounding on the front door. Tom Corbett opened it in his bathrobe. He looked annoyed.

The night had been filled with gathering the details of Danny T.'s death, the attack on 4 by Four, and of course, on himself. The police had shown up at Danny T.'s and found the door open and the man in his recliner covered in blood that had not yet congealed. His assailant must've slipped away right before they arrived. It being Swett Street, truly the wrong side of the tracks, nobody had seen anything. The state police Major Crime Unit had been called in. Nothing was likely to happen fast, though.

Bart had gotten Langdon the home address of both Corbett and Popa. Still wearing yesterday's blood-speckled clothes with an enormous cup of coffee, the rattled PI parked himself outside the house before the sun was up and waited with his thoughts for company.

He'd hoped that time to reflect would prevent him from doing anything stupid, but he felt one of those Dave Robicheaux moments coming on, a blackout fueled by anger and fear and not by chemicals. Dog left at home limping, hopefully okay. 4 by Four in the hospital with a knife stuck in him. Danny T., sprawled in his recliner, covered in blood, a gentle soul who'd never hurt a person in his life.

It was like a loop reel running through his mind. Dog. 4 by Four. Danny T.

Danny T. was dead. And it was somehow Langdon's fault.

He didn't believe Corbett was the killer. But the man knew something he wasn't sharing. His arrogant demeanor had rubbed Langdon wrong from the first.

"This is not the right way to go about this," Langdon said in the quiet morning air of the Jeep. "This is not the right way to go about this."

Dog. 4 by Four. Danny T.

Dog. 4 by Four. Danny T.

The lights in the house flickered on, and Langdon got out of the Jeep, the blackness in his soul the opposite of the rising sun.

"What are you doing here?" Corbett asked.

"Brought you donuts for breakfast," Langdon said, shouldering past the man. He tossed the Dunkin' bag on the kitchen island and sat down on a stool.

"I'm going to call the police." Corbett hovered in the doorway with his phone in hand.

"They're busy investigating the death of my friend. Don't think they'll have time for your whiny bitch behavior."

"What?"

"Yeah. Somebody stabbed my buddy multiple times before severing his jugular. Right after, my other friend was attacked in a hotel, and I had my hair styled with an arrow. So, forgive my impatience, but if you don't put that phone down, I'm going to shove it up your ass."

"What's any of this have to do with me? Why are you here?"

"Because, my friend, you signed up for a dating site, made plans to meet Annie Brown, and then she disappeared." Langdon drank two huge gulps of coffee. His eyes were red from lack of sleep and grief.

"I told you I know nothing of that."

"So you say. But a few days after I confront you, somebody opens up a can of whoop ass on me and my friends."

"This has nothing to do with me."

"This has everything to do with you."

"I'm sorry for the loss of your friend." Corbett had none of the smugness he'd displayed in his office on Monday. "But it wasn't me who signed up for that dating site."

"Where's your wife? Is she still asleep?"

Corbett sat down at the island across from Langdon. "She left me six months ago."

"You told me you were happily married."

Corbett shrugged. "I never said 'happily.'"

"She found out that you were having an affair?"

Corbett didn't reply.

Langdon wanted to punch the man in the face. But he also realized that this anger wasn't about Tom Corbett. "Who's the woman?"

"It doesn't matter. We're no longer seeing each other."

"Ah," Langdon said. "One of your creations. You molded the perfectly breasted woman and then cheated on your wife with her. What happened? Did she realize that you had issues that couldn't be fixed by cosmetic surgery?"

"Tiffany decided to give her marriage another go."

Langdon chuckled, a dry rasping sound like a cat with a hairball. "Hubby liked your creation as well, did he?"

"Why are you here?"

"I'm not quite sure, but it seems increasingly likely that you had every reason and motive to sign up for Patience and go on a date with Annie Brown. What happened? Did she laugh at you like Tiffany and your wife did, so you killed her?"

"They didn't… I didn't sign up for a dating site, Mr. Langdon. I'm perfectly capable of meeting women without paying for it."

Langdon reached across the island and grabbed a handful of robe, pulling the doctor's face inches from his own. "Then you best be telling me who used your credit card to do so."

"I don't know." Corbett's face quivered in fear.

"Think about it. Your brother? Your ex-wife? It could be that somebody at work overheard you giving your card over the phone when you were buying Viagra?"

"I don't have a brother. I canceled my old card the day that bitch walked out on me, and I don't need any help in that department. Please let me go."

Langdon released his grip and let Corbett settle back into his seat. He took a deep breath, pushing the blackness away. He'd best get his shit together or somebody else was going to die. "I want a list of everybody in the world you know. Relatives, friends, doctors, nurses, patients."

"I cannot give you a list of my patients. I'd lose my license and maybe worse."

Langdon contemplated this with a sip of coffee. "Fine. We'll start with the others. Get started. I'll wait."

Twenty minutes later, Corbett had regained a bit of his arrogance. "I'll be contacting the police, you realize, about your visit."

Langdon leaned forward and tweaked him in the nose. "Good. Tell them I did that as well. You want I should black your eye for evidence?"

Corbett went back to writing.

~ ~ ~ ~ ~

Gregory Popa lived in Lisbon Falls, about twenty minutes from Corbett's house. Langdon had decided tailing the man around was a better idea than confronting him but almost changed his mind when the stocky man walked out his front door and retrieved the newspaper from the box. He had a bandage on his hand. Langdon didn't imagine the life of an accountant led to many injuries and that this may've been caused by the bite of a dog.

"Good boy, dog," he said to himself.

Dog had been left home with Chabal for the day. Langdon had

told the canine it was to protect and defend Chabal, but, in reality, it was also to give him a chance to recover from his gimpy leg. He'd been to the firing range many a time with Chabal, and she always proved herself a better shot than him. Between dog and her SIG P365, Chabal was in good hands.

For the next half-hour, Langdon tussled with whether to confront Popa like he had Corbett. If the bandage was covering up bite marks, would that be enough proof to have him arrested for trying to kill Langdon? Probably not. He wondered idly if there were experts who could match his wounds to the teeth of dog. Probably not.

While he waited, he took a picture of the second of three pages of names of the people Corbett knew and sent it to Chabal to start researching. He wasn't quite sure what they were looking for. Membership to a serial killer club? But in this day and age, where everybody posts their meal and bathroom schedules on social media, it should be possible to find something.

At 8:30, Popa's car pulled out of the driveway. Langdon followed him to the parking lot on Bank Street in Brunswick and watched as the man went inside. It was only after an hour of sitting in his Jeep watching the front door of the accounting firm that Langdon allowed his thoughts to drift to Danny T.

He'd known the man for twenty-five years. Danny T. had dropped out of school in ninth grade to begin working on a fishing boat, only to be blackballed from the waterfront after cutting a full net to save a buddy's arm. This led to a series of dead-end jobs. He had few friends but knew everybody in town. He was probably 100 pounds overweight. All this aside, he'd been the salt of the earth.

They'd argued sports as a common ground, and when Langdon needed information about the underbelly of Brunswick, it was Danny T. who provided it. And now he was dead. Most likely because Langdon had him out digging for information about the missing people. Because he'd brought out Graham, who Langdon now knew was Graham Fuller, as an eyewitness against the man who'd potentially abducted Liam Couture.

Graham hadn't been out back of the deserted gas station, according to the officers who were sent to look for him. No belongings, no bedroll, no makeshift tent. There were signs that he'd been there. Ashes from a fire. Empty soda and booze bottles. But he was gone.

Chabal texted asking if he could talk, so he called her.

"How you doin'?" she asked by way of a greeting.

"Been better," Langdon said. "You get any sleep?"

"I might've dozed off for a bit but not much."

"Dr. Corbett was kind enough to provide us with a list of people he knows who may've stolen his card number."

"I saw that. Not sure what you want me to do with that. I did contact that Church of Satan. Filled out an online form when I got home from the hospital, and the Reverend Allen something-or-other just called me back. He said that the sect that opened a Grotto in Maine was led by an outcast named Pan Nergal, who'd strayed far from the teachings of the Church of Satan. They'd expelled Nergal from the Church and, thus, did not keep in contact with him or his followers."

"Strayed?" Langdon snorted. "Did the Reverend say in what way they'd strayed?"

"He only said that they believed in witchcraft and human sacrifice."

"Oh, is that all?"

"You know, some people are just batshit crazy."

"Okay," Langdon said. "I don't know what to do with the list I sent you. Let's give it some thought."

"Where are you now?"

"Outside Popa's business."

"You want me to come spell you so you can grab a nap?"

"Not yet. Maybe later this afternoon."

"Star called to say he was opening the bookshop," Chabal said. "Didn't want to be sitting at home with nothing to do but think about Danny T. being murdered. You want I should have him close down so he can help us out?"

"No. We're not going to put anybody else's life in danger."

"Okay. You hear anything more about how 4 by Four is doing?" she asked.

"No. I'll check in with Bart about that and some other things after I get off the phone with you."

"Let me know."

"I will."

"Anything else you want me to do?" Chabal asked.

"Yeah. See if you can get hold of Tom Corbett's wife, MaryAnne Corbett. Might be using her maiden name. I'll text you the phone number. Probably be more willing to speak with you than me."

"She might be using her maiden name?"

"Yeah, turns out she split on the good doctor about six months ago. He said he has no idea where she is and doesn't really care. She might be willing to share some dirt on Dr. Corbett."

"Got it. I'll do that first."

"Be careful."

"Love you," Chabal said.

"I love you, too, babe. Let me know if you find out anything more."

Chapter 17

Annie banished the demons of sleep and prepared to face the monsters of the waking day. Pixel by pixel, she replaced the Overlord of the night with Mama Brown on Christmas morning, opening the painting of their home that Annie had created for her. The look on her face was forever imprinted in Annie's soul, the look of love, pride, and serenity. This was equaled by Papa Brown's face the day she'd won the regional championship high jump competition. These two visages Annie carried with her every day.

Her third male lover filtered into her thoughts. Not the first, Eric, who'd been a disaster. They'd sat next to each other in class, began to study together, which led to heavy make-out sessions, and finally, Annie had succumbed to having sex with him. He'd been clumsy, she'd been awkward, and soon afterward, they stopped making out, studying together, and sitting next to each other in class.

The second man was when she was home for the summer. Kevin had been perfect, and it'd been seven weeks of delicious love. But then he'd returned to his college on the West Coast, and she'd stayed on the East Coast. They tried to keep up, but that had dwindled, and, when he didn't make it home for Christmas vacation, they gave it up and moved on.

Annie married the third man she made love to. George. For eleven years, it'd been like a fairytale. George was a writer. She was able to paint and sell her work at craft shows and a few local galleries. His income was such that they lived a comfortable if not lavish life. He was the rare writer who made money.

For this particular memory, Annie focused on a trip they'd taken to Paris. They'd followed the journey of Hemingway for the almost decade he'd lived there, sitting in the *Les Deux Magots*, now a tourist trap, and envisioning all the wonderful writers and artists he'd crossed paths with, including Picasso, who was a hero of Annie's. They'd go out late to the jazz clubs, make love in the afternoons, and drink white wine with lunch. The blooming flowers, the delectable food, and the passion that was Paris instilled in Annie a happiness she'd never thought possible.

Annie opened her eyes before her thoughts could turn to the death of George in a boating accident. It felt earlier than normal. Something was off.

"Good morning, Pumpkin Pie," the Overlord of the day said.

Or, as she thought of him now, the Wendigo, not that she even knew what a wendigo was, but that appeared to be the first time he hadn't lied about who he was.

"Good morning," Annie said. She knew what would follow if she didn't reply in kind.

"I have a treat for you today," he said.

The Wendigo put the collar around her neck and unbuckled her ankle and wrist restraints. She pulled the monk's robe over her head, pulling the leash out the top and handing it to him. Twice she'd tried to attack him, with the thought of slowing him down so that she could run. He was too fast. Too strong. Perhaps she was slow from being chained up all night. The punishment had been unpleasant. Extremely unpleasant.

The first time he'd strapped her back to the table, naked, and slathered her with peanut butter. He'd then loosed a barrel of rats at her feet. At first, they'd been shy, afraid of the vibrations and muffled sounds she made. Gradually, they became bolder. She could feel, but not see, the first rat coming up the incline of the table, between her legs. When it reached her private area, the rat paused and then climbed up her. Annie could feel his feet, his belly, his tail as it slithered across the soft fur of her lady parts on his way to the peanut butter slathered on her belly, breasts, chest, and face.

And then there were more, a stampede of rats crossing *down there*, her legs, bounding onto her body, licking at the peanut butter on her belly, her breasts, her face, vying with each other for the best treats. Their tiny feet dug into her skin. She could feel their teeth gnashing as they slurped up the peanut butter. She was covered with writhing rats feasting off the platter that was her body.

As the peanut butter vanished, they became more aggressive, their teeth digging into her flesh, breaking the skin. Then the Wendigo brushed them from her body with a broom, shooing them away, commenting that it was he who'd feast upon her body, not the vermin.

"I said that I had a treat for you," the Wendigo said, interrupting the traumatizing memory.

Annie shuddered. It was as if she could still feel the rats crawling and gnawing at her. "What is it?" she asked.

"I'm going to allow you to make a phone call. To your friend. Madison Campagna."

"What? Why?" Annie stood, the feeling returning to her limbs, and began to shamble toward the table and her breakfast, which today was a stack of pancakes she knew she'd have to eat all of.

"Sit. Eat." The Wendigo pointed to her chair. "I will tell you as you dine."

Annie did as told.

The Wendigo lay a photograph on the tabletop. It was Mama and Papa Brown sitting on their front porch in their rocking chairs. They looked older. Worn. It was for this reason that Annie knew it must be a recent photograph.

"Do you know Madison's phone number?" the Wendigo asked.

Annie wanted to lie and say no, but the question caught her by surprise as she looked at her parents. They looked so frail. So old.

She knew that her face, her eyes, would give away any lie. "Yes."

"Good. I think it best if we do not use your cellphone." He lay a nondescript cell phone on the table.

Annie looked at it. She assumed it was one of those phones they called burners, bought anonymously at Walmart for twenty bucks and disposed of when one wanted to keep their identity secret. "Why do you want me to call Maddie?"

"To tell her that you're fine, of course." The Wendigo reached out and stroked her cheek with his thumb. "After you've finished your pancakes, that is."

"Why would I tell her that?" she asked, a tinge of defiance creeping into her voice.

"She's hired a private investigator to find you. A chap by the name of Goff Langdon. The man is a bumbling fool but has become, how shall I say? Annoying. Like the solitary mosquito in your tent when you're camping."

Of course, Annie thought, Maddie would be the one to think outside the box. To hire a PI and not just leave it to the police.

The Wendigo used her spoon, the only utensil allowed her, to carve out a piece of pancake, holding it up for her to take a bite.

"Why would I lie and say that I'm fine?" she asked.

He gently pushed the spoon of pancake into her mouth. "So that the PI will stop buzzing around," he said.

"But I'm not fine, am I?" she said as she chewed.

The Wendigo tapped the photograph of Mama and Papa Brown with his pinky. "They seem like nice people. You told me that they adopted you. What happened to your biological parents?"

"They died in a fire."

"Methamphetamine addicts, I believe you said."

Annie stared at him. Had she told him that, she wondered? It was all such a blur, hard to discern what was real and what was nightmare or the torment of her mind as she awaited her fate.

"Blew themselves to kingdom come," he said. "Is that correct?"

Annie nodded yes.

"Terrible way to go, in a meth fire, being burned alive." The Wendigo eased another spoonful of pancake into her mouth.

A piece tumbled in Annie's mind, a memory flittering on the edges, a memory of who she was, just out of reach.

"Being burnt alive is pretty bad," the Wendigo said. "But I know of worse ways to kill somebody than that."

"I know," Annie said, the defiance in her rearing up. "You're going to kill me, cook me, and eat me."

The Wendigo smiled. "Ah, yes, that does sound horrible. But it won't be that bad, really." He stroked her cheek with his thumb. "As you'll be dead for the worst of it."

"I won't call Maddie and tell her I'm okay. I won't lie to her."

"Oh, but you will, Pumpkin Pie."

"Fuck you. Do whatever you want to me, but I won't be a part of my own demise."

"Not to you, Pumpkin Pie. I already have a plan for you."

"What?"

The Wendigo tapped the picture of Mama and Papa Brown with his pinky again. "Let me tell you what is worse than being burned alive," he said. "And then I'd like you to make a phone call."

Chapter 18

The jarring ring of his cell phone woke Langdon from sleep. It took him a moment to orient himself. He was in his Jeep. The sun was lightening the sky in the east. He'd backed into an old trailhead just down and across from Popa's driveway. Langdon had finally let himself drift off to sleep around 3:00 a.m.

He looked at the phone. It said 'Maddie Campagna.' "Hello."

"Langdon? It's Maddie. Maddie Campagna."

"Good morning."

"She called me just now."

"Who?"

"Annie."

Langdon processed that. The woman was alive. That was the good news. "What'd she have to say?"

"Annie said that she was doing fine. She just got fed up with everything. Her job. Her trouble finding a suitable man. Being stood up at Sugar Magnolia's was the last straw. She said she walked into the bus station and went south until the mood struck her and got off somewhere on the other side of the Mason-Dixon line, wouldn't say where exactly, and was taking some time to figure things out."

"How'd she sound?"

"Terrible. Scared. Tired. Frightened. Her voice was cracking the entire time."

"What'd you say to her?"

"I told her that her parents were heartbroken. That they'd taken her dogs in and were taking care of them."

"And?"

"Annie started crying, and then the call ended."

"No matter how terrible this is," Langdon said. "The truth of the matter is that this is a good thing."

"A good thing?"

"We now know that she is still alive. And that whoever has taken Annie is getting scared. That means I'm getting close."

"You don't think that it might be the truth, do you?" Maddie's voice quivered. "That Annie may've just snapped and gone away?"

"Annie's your friend, Maddie. What do you think?"

There was a pause and then a sigh, followed by a sob. "No. Annie would never do that. Or, I don't think so, anyway."

"She didn't call from her own phone, did she?"

"No."

"Did Annie say anything else?"

"I'm pretty sure that was all of it."

"Could you hear any noise in the background?"

"No… wait. There was a crackling, not from the phone, but from—I think it was a fire. It sounded like there was a fire burning in the background."

After hanging up, Langdon got out of the Jeep to pee against a tree. He could use a cup of coffee, but his Thermos had gone dry sometime after midnight.

Why had Annie called? The abductor couldn't really think that they'd believe the cock-and-bull story of Annie having just run off to find the meaning of life. It might back the police investigation off a bit, as they had enough on their plate already, and most missing person cases involved the individual having voluntarily gone off on their own and magically reappearing sometime later. It was possible this would move it to the back burner for them.

Langdon lumbered his way back to the Jeep. He wasn't getting any younger, so spending the night in the front seat on a stakeout wasn't something his body was willing to abide by. The thought that had been tickling his brain all night long kept nagging at him. What if Annie Brown was in Popa's house right now? Locked in the basement or some special room for just that purpose.

His phone rang. Call from Bart. "I take it you spoke with Maddie Campagna," Langdon said by way of greeting.

"I'm not on the case, you know that," Bart said. "But the lieu told me."

"What's the official police stance?"

"Nothing yet."

"What do you think the unofficial stance will be?"

"Back burner. Put our resources behind MCU looking for who killed your buddy."

Langdon drummed his fingers on the steering wheel. "You find the homeless guy? Graham?"

"Nope. Disappeared off the face of the earth."

"Any word on 4 by Four?"

"Visitors are going to be allowed in later this morning. Ten to twelve."

"You going over?"

"Yep," Bart said. "How about you?"

"Sitting outside Popa's place in Lisbon right now. Any chance you can get a search warrant for his house?"

Bart's guffaw was like a small explosion through the cell phone. "For what?"

"Well, if purchasing and using heroin isn't big enough, how about gut instinct? The guy is dirty. I can tell. He's hiding something about both Liam and Annie."

"That's the beauty of being a PI," Bart said. "You don't have to follow all those rules and protocols."

Langdon had been contemplating doing just that.

~ ~ ~ ~ ~

Chabal woke up in an empty bed if one were to discount dog, who was standing over her, wondering if she was hungry, and if so, shouldn't they eat breakfast? Langdon had insisted that he was going to keep watch over Popa the entire night, in case of any middle-of-the-night outings or early morning visitors. She looked at her phone. No messages. He'd promised to text or call with any updates.

A cup of dry food with a squirt of salmon oil for the canine and a cup of steaming coffee for her and they were both happy. Dog went outside to take care of business and chase away any squirrels, and Chabal went to her computer and picked up where she'd left off last night. She was compiling a profile on each person from Dr. Corbett's list, but so far, she had come across nobody who'd previously been suspected of being a serial killer.

She texted Langdon. Good morning.

There was no immediate response, so she went back to the computer, deciding to dig into Popa some more. After all, that seemed to be the one lead, tenuous as it may be. The man had grown up in Durham with his parents, gone to school at UMO, and then returned to the area, renting in Topsham before buying a house in Lisbon about ten years back. He was thirty-seven years old, was a CPA, had bought the current business twelve years ago, and had never been married. Three speeding tickets over the years, nothing more serious, was a member of the Knights of Columbus.

And then, there it was. Gregory Popa had several times been the state champion of the Maine Archery Club. One year, he'd been third in the nationals.

Her phone rang with a call from Langdon. He filled her in on the call from Maddie and the talk with Bart. She could hear the tiredness in his voice.

She told him about Popa being an expert with the bow.

"That bastard is the one who tried to kill me," Langdon said.

"The evidence does seem to point in that direction," Chabal said. "But we need more proof."

She was trying to dampen his anger. Langdon was one of the most laid-back people she'd ever known in her life. Not much upset him. He just went with the flow. Up to a point. On occasion, she'd seen his temper erupt into a black rage that couldn't be quelled until it'd run its course. She could hear that fury igniting now as the realization that his friend had been murdered and others he cared about were in harm's way.

"You're absolutely right," Langdon said in a low voice. "Bart's going to swing by and pick you up. Leave dog at home mending his leg. Bring your pistol."

"What for?"

"I'm going to do a little B & E at Popa's house after he leaves for work. Bart's getting off duty in ten minutes and is then going to tail the man. You're going to be my lookout."

As Chabal hung up, there was a knock at the door. Bart was here sooner than she expected. Strange, he usually came through the mudroom and not the front door. Dog started barking, having come back inside, and was even more surprised by the early morning intrusion than Chabal.

They rarely locked the door, even at night, but last night, home alone, with a murderer tramping the streets of Brunswick, it seemed a good idea. Chabal turned the latch, opening the door wide to let Bart in, but only, it wasn't the cop. It was a tall man with dark hair, hard eyes, and a gaunt frame.

Chabal was aware that she had on a bathrobe over her nightwear and no bra. She pulled the robe a bit tighter. Her pistol was in the drawer under the bed, easy to access at night, but useless here at the front door.

"Sorry to bother you. I'm Dr. Tom Corbett. Are you Mrs. Langdon?"

"Yes. What can I do for you?"

Dog was barking at the screen door, trying to push his way out, the fur on his back end standing straight up.

"Is your husband home?"

That was a loaded question, Chabal thought. To say no would indicate she was here alone, but to say he was here would be even more complicated. Luckily, Bart would be here in a bit, if she could just stall.

"No," she said. "He should be back any minute. He ran out to grab bagels."

"May I come in, Mrs. Langdon?" Corbett reached his hand up to the screen door as if to pull it open.

"I'd rather that you didn't. I'm not dressed."

Corbett paused. "He's not coming back soon, is he?"

"What do you want, Dr. Corbett?"

"I've been helping your husband on a case he's working on." Corbett smiled genially.

"I know all about it. Is there something I can do for you?"

"I'm sorry to startle you this morning, Mrs. Langdon. I just had a thought. There is a doctor I know just down in Falmouth that I didn't put on the list that your husband asked me to compile."

"You could've given him a call, texted, or emailed."

"Yes, yes, of course. But I wanted to make sure he understood the importance. You see, this man and I know each other quite well, and the thing is, he is about as tall as me. And thin. With dark hair. People have mentioned that we could be doppelgangers."

"That is very interesting, indeed," Chabal said.

Dr. Corbett stood waiting for more. There was none. "Very well, I will send your husband his name and contact information."

"Thank you, Dr. Corbett."

He turned to go, stepping down from the small porch, and then stopped and turned back. "Have you ever considered getting any work done, Mrs. Langdon?"

"Work?"

"I could create a gorgeous pair of breasts for you. I know just what we'd do. To complement what you already have, of course."

Chapter 19

Langdon crossed the road and went into the thin band of trees on the other side that separated Popa's home from his neighbor's. The man had left in his BMW about twenty minutes earlier with Bart tailing him. Chabal was in the Jeep with cell phone ready in case any unexpected visitors stopped by.

She'd told him and Bart about the visit from Corbett. Langdon was simmering inside. He realized that it was most definitely a message from the doctor that he also knew where Langdon lived. The question was, did that make him the bad guy? Well, yes, Langdon grinned wryly as he worked his way closer to the house. The man was a real piece of work. He was arrogant, crass, cheated on his wife, and who knows what else, but was he the man responsible for the disappearance of Liam Couture, the abduction of Annie Brown, and the death of Danny T.?

Corbett had in no way threatened Chabal, but he had commented on giving her a boob job. What was the purpose of that churlish comment? It was possible that he was just promoting his services, no matter how odd that was, but Langdon thought that it was retaliation for going to his house and forcing him to produce a list of people, and yes, Langdon had been threatening him.

As Chabal had finished recounting the early morning incident, Langdon's phone had buzzed with a text from Corbett. It was the promised name and contact information of Corbett's doppelganger. And, in fact, the man was. Jasper Ansari. Corbett hadn't sent a picture, but it was easy enough to Google the man, and he did indeed look quite a bit similar.

Tom Corbett's profile picture on Patience had been shadowed and not very clear. The police were currently trying to do a facial recognition but had not yet gotten anywhere, and according to Bart, the case might soon be headed to the back burner. The name Tom Corbett and his address had been used, but the email was not his, at least according to him, even though it'd been opened in his name.

There was no proof of any kind that Annie had even met a man that night she disappeared. Unless you took Corbett's steadfast denial as such, though that still fell under the dubious, as in, how do you prove a negative? Maybe somebody had yanked her from her home or carjacked her on the way to or from such a date. If Corbett had just admitted that it was him who'd signed up for Patience, met Annie online, made plans to get together, and then changed his mind or she'd been a no-show, there wasn't a damn thing that would say otherwise.

It stood to reason that Annie Brown had looked Corbett up and discovered better pictures of him, that he was a doctor and whatnot. They might've even had a Zoom conversation. In which case, it was either Tom Corbett or somebody who looked very much like him, so Annie couldn't distinguish the difference between computer images versus video meet and greet. Of course, they might not have Zoomed. All this was conjecture because Annie was missing.

Maddie was meeting him back at his office with the Browns later in the day to discuss the latest development, the phone call from Annie. He knew that she was skeptical about the nature of the call. Langdon was interested in what Meg and Harold Brown might think and if anything more could be gleaned from the two friends' conversation.

Langdon left the protection of the trees from the rear of the house. There was a large shed that he worked his way around before approaching the back door. There were no signs of security cameras. He couldn't see any indication of an alarm system, but better safe than sorry. He found the phone line coming into the house and cut it, trying to make it look jagged, like maybe a squirrel chewed through it. There wasn't much chance that Popa or the police would believe that, but it'd at least cast a shadow of a doubt, much like the phone call from Annie had brought her kidnapping into question.

Once back at the sliding glass door in the rear of the house, Langdon was happy to see that it was an outside slider, much easier to gain entry through than an inside one. The L-shaped latch pivoted upward to fit into a bracket that was little more than a hole in the wall. Langdon inserted a pry bar between the door frame and the door at the bottom, diagonal from the latch, and lifted. By tilting the door outward, the latch was lowered, and the door unlocked, allowing him to slide it open.

The alarm went off. *Whir-whir-whir-whir*. Grating.

This was not unexpected. By cutting the telephone wire, he'd cut the transmission of the illegal entry unless, of course, Popa had a wireless system. In which case, Bart was keeping tabs with a buddy at the Lisbon police department, who would notify him of any break-ins, who would, in turn, text Langdon to get out. It wasn't likely that the response time would be under twenty minutes unless they were very unlucky.

Whir-whir-whir-whir.

Langdon stepped inside and shut the door. The alarm was annoying but something he'd have to live with. He scanned the kitchen for any videos. There didn't appear to be any. He moved his way to the stairs and upstairs until he found Popa's bedroom and began tossing the house, putting everything back, but not too carefully. He wanted the man to know that he'd been violated but leave that shadowy gray area for the police.

Whir-whir-whir-whir.

There was a box of tissues and lube on the table next to the bed. Classy, Langdon thought, trying to banish the image of the man masturbating.

Langdon's pocket vibrated. Text from Bart. He's headed your way. 20 min.

K. Let me know about Lisbon PD.

Got it.

Time to pick up the process, Langdon thought. If he was right in thinking that Annie might be in the house, the basement was the most likely place. If she was here, or there was evidence of Popa's guilt in the house, the man wouldn't want the police showing up any more than Langdon would if he were wrong. Finding nothing in the man's bedroom, Langdon went back downstairs to check the basement. The door was off the kitchen. It was a typical interior door with no special locking mechanism.

Whir-whir-whir-whir.

The stairs were carpeted, allowing him to move down them quietly. It was possible that the others—and Langdon knew there must be at least two more from the attacks the other night—could be downstairs. Thoughts of the Grotto—a group so extreme that The Church of Satan had banished them—swirled through his mind. The Wendigo. Cannibalism. Sacrifices. People dancing around fires at night, speaking in tongues. He took out his Glock as he reached the bottom step.

Whir-whir-whir-whir.

The first room he looked in held workout equipment. He moved on to the second room. It was filled with archery accessories. Bows, arrows, quivers, targets, gloves. Langdon wondered if it was possible to match the arrow recovered in the woods behind his own house to the arrows here or whether one of these bows had been used, much like a bullet could sometimes be matched to the barrel of the gun from which it'd come.

Whir-whir-whir-whir.

Things to be noted, he thought, but he was running out of time. He looked at his phone. He had nine minutes. Best check the last door and then get out. There was a leather recliner facing a theater-sized television. Next to the chair was another chair with a box of tissue and lube. Fantastic, Langdon thought, the guy has multiple jerking-off stations in his house. He turned on the television and hit play on the old-school VCR as he went over to the record player in the corner. The guy lived in the past, Langdon thought. He turned it on and dropped the needle on the record on the turntable. Loud classical music filled the room. Bach, Beethoven, Mozart, or something like that, Langdon thought, not being much of a classical music fan himself.

Whir-whir-whir-whir.

He turned back to the screen and froze. There was a naked man strapped to a tabletop. The video zoomed in on the terrified eyes of the man. Then the video cut to the man hanging upside down. A man stood to the side of him, holding a gleaming knife. He was wearing a monk's robe, back to the camera. There was no sound to the video, only the classical music loudly blaring from the turntable behind Langdon. And the alarm.

Whir-whir-whir-whir.

The video again zoomed in on the captive man's face, his quivering jowls, saliva drooling from his lips, perspiration on his brow, his cheeks bulging from whatever was stuffed in his mouth, and the bulging eyes. The man in the monk's robe, his head shrouded in the hood, raised the gleaming blade, stepped forward, and cut his throat.

Langdon's phone buzzed. Text from Bart. Almost there. Get out.

The television screen flickered and then there was another person buckled to the tabletop. This time it was a naked woman.

Langdon's phone buzzed. Text from Chabal. He's here. I hope you're out.

Langdon went to favorites and hit her number.

"You out?" she answered.

"Send Bart in. We have our man. Or, at least one of them."

"What'd you find?" Chabal asked.

Before Langdon could reply, the voice of Bart came over her phone. "You got to get out of there. If you got anything, it won't be admissible in court."

Langdon had had that thought. But his feet seemed rooted to the floor. He heard the door open upstairs. "I have to go," he said. "Popa's home."

It took only seconds until footsteps came down the stairs. Langdon was waiting for the man sitting in his recliner, the classical music wafting through the air as video images of naked men and women being killed played on the television screen. He had his Glock out and trained on the door.

Popa came through the door. His face was ashen around the edges of his thick beard. He stood in the opening, staring at Langdon for about twenty seconds. He held no sort of weapon. His eyes flickered to the television, then back to Langdon.

And then he turned and ran. Langdon came out of the chair and went after him. The man tripped and fell halfway up the stairs, and Langdon grabbed his foot and pulled him back down, smashing the pistol into his face as he slid past him to the basement floor.

Langdon took two steps back down and kicked Popa in the face as he went to rise to his feet, knocking him backward into the wall, where he crumpled to the floor. He was bleeding from a cut on his chin and sobbing in anguish.

Langdon grabbed his beard and dragged the man back into the television room, Popa's hand grasping his as he begged him to let go.

"It's not what you think," Popa whined, his eyes drawn to the screen where a young man was getting his throat slit.

"Yeah, how about you tell me what it is, then?" Langdon said. He picked up Popa and tumbled the man into the recliner. "It looks like people getting killed, is what it looks like. Some sort of snuff film, and you're getting off on them being murdered. Butchered."

"That's not true," Popa said as he sat staring at the carnage of the bloodletting on the screen. "I didn't want to be part of it. I tried to leave. He wouldn't let me."

"Yeah, so much so that you filmed it all and then sit here and whack off to people getting killed. You're sick and perverted and are going to burn in Hell."

Popa's eyes flickered over to Langdon. "Please. I know it's wrong. But I'm not hurting anybody. It's him. He's the one."

"Far as I can tell, you're there participating in the whole shitshow, not stopping anything, and in fact, *filming* it, then coming back here and getting your jollies off watching what happened. You are a twisted and perverted fuck, and to even call you a human being would be too kind. Don't tell me you're not hurting anybody."

"He makes me do it," Popa said.

"Bullshit." Langdon stared at the man for a long moment. "You know, he's setting you up."

"What do you mean?"

"Whoever is yanking your chain knew we'd be able to trace that credit card to your Aunt and then to you."

"He wouldn't do that."

"You tried to kill me in the woods with a bow and arrow," Langdon said. "I bet he told you to do that as well. Knowing that we'd find out about your archery accomplishments. He set you up to take the fall."

"That's not—"

"Yeah? Tell me how it all happened," Langdon said.

"I can't."

"Because you know in your mind that you are wrong. That you are depraved. A deviant. You have no defense."

Popa started sobbing. "I don't want to be like this. It just happened."

"Tell me how."

"It started off innocent enough," Popa said. "He came to me and asked me if I'd like to get together with the others. The children of the banished Grotto of the Church of Satan. Our parents were the founding members of that group, but over time, it waned. Several of the members became increasingly radical, causing many to drop out and return to normal society. His father was the worst. But when he came to me and told me that seven other children had agreed to meet for coffee, I went as well. It was like a support group, you know, for children of the Wendigo Grotto."

Bart stepped into the room with his pistol trained on Popa. Chabal followed him through, gun also drawn and aimed.

Popa's eyes darted their way and then back to Langdon. "We decided to get together once a month, taking turns hosting. At first, it was just to talk, but then somebody started up a conversation about Wicca. It was about the science of controlling the secret forces of nature. That appealed to all of us. You know, because of the forces outside of our control when we were children. The things we saw, were involved with, and participated in. A few of the others dropped out. We wanted to control those forces, not be victims to them. Harness the natural power of nature. Get in touch with our five senses. We started meeting weekly, having rituals, white magic for healing, right-hand magic for good—none of that Satanic bullshit."

Popa covered his face with his hands. After a bit, Langdon prodded him along. "To do good where your parents did evil?"

"Yes. That was all. We were Wiccans practicing healthy magic to banish the negative pressures in our lives. And then it shifted. Just a bit at first. We'd sacrifice chickens and stew them up during the supermoons. He suggested that the moon was the source of our magic, of our power, of our possible redemption. And chickens? It was no big deal. Then he—"

"Who is he?" Langdon asked.

Popa looked up, surprised, almost as if he'd forgotten there was anybody else in the room."

"The Wendigo." Popa again pressed his hands to his face.

"Then he what?"

"He suggested that our power was waning, that we needed to up our game. He said the supermoon demanded a human sacrifice. That is when Jill dropped out, said no way, and left. Three days before the supermoon, he called us to the barn, and there she was, naked, shackled to a tabletop. I wanted to walk out the door and never come back, right there and then, but I was too scared to leave. After all, that's what Jill did, and where did that get her?"

"And it turned you on, didn't it?" Langdon asked. "Seeing her helpless, restrained, afraid—it excited you, didn't it?"

Popa stared and then nodded his head up and down twice. "I tried to fight the evil inside of me, but it was too powerful."

"Go on," Langdon said.

"The night of the supermoon, he slit her throat, bled her out, and made a stew of her. We all refused to eat any, but the Wendigo didn't mind. Eventually, he began to say that he was the power, the spirit, and that he would lead us to salvation by gorging on human flesh."

"How many of you are there?" Bart asked. "Still participating?"

"Three. Plus the Wendigo."

"Where is Annie Brown?"

"In the barn."

"Where is the barn?"

Popa suddenly started to twitch, and then a shudder ran through his body. Langdon stood up as spittle leaked from the corners of the man's mouth. His torso was wracked with convulsions. Fuck, Langdon thought, stepping forward just as the man spewed forth a projectile of bile, blood, and vomit and fell to the floor. His limbs flailed, his body convulsing as if an alien were about to burst from his stomach.

"Who is the Wendigo?" Langdon yelled, leaning over the man.

Popa's looked for a split-second at Langdon, looked as if to speak, and his special body concoction of mud mucus glopped from his mouth like an erupting volcano before he passed out.

Chapter 20

Langdon and Chabal had spent the rest of the day and into the night with the police. First, Brunswick PD, and then the Staties took over. The preliminary assumption of the cause of death was by poison but testing would follow. Langdon figured the man had taken the suicide pill when he'd covered his face in his hands.

The story concocted was that Popa had contacted Langdon wanting to confess. When Langdon and Chabal had arrived, the alarm was going off and Popa was in distress. Langdon had struck the man to prevent him from hurting himself and then had texted Bart about the situation. Popa had taken him and Chabal down to the basement to share his guilt via video. Bart showed up, and then Popa killed himself.

This all was basically true, Langdon thought as he drove into his office in the bookshop the next morning. Maddie Campagna and the Browns were coming by at ten to get an update on the case and what progress had been made. He welcomed the opportunity to get their input on Annie's mysterious phone call. The truth was that, despite Popa's damning confessions, they were dead in the water. Popa had been their strongest lead to find the people who'd taken Annie. Now, he was no more.

Yes, Popa had given some information. He'd said there were three members of the Grotto, now two, plus the Wendigo. Annie was being held in a barn. But he'd not said where and hadn't given any names. The lead candidate for this mysterious Wendigo was

Dr. Tom Corbett. Or, this other doctor, down in Falmouth, Jasper Ansari. The doppelganger.

Langdon passed Bowdoin College and then the Mall, both on the right. Before him lay the downtown. It was a good town, he thought. Not a place that deserved the likes of Gregory Popa and this Wendigo beast. Just past The Coffee Dog Bookstore, he turned left to go into the all-day parking behind the bookshop. He and dog, the canine's leg doing much better, walked back and crossed over Maine Street to get two coffees, deciding upon a couple of pieces of coffee cake as well. That would make Starling happy.

A few people said hello and good morning to him, and he wondered what they'd think if they knew that somebody was abducting, torturing, killing, and eating people in their town. Or anywhere, for that matter. He couldn't imagine telling Annie's parents or Maddie the fate that was looming over her. He had until the supermoon to find her. May 26th. The Super Flower Blood Moon. The partial eclipse was slated to happen at 5:30 a.m. That, he figured, was the final deadline to find and save Annie.

"How you doing, Boss?" Starling asked as he came through the bookshop door, which was propped open for business.

"Been better, my friend, been better." He handed Starling the coffee and cake. "How's the store been doing?"

"I think the *Bath Daily News* story mentioning that you, prominent, and I quote, prominent local businessman Goff Langdon, getting attacked in the woods with a bow and arrow, sent people scurrying in here the last few days. I think they were hoping to see you but settled for buying a book or two instead."

Langdon went to the computer and brought up the past few days' totals. He whistled. "You're going to need all hands on deck today. Especially if they mention me being involved in the death of another prominent local businessman."

"Yeah," Starling said. "Do tell."

At that moment, Maddie Campagna and the Browns, Meg, and

Harold walked through the door. Langdon ushered them back to his office, kicking himself for not having gotten them a coffee as well. He had to pull a third chair across from his desk, bidding them to sit, before sinking into his own chair.

"My daughter didn't just take off," Meg Brown said.

"She's too responsible for that," Harold added.

"I believe you," Langdon said.

"What are you doing about it?" Meg asked, barely coherent and then losing her composure completely, covering her face with her hands as she started bawling, and her husband put his arms around her protectively.

Langdon grabbed a box of tissues and slid them across the desk. "I'm doing everything I possibly can," he said gently.

"Have you found anything new?" Maddie asked. Her skin was pale and her eyes red, showing the stress that they'd all been under.

"I found one of the people behind the abduction of Annie," Langdon said. "Unfortunately, he's dead."

Meg gasped. "Who?"

"Did you kill him?" Harold asked. His eyes suggested that he'd like to have been the one doing the killing.

Langdon shook his head. "I believe he poisoned himself."

"Who was it?" Meg asked, her voice high-pitched. She cleared her throat. "I'm sorry, who was this person?"

Langdon sighed. He had so much to tell them, and it meant so little. He was no closer to finding their daughter than before he'd shaken Popa loose from his hole. "His name was Gregory Popa. He was an accountant here in town."

"Did he say anything before he died?" Maddie asked. She seemed to be the voice of reason, Harold comforting Meg, who had, again, broken down crying.

"Not much," Langdon said. "Though he did give me a few things that I might be able to follow up on." Very little, Langdon thought. But he knew that any bit of hope would help, that Maddie and the

Browns desperately needed something to cling to right now.

"Like what?" Maddie asked.

"The Grotto had other members, four of them in total responsible for kidnapping Annie," Langdon said. "Three now. And Annie is being held in a barn."

"Why are they doing this?" Harold asked, his voice hoarse and tinged with fear and anger.

Langdon sighed. "They believe themselves to be Wiccans. Some would call them witches. Many Wiccans believe in good magic and harnessing the invisible force of nature. This group seems to want to do so for… nefarious purposes."

"Wiccans?" Meg asked. "Nefarious purposes?"

Langdon took a deep breath. "Fifty years ago, a group established a… religious cult locally that they called the Wendigo Grotto. A wendigo is a mythical Native American creature that… I think they mean to sacrifice Annie." He figured they didn't need to know at this point that she'd then be bled out and eaten. "I believe that this Wendigo Grotto has resurfaced."

"What do you mean?" Harold asked.

Langdon would rather be shot at, beaten, or just about anything other than having to have this particular conversation. "They, uh, believe in the power of nature, and especially the full moon when it is at its closest point to Earth. I believe they plan on sacrificing Annie, uh, during an eclipse of the Super Flower Blood Moon."

"When is that?" Harold asked.

Langdon coughed. "The morning of May 26th."

Three blank faces stared back at him.

"Sacrifice her." Eleven days from now." Harold repeated mechanically.

"What makes you think this?" Maddie asked.

Langdon chose to answer Maddie's question. "Popa had a video in his basement of this happening to others before. And he brought up the supermoons as a source of their power. Their magic. The ability to harness the forces of nature for their evil intentions."

"There's a video?" Maddie asked, a shocked look on her face. "Could anybody be identified?"

Langdon shook his head. "I only saw a bit of it, but only the victims were visible. The police are analyzing it now. I don't know any more."

Meg had her hands over her face stifling sobs.

Harold drew her closer. "Was Annie on the video?"

"I don't believe so."

"But the police will know?" Meg sobbed.

"I doubt they'll be able to tell you much," Langdon said. "Not yet, anyway. But, by all means, you should try."

"Is there anything more you can tell us?" Maddie asked.

"That's all I know," Langdon said. "We'll get her back safely, I promise."

"You can't promise anything of the sort," Meg said, her voice cracking and choking.

"You have no more leads?" Harold asked.

"What about that doctor?" Maddie asked. "The one who met Annie on that dating site, who she was going to meet for dinner?"

"He claims that he knows nothing of it," Langdon said. "That his information and credit card number were stolen without his knowledge."

"Like identity theft?" Maddie asked. "Do you believe him?"

"I don't know."

~ ~ ~ ~ ~

At noon, Langdon and Chabal walked into the diner. Rosie, the owner, was hosting a celebration of life of sorts for Danny T. The only family the man had had were mostly the patrons of the diner, and it seemed appropriate to gather in the place where Danny T. had spent so many of his waking hours the past twenty-nine years.

Richam, Jewell, Starling, and 4 by Four were crammed into one of the booths in the middle.

"I didn't realize you were out of the hospital," Langdon said, pulling two chairs over so he and Chabal could sit at the end of the booth.

4 by Four made a face. "The doctors were none too happy, but I've spent enough time there in the last year. Even if some of the nurses are mighty fine, I think I might've gotten a date with one of the doctors. She gave me her number."

Richam sniggered. "Yeah, well, I was there, remember? She told you to give her a call if you had any complications."

"That's a fact," 4 by Four said. "And I plan to have complications."

Jewell glared across the table, but then her expression softened. "You just never stop, do you?"

"Can't blame me if the ladies love me," 4 by Four said.

Langdon looked at his friend with the bruised face and bandaged leg. He thought of him going home alone after the celebration of life for their dead friend. "Glad to see you out."

"What happened yesterday?" Richam asked. "Star told us some."

Langdon told them the bare bones of the previous day's exploits. Too many times in the past, he'd drawn his friends into his PI work and endangered their lives. Now, Danny T. was dead, most likely due to his involvement in the most recent case.

"Gregory Popa," 4 by Four shook his head. "I sat next to him just a couple months back at a luncheon for the Downtown Association."

"What can we do to help out?" Richam asked.

Jewell gave him a look across the table.

"Nothing," Langdon said.

"C'mon," Star said. "We always help out when you catch a big one."

"Not this time." Langdon thought of Danny T. The shadowy figure of the Wendigo flitted through his mind. A person who abducted, tortured, killed, and ate people. Even worse, somehow, than the BTK killer who bound, tortured, and killed. He wondered if the papers would take to calling this person the ATKA killer. "Not this time," he repeated.

"We can ask around, do some research, something," Star said.

"Can I get your attention?"

All eyes swiveled to the source of the voice, where Rosie, five feet tall and almost as wide, stood on the counter. She had to be close to seventy and always had a sheen of perspiration on her face. She was one of the kindest people Langdon knew and had been Danny T.'s closest friend.

Rosie looked around at all the faces before her. "We're gathered here today to celebrate the life of one of our own, taken before his time. Today, the food, and the memories, are free. Feel free to share in both."

Jewell surprised them all by stepping forward and clearing her throat. "I have a memory I'd like to share," she said.

The crowd murmured for her to go ahead.

"It was just about twenty-five years ago," Jewell said. "My husband and children and I hadn't lived in this country very long. I didn't know Danny T. all that well before the day I'm going to share, but I sure did come to embrace him after it. Langdon had left his daughter for me to watch along with my two, Tangerine and Will. We played in the backyard in the snow and had just come in when Langdon called me, worried about something, some man, some monster. But he was too late. The man was already at my door. I took an old pistol from the closet and braced that man, but he took it from me and knocked me to the ground. He was going to hurt my children. Our children. Langdon and Danny T. came careening down the driveway, and Langdon charged at the man who knocked him down as well. And then started kicking him. He was going to kill us all, and then Danny T. drove the car straight at this monster by the name of Shakespeare and made him run for his life, saving all of us. We wouldn't be here today if it weren't for the bravery and heroics of Danny T."

"Three cheers for Danny T.," Rosie said.

As the gathering broke into hip-hip-hooraying, Langdon joined them, his own thoughts flashing back to that day. Jewell had embellished the memory slightly, whether in honor of the dead or because time had changed it, he wasn't sure. Danny T. had indeed made an attempt but, in reality, had panicked and run into the side of the house and parked the car in the living room. Maybe that had been what drove Shakespeare off, or maybe the man had just taken it as his cue to skedaddle, but either way, Danny T. had acted the hero that day.

~ ~ ~ ~ ~

Jasper Ansari agreed to meet with Langdon at a bar just down the street from his office at six o'clock. That had given Langdon and Chabal some time after the celebration of life to dig into who exactly this Tom Corbett doppelganger was. He worked out of a practice in Falmouth and was affiliated with Maine Medical Center in Portland. Jasper practiced internal medicine, which seemed to just be a doctor who treated adults for general symptoms across a wide spectrum.

He was forty years old, had never married, and lived in a beautiful house in the Falmouth Foreside. Jasper was a member of the gym, played racquetball, and owned a sailboat. Langdon and Chabal were unable to find out any marital history on the man at all, which was odd, and the only family member they could find was a brother in Oregon.

Langdon was at a high-top round table in the corner facing the road when Jasper came in. He was the spitting image of Tom Corbett. His lanky form seemed almost emaciated, and he was six inches over six feet at least. Langdon waved to him as he came through the door. As he approached, Langdon noted that, up close, his face differed a bit from Corbett's. His nose was larger and hooked like the beak of a falcon with a thin scar on his right cheek.

Jasper approached the table warily, like a tiger advancing on its prey.

Langdon stood and held out his hand. "Jasper. I'm Langdon."

The man grasped it and shook it firmly before sitting down. "What's this all about?"

What was it all about, Langdon wondered? He didn't really have an iota of evidence that this man was in any way involved. "I'm searching for a missing woman."

"Somebody I know?"

"Possibly." Langdon was stretching the truth there.

"Who is it?"

"Annie Brown." Langdon didn't see the least sign of recognition on the man's face.

"Don't know her. She related to Karen Brown?" Jasper's words were clipped and precise.

Langdon shook his head. "Not that I know of."

"She from Falmouth?"

"Cape Elizabeth."

A waiter came over to them, and Langdon got a beer and Jasper ordered a martini.

"I don't understand why we're meeting," Jasper said.

Langdon thought it interesting that the man had agreed to meet with him at all. "Annie Brown was supposed to be going on a date up in Brunswick with a man she met on a dating site. She hasn't been seen since."

"What's that have to do with me?"

"Have you ever used the dating site called Patience?"

Jasper leaned forward over the table. He interlaced his fingers and settled his craggy jaw onto the bridge made. "Are you suggesting that I kidnapped this woman?"

"Did you?"

Jasper barked out a hoarse laugh like coarse sandpaper. "I'm not in the business of abducting women. I'm a doctor. I help people."

The waiter delivered their drinks. Langdon took a sip off the foamy top of his beer. "Are you in a relationship with anybody currently?"

"In a relationship?"

"Dating. Engaged. Married. Man or woman."

"Are you?"

"My wife's name is Chabal."

"That's a strange name."

"Combination of things," Langdon said. "Her mother was an odd woman."

"Perhaps I'll wait to hear the story directly from her, now that we're old friends," Jasper said drily. "Maybe we can go on a double date."

"So you are in a relationship with somebody?"

"Perhaps you can tell me what you suspect me of and why, exactly?"

Langdon pondered that. It was a piece that he knew he'd most likely have to share. "Do you know Tom Corbett?"

"Dr. Tom Corbett?"

"Yes."

"Of course. We've done several conferences together. Just last summer, we were down in Boston for three days."

That, Langdon thought, at least confirmed that the two men knew each other, if only professionally. "Would you say that you were friends?"

Jasper shrugged. "We got a few drinks together. I've seen him once or twice since. Met for lunch in the Old Port a couple months back. Why? Do you suspect Dr. Corbett is involved in abducting this woman? Tom's a good guy. He'd never do something like that."

"How do you know?"

"He seems to be a generous man. A kind man. He's a doctor."

Langdon chuckled. "He does boob jobs. Why is it that you go to the same conferences?"

Jasper suddenly sat back. "We look alike. Dr. Corbett and me. Everybody always says we're like twins."

"Have you ever used the dating site called Patience?" Langdon asked.

"Yes. For about four months. In the fall, I met the woman I'm dating now on Patience, and I stopped using it."

Langdon wondered about the implications of all that. It was certainly something to think about.

Chapter 21

Annie woke up that morning not feeling terrified. Rather, she felt satisfied. Content. Maybe even elated. This was a strange emotion for her waking from a night's sleep. Especially as the tendrils of flames and screams still echoed in her waking mind.

Instead of banishing the nightmare to be replaced by warm memories of Mama and Papa Brown, she did something quite different. Annie's mind trickled backward into her dreams. There'd been a fire. It was nighttime. She remembered the moon shining brightly overhead. It was a cool night, and the blaze—was it a bonfire?—felt good. It brought warmth.

A little girl was standing in front of a building, holding a stuffed animal, her thumb in her mouth. It was a dog, worn and beaten with floppy ears, and the girl held the stuffed dog by the tail. Annie remembered the dog, her only friend, Sally, the stuffed dog. Why had she called it Sally, she wondered? Annie plummeted down and settled into the little girl so that she was seeing the inferno, and yes, it was more an inferno than anything else, through her own eyes.

Now, Annie was able to hear the calls for help, the screams of pain. She could feel her mouth crease, and she realized she was smiling. It wasn't in malice so much as in satisfaction. Annie understood that the bad things would no longer happen. The Overlord was burning. He and his evil partner, Annie's mother, had been relegated to their fate.

Annie hit the rewind button, working the dream backward. She was in her bed asleep when a noise awakened her. She grabbed Sally and shuffled into the bathroom, fearful of waking the Overlord. She heard voices drifting from the shed behind the trailer and knew that the Overlord and her mother were out there cooking. That's what they called it, but she never saw any food. Annie assumed that they went out there to cook so they wouldn't have to share with her, not that they would anyway.

With them out of the house, Annie felt safe to go to the refrigerator and see if there was any food. There wasn't. What were they cooking in the shed? Annie went to the window and looked out. The moon was shining brightly but it was still dark, still scary, with shadows and evil lurking. But she was hungry. Her tummy rumbled. Maybe they wouldn't notice if she snuck in and took some of what they were cooking.

There was a flashlight in a bowl by the door, but it didn't work. Fucking battery must be dead, the Overlord had said. On a shelf was the lantern they used when the power went out. Annie had seen how the Overlord took the glass top off, struck a match, and lit the wick before putting the glass back on. It took her seven tries to light the match, but she managed to hold it to the white tongue coming from the base of the lantern, and then put the glass back on. She noticed that she'd burnt her thumb but didn't think much of it. Pain was just part of her being.

She had Sally in one hand, so she had to put the lantern on the floor to open the door and then pick it back up. She didn't bother closing the door behind her, as she figured she'd be right back. Annie walked carefully around the side of the house, avoiding the rusted-out car, the wheelbarrow without a tire, steering clear of the thistles. She noticed there was no snow on the ground, but it was still cold, very cold. She should've put her jacket on.

The windows of the shed were painted black. Annie had tried to look through them before, in the light of day, but to no avail. This she knew, so didn't bother to try. With tentative steps, she approached the door. She was scared. So very scared. But her tummy rumbled again, and her hunger won over the fear. Quietly, carefully, she set the lantern down by the door, clutching Sally to her.

With a trembling hand, she reached out and slowly turned the knob and opened the door. Just a crack. She tried to look through but was unable to see anything. Annie took a deep breath and opened the door wider. There were strange creatures inside in yellow spacesuits and with large black masks covering their faces. Two of them. Their hands were blue. Annie shrieked, and the two monsters swung their snouts to look at her. She stepped back, falling backward and kicking out her legs, knocking the lantern into the opening of the door.

There was a *whoosh* as Annie scrambled away from the strange creatures in her back shed, and then the ground shook underneath her with an explosion and flames shooting out the open door of the shed. At first, Annie thought that the shed might've been an alien rocket ship that had blasted off. She realized her knees were scraped and bleeding from crawling and stood up, turning slowly back to see the blaze, the bonfire, the inferno raging behind her.

She still held Sally in her hand, and she brought the stuffed dog up, the tail under her nose and her thumb in her mouth.

And then she understood. She'd killed the Overlord. She was free. A smile creased her face.

"What are you smiling at, Pumpkin Pie?" the Wendigo asked.

Annie opened her eyes. She wondered what had happened to Sally, her stuffed puppy dog, yet even without her, she wasn't scared any longer. She'd killed the Overlord.

"I was wondering how I was going to kill you," she said.

The Wendigo burst out a coarse guffaw. "Finally, Pumpkin Pie, you are coming to understand that hatred is not wrong. Vengeance has its place. You *should* hate me. You *should* want to kill me. After all, I have you strapped naked to a tabletop and plan on bleeding you out, stewing you, and then eating you. Yes. You should want to kill me. It's your nature. It is our nature. It is human nature. Don't try to bury it or push it away. Let it flow. Feel the power. It's the sixth sense."

"You look tired," Annie said. It seemed that as the time of her death approached, the Wendigo was becoming more beastly, transforming from human to monster. "Did you sleep poorly?"

The Wendigo gave her a searching glance. "I slept fine." He put the collar around her neck and then unstrapped her restraints, gave her the monk's robe, pausing to allow her a minute for the feeling to return to her limbs, and led her to the table for a breakfast of French toast.

"I sense something has happened. Tell me," Annie said.

The Wendigo slapped her hard on the side of the head, the force of the blow crumpling her to the ground. She didn't mind. Annie had gone back to a time when she embraced pain. Used ache and agony as her secret power. She had killed the Overlord.

"The police are closing in, aren't they," Annie said, rising back to her feet. "I can tell you're worried."

The Wendigo looked like he might hit her again, but stopped and smiled instead. "Not the police, my dear, but a bookstore owner who plays at being a private investigator has proven to be more formidable than I would've thought."

"What's his name?" Annie sat down at the table. She felt that the tables had been turned, that the power had shifted. To her.

"He's nobody."

"Tell me. Is it that man Langdon you mentioned before? What does it matter? Soon, we'll be together, the same being."

The Wendigo sat down across from her, his dark eyes reflecting his soul, and laughed again. "I do believe that you have opened your heart to Satan. Yes. The man's name is Langdon. He has a tasty-looking wife named Chabal. He'll soon regret ever having stuck his nose into my life. Yes. Yes, he will soon regret it very dearly indeed."

"Langdon and Chabal," Annie said. "Are they close to finding me?"

"No. If they were, they'd already be here. But we may have to move you somewhere else, just to be safe."

Chapter 22

"Ugh," Chabal said. It was Wednesday afternoon and the third day of poring through property assessment records. "My eyes are going buggy."

Langdon chuckled. "Remember the days when we used to have to go to the town office and get them to bring the big paper maps out to us? You should be glad everything is online now." Instead of going into the office, they'd decided to work at home and were on their computers. Dog thought this to be rather boring and was moping on the couch.

"Who would've thought there were so many barns and sheds in the greater Brunswick area?" Chabal stood up and stretched. "But it is kind of creepy that I can pull up anybody's home and see the estimated value. Did you know that Jewell and Richam's place is valued at almost a million bucks?"

"Wow. Good for them. It *is* a beautiful location."

They'd started with the list of names supplied by Dr. Corbett and then moved on to whoever had a second structure on their property that was not a residence.

"What time's your appointment with the good doctor, Tom Corbett?" Chabal asked.

"He said he'd meet me at his office at six." Langdon also stood up and stretched.

"I could use a break from screen time. And we got a couple of hours until we have to be out the door."

"Jasper Ansari has his... what do you call a racquetball event? Game? Match?"

Chabal snickered. "I don't know. Let's go with game. He's in a league and plays at five. He and the boys like to have a few beers afterward, or so I'm told. Thought I might say hello."

"You're telling me you're going to go pick up a guy in a bar?" Langdon raised his eyebrows. "You know we're married, right?"

"If you were paying attention," Chabal said. "I was saying that we have some time to kill. Can you think of some way we might occupy ourselves?"

Dog had thought the day was a bust but was even further disgusted when they closed the bedroom door on him.

"I still don't like the idea of you going down to Falmouth to flirt with some doctor," Langdon said as he nuzzled her neck and slid his hand down the back of her pants.

"I'm just chatting him up to see what I can find out." Chabal ran her hands up the inside of his shirt and then lifted it over his head while he pushed her pants down to the floor. "And don't you be getting any ideas about signing me up for a boob job with Dr. Corbett."

Langdon laughed, his hand trailing up her back and releasing her bra. "No worries there. I'm happy with what I have."

"Liar," Chabal said. "But you're sweet."

Langdon rather thought it was quite a delicious diversion.

~ ~ ~ ~ ~

Chabal sat in the tavern next to the Falmouth Racquetball Club on Route 1. She'd discovered that Jasper Ansari was a member of the club and played in the Wednesday night league. A little more digging had led her to one of the gang's Facebook pages where she'd seen pictures of the same bar, which turned out to be right next to the club and was evidently a favorite destination for cocktails afterward.

She was not disappointed, as she saw him come through the front door with another man, grabbing the table catty-corner to her at the bar. He wasn't a bad-looking man, Chabal thought, very tall, lean, and with a charming smile. His glasses were black with a thick frame that looked more hipster than stodgy.

Chabal checked herself in the mirror behind the bar. Now in her mid-50s, she was critical of her aging body, but people all commented that she looked extremely young for her years. She thought that might have to do with her height but welcomed the compliments all the same. Her blonde hair cascaded just to the shoulders, styled and dyed every four weeks to keep the gray at bay. Sure, there was just a hint of a wrinkle at the corners of her eyes and maybe a bit of extra flesh under her chin, but you had to look closely to see either.

What Chabal did know was that when a group of men congregated in a bar, they couldn't let pass the opportunity to talk to a member of the opposite sex. This had intrigued her for some time, as she was sure many of them were happily married. Others, she knew, wouldn't typically be interested, but for the age-old equation of a pack of guys plus sufficient liquid courage nearly always equaled the flirting game soon afoot. It must be hardwired into their genes, this need to flirt with and garner the attention of any female, beating out the attempts of their friends.

The man with Jasper came to the bar and got a pitcher of beer and four glasses as two other men sat down at the table. She caught him looking at her out of the corner of his eye, and she smiled coyly without looking at him. When the man returned to the table, she could hear him whispering to his buddies. As there was no call to whisper in the tavern, Chabal had to assume it was about her.

Jasper came for the second pitcher of beer just ten minutes later, sliding into the stool next to her. "Meeting somebody?" he asked, sliding the empty pitcher across to the bartender.

Chabal looked at him with surprise. "No. Why?"

"Just thought a pretty woman in a bar must be meeting somebody."

His voice was a bit high-pitched, and she noticed the hook to his nose. "Just having a glass of wine."

He looked at her almost empty glass. "Can I buy you a drink?"

"Sure."

Jasper motioned the bartender to refill her glass as he took the fresh pitcher of beer and went back to the table. Chabal watched as he poured himself a pint, set the pitcher on the table, and said something that brought laughs from the table before moving back to the stool next to her.

"My name's Jasper," he said.

"Annie," Chabal said. She watched his face for any sign of recognition. She saw none.

"Do you live around here, Annie?"

They engaged in a few minutes of polite chitchat. He pretty much told the truth as far as she could tell, other than saying he wasn't currently involved with anybody, which directly contradicted him telling Langdon he had a girlfriend he'd met through Patience. For her part, Chabal had concocted a story about being recently divorced, working in the school system in Brunswick, and having to sell the house she couldn't make payments on.

"Quite some happenings going on in Brunswick," he said. "First, the murder of that guy, and then the suicide. What's going on in your town?"

Chabal shrugged. "I've been busy and haven't really followed any of it. I read about the man killed but didn't hear about a suicide."

Jasper leaned over conspiratorially, his arm pressing into hers. "Guy by the name of Popa poisoned himself. I knew him, in fact. Seemed like a decent enough person. Can't imagine why anybody would ever do that."

Chabal suppressed her urge to cringe away from his close proximity. "That's terrible. How'd you know him?"

"Oh, we just crossed paths a time or two. Maybe we should talk about something not so gloomy."

Chabal had to listen to him talking about being a doctor, sailing adventures, and how carefully he manicured his yard. After a bit, the other three men left, saying goodbye to Jasper and punching him in the arm like they were in seventh grade.

They always said that serial killers could pass off as the Boy Scout next door, Chabal thought, but she was having a hard time believing this man to be a killer. Not just a killer, but a sadistic and demented degenerate. Arrogant, yes. A womanizer, possibly, but not a sadistic beast.

"Would you like another drink?" Jasper asked.

"I should be getting home as well," Chabal said.

"Can I get your phone number?"

Chabal gave it to him. She wasn't sure about the wisdom of giving out your phone number to a man you believed might be a raving lunatic serial killer, but that was the game being played, and she meant to see it through.

"I'll walk you to your car," Jasper said. "It'd be the gentlemanly thing to do."

~ ~ ~ ~ ~

"What were you doing coming to my house?" Langdon asked. He was sitting in Dr. Corbett's office at Cooks Corner in Brunswick. The rest of the staff were gone.

Corbett grinned wickedly at him. "I came to give you information to help you solve your case, that missing woman. I thought, seeing as you came by my home, that we were that kind of good friends."

Langdon stared at the man, trying to see past his smug smile. Could he be the Wendigo? "Do you make it a habit to offer breast enhancement surgery to a woman you've just met?"

"Every day, my dear chap, every day. As a matter of fact, that's what I do. Women I've never met come in wanting… something more, and I provide that."

Langdon felt like this interview was slipping away from him. "I don't imagine house calls fall into the realm of normal." It sounded petty, with a hollow ring even to his own ears.

"I'm sorry that you felt offended or threatened," Corbett said. "I was merely trying to help. As far as letting your wife know that I could help her out, well, that merely falls under the Hippocratic Oath, now, doesn't it?"

"The Hippocratic Oath? Doesn't that involve the privacy of patients? First, do no harm, that kind of thing?"

"Amongst other things, yes. But it also states that a doctor has an obligation not just to their patients but to all of society, poor and rich. Those of sound body and mind, as well as the infirm."

Langdon stared at the tall man with the intense eyes and felt his stomach turn over. "You're saying that it is your duty as a doctor to enhance my wife's breasts?"

Corbett leaned back, and his face creased into a wide smile. "Exactly. If I saw somebody with a cancerous tumor, it'd be an obligation to mention to them that they should do something about it. My particular expertise happens to be breast enlargement."

"You deal in outward appearances, right? That's what cosmetic surgery is all about, Corbett, not health."

"They are intertwined in this natural world of ours," Corbett said. "Perception, diet, medicine, emotion—they are all woven together to create a healthy body and mind."

This guy is cracked, Langdon thought, at the same time mentally checking himself. He'd allowed the doctor to lead him away from his intended path. "Have you had any more thoughts on who may've stolen your private information?"

"You know as well as I that it was most likely a hacker, somebody in Asia that I've never met, or maybe Russia, who breached the security somewhere where I've used my card in the past year."

Langdon shrugged. "The police haven't been able to find any place that's been hacked where you've used your card recently." This was true, to the best of Langdon's knowledge, which was limited. "But I find it highly unlikely that somebody from Asia got access to your card number and then used it merely for a monthly fee from a dating service. Your bill would have been right up to your limit, or at least you'd have gotten a text or call from the credit card company about unusual charges."

Corbett sighed. "That does seem a bit far-fetched. How about Dr. Ansari? Did you go speak with him?"

"Why have you focused on him?"

Corbett looked surprised. "Because he looks like me. It seems that would be a benefit to impersonating me, doesn't it?"

"Do you know anybody who owns a barn?"

"A barn?"

"I have reason to believe that Annie Brown is being held captive in a barn."

"Not off the top of my head," Corbett said. "I don't really interact with the farmer crowd."

Chapter 23

Langdon, Chabal, and dog were at the Lenin Stop having a cup of coffee. They'd gotten home Wednesday night and shared notes, and then spent all day Thursday grappling with the complexities of the case, trying to come at it from every possible angle to make sure they hadn't missed anything.

All they knew was that somebody using Tom Corbett's name, information, and credit card had signed up for the dating site Patience and had made plans to meet with Annie Brown. It could've been him. Or, perhaps, it was his doppelganger down in Falmouth, Jasper Ansari. Or somebody else entirely.

The case of Liam Couture, who'd been lured to Brunswick to buy an ATV and then disappeared, appeared quite similar. The credit card for the advertisement was almost certainly stolen. This had been linked to Gregory Popa, who was now dead, so there were no further leads there other than what he'd let slip before the poison had killed him. Bart had told Langdon that it didn't appear that Liam was one of the victims in the video, and he wasn't even sure if the killings on film were local or just some sort of snuff film, but Langdon still couldn't shake the feeling that the man was dead. If there was anybody still to be saved, it was Annie Brown.

Right before he died, Popa had mentioned that Annie was being held in a barn. Corbett didn't have a barn. Jasper had a large shed. They'd been through the town records to find everybody in Brunswick who did have a barn. And then the surrounding towns. They'd cross-checked that list with the one that Corbett had supplied of people he knew and come up with two hits. Langdon had investigated both of them on the sly with no results.

"We need to do 24/7 surveillance on Corbett and Jasper," Chabal said.

"How?" Langdon asked. "We don't have the manpower."

"Bart says the police stance is a no-go?"

"They got two officers keeping tabs on things but not actively. The Staties are running the investigation on Danny T.'s murder, but they don't seem to believe it's connected to the disappearance of Liam or Annie."

"That's effed up," Chabal said. "How can they be so obtuse?"

Langdon shrugged. "Lots of people go missing."

"And they couldn't find a connection to a missing woman named Jill? Who Popa said the Wendigo ate?" Chabal looked around, realizing that her voice had risen and that she was in a public space.

"There's no record of any woman named Jill gone missing in the past twenty years."

Chabal leaned forward. "How about Popa's confessing all of this to us before offing himself? And the fact that Annie's being held in a barn where, we're pretty sure, she'll be sacrificed in a week when the supermoon eclipses?"

"Eclipses?" Langdon said. "Is that a thing?"

Chabal gave him the *look*.

"They're going with Popa was insane," Langdon said. "Batshit crazy. The fact that Annie called Maddie to let her know she was okay seems to have reassured them that they can back off. People are reported missing all the time and almost always show up somewhere just fine."

"Don't think most crazy people carry a kill pill of cyanide with them," Chabal said.

Langdon sighed. "If I'd only realized what he was doing when he covered his face with his hands, we might have found Annie by now."

"Be nice if we got some help from the police."

"Bart has no official place in the investigation, but he thinks the official stance is that it was a random act of violence by a deranged man who then killed himself."

"And the videos from Popa's basement?"

"A collection of snuff films from around the world with, we think, some local ringers mixed in. Sick, yes, but the killers? The boys in blue aren't so sure."

"Bullshit."

Langdon shrugged. "Under investigation. Probably take the techies a while to work their way through that mess."

"Too bad Jackson isn't in charge of MCU anymore," Chabal said. "He'd believe us." Jackson Brooks was a friend of the State Police who had run the Major Crime Unit in Maine for many years.

"He probably still has some clout. I'll check in with him."

Langdon's phone buzzed in his pocket. It was an incoming call from Maddie Campagna. "Hello, Maddie," he said.

"I had another call," Maddie said. Her voice was high-pitched and excited. "From Annie. She gave me the same run-around as last time. Said she was down in Chapel Hill doing some painting. Said she pretty much had a nervous breakdown, but she was recovering."

"Did you record the call using the app we downloaded on your phone?" Langdon asked.

There was a pause. "No. I forgot. It took me by surprise."

"Did she give you her new phone number or address?"

"No, but I think she slipped up or tried to give me a tip. I asked what her address was, and she said she couldn't tell me that, just that she was in Falmouth. Falmouth. Not Chapel Hill. Falmouth. Like Falmouth, Maine. And then there was a rustle, and she gasped, and the phone went dead."

Langdon didn't know what to say to that but felt it demanded some sort of response. "Wow." Pretty lame, he thought. Some PI. Wow.

"That narrows it down some, doesn't it? I mean, Falmouth is a big place, but that should help, shouldn't it?"

"More than you know," Langdon said. "Did she say anything else?"

"No, that was pretty much it."

"We're getting closer, Maddie. Don't worry, we'll find her." For the first time, Langdon began to believe that might even be true.

"Is there anything I can do?"

"I'm working on some things today that might pay off. How about we get together sometime tomorrow, and I can bring you, Meg, and Harold up to date on how things are going."

"Your office at nine in the morning?"

"Sounds good."

"Langdon? She's going to be okay, isn't she? I mean, you'll find her, won't you?"

"I'll do my best."

"Thank you." Maddie hung up.

"Wow?" Chabal asked him.

"Annie called again and let slip that she was in Falmouth, and the phone call ended."

"Wow."

"Yeah. Dr. Jasper Ansari."

"Barn and shed are pretty close to the same thing," Chabal said.

"Might be a good idea to go have a look."

"I imagine Dr. Ansari is at work all day."

"No time like the now." Langdon stood up. "Maybe when we get close to his house, you can give him a call and make sure he's in his office."

They went around the corner of the building to the back parking lot where the Jeep was parked. Dog seemed to sense the excitement of the moment and bounded along, but then again, he was always up for an adventure, even if it was just a ride to the post office.

Jasper Ansari lived in a large colonial in Falmouth Foreside. He didn't have an ocean view as some of the really wealthy people did, but his house was the last one on a circle that backed up to the Falmouth Forest Preserve. Langdon did a slow drive past.

"Want I should call the office now?" Chabal asked.

"Not yet," Langdon said. "I'm not sure where to park."

"Side of the road?" Chabal said sarcastically.

"This is the kind of neighborhood where an old Jeep parked on the side of the road gets ten phone calls to the police."

Chabal nodded. "You got a point there." She tapped away on her phone.

"What do you think?" he asked after a few seconds.

"Actually, if you go back to Route 1, there's a nursing home with a parking lot that we could probably fit into inconspicuously."

"Route 1?"

Chabal laughed. "Yeah. I'd say it's no more than a half-mile, maybe less, through the woods."

"Hmm. Sounds like a plan. Luckily, we have dog with us to find the way."

They both laughed. Dog looked from one to the other, trying to figure out what was going on. His mournful eyes suggested he knew they were mocking him.

"At the very least, he'll protect us from any killer squirrels," Chabal said.

Langdon rubbed the dog's head. "We're joshing with you, buddy. We know full well that you saved me the other night out on the Commons. Once again."

"Our ferocious attack dog."

Langdon chuckled and then grew somber. "Let's not forget that we're dealing with a killer here. Most likely a serial murderer, at that."

"Three of them," Chabal said. "Not just Jasper, but there's two more, according to Popa."

There was a good spot to park at the nursing home. They were able to slide into the trees at the back of the facility without being spotted, or at least, so they thought. GPS was a marvel, leading them through the forest to the back of Jasper Ansari's home. There was a swimming pool that was fenced in, but the rest of the area was open, including the large shed that looked like it could almost be considered a barn.

Chabal called the office, spoke for a minute, and hung up. "Dr. Ansari is on vacation," she said. "Took today off and all of next week."

"Hm," Langdon said. "That's quite a coincidence. I question him about missing people, and he goes on vacation. Did he happen to invite you along the other night when you were cavorting with him?"

"I think I'm glad he didn't."

"What?"

"If Jasper is the Wendigo, this vacation might've been already planned. Prepping for the big day Wednesday A.M. I'm not sure I want to be invited to that meal. Or be that meal."

"True. I'm betting they do some crazy-ass rituals all of Tuesday night leading up to the sacrifice."

Chabal's face was pinched tight and white. "What'd Popa say? Then they'll slit her throat, bleed her out, and make a stew of her."

"So, the ritual probably goes on for another day or two while they cook her, and then the Wendigo eats her to gain her power."

"Giving him the weekend to digest," Chabal said. She looked like she might vomit.

"How about you try his cell phone," Langdon said. "The number he gave you the other night."

She scrolled through, found the name, hit call, and put it on speaker. It went immediately to voice mail, saying that Dr. Jasper Ansari would be out of cell phone reception for the following week. If it was an emergency, please call the office number, and somebody would help.

"I thought doctors always have to be reachable," Chabal said.

"I'm betting the office has a way to reach him."

"Not that they're going to share with us."

"We don't want to talk to him," Langdon said. "We just want to make sure he's not here."

"Watch my back," Chabal said.

She left the cover of the trees as Langdon pulled his Glock. He knew better than to protest, ask, or even suggest that he should be the one taking the risk. He was able to suggest, however, that dog stay, and the canine actually listened to him. One for two wasn't bad.

Chabal eased her way past the shed, which had no windows, which seemed odd since it was about thirty feet long by twenty feet wide. With a bold step, Chabal stepped from the cover of the shed and crossed an open space of forty feet to the back of the garage. Here, she slipped from his sight as she went around the corner.

Chabal was gone no more than five seconds before she came back into view, sat down with her back to the wall, and pulled her phone out.

Langdon's pocket buzzed. Chabal was texting him. No car in the garage.

He texted out his reply. Meet you at the shed.

Chabal stood up, pulling her SIG from the holster, and Langdon left the cover of the trees, dog padding along behind him. He felt like eyes were watching him. Wiccans. Witches. Wendigos. Even if Jasper wasn't here, wouldn't one of the others be here guarding Annie? Keeping watch. His eyes swept the back windows of the house as he walked around the shed. There was no sign of movement. No sound.

It was as if the air had been sucked from the sky, and a black cloud crossed over the sun. Even the birds grew quiet. They reached the door to the shed at the same time. He turned the knob. It was unlocked. Langdon pointed to the house, indicating that Chabal should keep watch there, and then swung the door wide, stepping inside with pistol leveled. Dog ran past him, excited at what might lie within.

It was empty. Well, not empty, but there were no signs of life or recent habitation. There was a riding lawnmower. Weed whackers, rakes, shovels, and other lawn equipment. A circular table was in one corner with poker chips and a deck of cards on it.

"Come on in," Langdon said to Chabal's back.

She turned and stepped inside, drawing the door closed behind her. "Doesn't look much like a torture chamber to me," she said.

"No. Dr. Ansari might be a bit anal, but there are no obvious signs that he's a people eater."

"Suppose that while we're here, we should look for clues," Chabal said.

"Like a huge stew pot?"

"Something like that."

"You got this side, and I'll start over there."

It was innocuous lawn equipment and storage of stuff that the man probably should've just thrown away. Dog wasn't sure what all the fuss was about.

It was under the upside-down wheelbarrow that Langdon found the shoe. A woman's high heel. A strange item to be in the shed of a bachelor. Two shoes might've been something left behind by an ex or a one-night stand, possibly. One shoe? That seemed to be more suspicious.

He took it with him when they slipped back out the door, around the side, and into the forest.

"What do you think?" Chabal asked.

"I'm thinking that Maddie Campagna might know if this shoe is Annie's." Langdon took his phone out, clicked on recent calls, and hit the woman's name.

"Did you find something out?" she asked by way of greeting.

"I found a shoe. Was wondering if you might be able to take a look at it, tell me if it's Annie's."

"I'm at work now. Can you send me a picture?"

Langdon realized he didn't know what she did for work. And sending a picture made a lot of sense. So he put her on speaker, had Chabal hold the shoe up, snapped the photo, and texted it to Maddie. "On the way."

There was a long silence. "It's Annie's shoe." Maddie's voice was barely audible. "Her favorites. The ones she would've worn to go out on a first date. Where'd you find it?"

"In Falmouth," Langdon said.

"Where in Falmouth?"

"I can't tell you right now, but we're getting closer."

"Please find her."

"I will."

"Thank you."

~ ~ ~ ~ ~

Langdon and Chabal sat in a conference room of the Major Crime Unit in Gray. Jackson Brooks sat across from them. He was about the same age, had dark features, black hair cut short on top, blue eyes, and wore an expensive suit.

Langdon had called Bart first, who in turn suggested they contact Jackson Brooks, who used to head up the MCU for the State Police but had been transferred after the last case involving Langdon. Langdon was old friends with Jackson going back some thirty years, but the relationship had been based more on work than anything else. He'd been meaning to check in with him anyway, and now, here they were.

"Nice suit," Langdon said drily.

"Thanks," Jackson said. "Couldn't wear the good stuff when I was with MCU. Never know when you might get blood or worse on the threads and ruin them." He'd always been a bit of a dandy but was extremely good at his job.

"Wished you hadn't transferred over to the Computer Crime Unit," Chabal said. "We could use you here at MCU for the case we're on."

"The missing Annie Brown?"

"Yeah, that's the one." Langdon showed his surprise. "What do you know about it?"

Jackson smiled, flashing brilliant white teeth. "You think us coppers never talk to each other? As a matter of fact, what do you think I'm doing here at MCU?"

"Thought you picked here because it was close to both of us?" Langdon said. They'd thought it best to call Jackson first with the new evidence they'd found before turning it over to the MCU, which seemed to be stonewalling them.

"No, brother. I picked here because I'm on the Annie Brown case."

"Don't you do computer crimes now?" Chabal asked.

Jackson chuckled. "Like fake dating profiles to lure unsuspecting women to be abducted?"

Langdon thumped his forehead with the heel of his hand. "Duh."

"I thought the police had bought into the phone call from Annie saying she was down in North Carolina," Chabal said.

"Of course not. We got Missing Persons, MCU, and CCU all working on this one. We just figured to lay a bit low, let the lack of media attention lull the sicko into false security. Hell, I thought about not wearing my Kiton to work anymore in case I get a chance to blow this mo-fo away."

Langdon figured that Kiton was the brand of his suit. "Why didn't you contact me? You must know we've been working the case."

"Bart's been keeping me in the know."

"Son of a bitch didn't mention that to me," Langdon said.

"I asked him to keep it on the down-low," Jackson said. "On account of just about every time I get involved with you on a case, it gets real messy. As a matter of fact, I'm pretty sure that's why the Colonel squeezed me out of MCU. My association with you almost let that guy off the hook last fall."

"Sorry about that," Langdon said.

"No worries." Jackson laughed. "The computer stuff is a nice change of pace. And I get to look good instead of wearing rags."

"Why'd you agree to meet with us now?"

"When you called, I knew you must have something good. So, let's have it."

"You know about Corbett's doppelganger down in Falmouth, and that Maddie Campagna got another phone call from Annie?"

"Yep. I spoke with Miss Campagna earlier on the telephone and will be stopping by her law office this afternoon."

Langdon shook his head. Maddie had failed to mention this to him. He sorted through the concocted story he'd been working on ever since getting in touch with Jackson. "Me and Chabal went down to visit Jasper Ansari today. He wasn't there, but while we were on the front porch, dog wandered off. We found him out back with a shoe in his mouth. A woman's shoe. We sent a picture of it to Maddie, who confirmed that it was one of Annie Brown's favorite shoes."

Jackson leaned back in his chair and gave Langdon a long stare. "Dog just happened to be wandering around the backyard of a suspect's house and found a vital piece of information regarding the missing Annie Brown?"

Langdon held out his hands to the sides, palms up. "He's quite the sleuth."

Jackson looked at Chabal. "And you're ready to swear to this in a court of law?"

"I don't have a problem telling the truth," she said.

"You have this shoe with you, I take it?"

Langdon pulled the shoe from the bag he'd put it into and lay it on the desk. It was powder blue. Chabal had said it was one of a pair of pumps. Langdon wasn't sure what that meant, as she was not a high-heel wearer, so he had no real cause to know.

"I'll get forensics on it."

"We called Jasper at his office, and the person who answered the phone said he was on vacation through next week," Chabal said. "Out of reach, she said."

"Is that so?" Jackson smiled. "We'll see about that."

Chapter 24

"Where'd you find the shoe?" Maddie asked. She was sitting across from Langdon in his office along with Meg and Harold Brown on Saturday morning. "That nice police officer, Lieutenant Brooks, came by my office yesterday asking all kinds of questions."

"I'm sorry, but I just can't tell you right now," Langdon said.

"He was also asking me if I knew Doctor Jasper Ansari. Does this have something to do with him?"

"Do you know him?"

Maddie flipped her hair back from her eyes. "No. I mean, after Jackson left, I Googled him, of course. He has an office in Falmouth. And lives there as well. Where Annie said she was. Where you said you found the shoe."

It didn't escape Langdon's attention that Jackson Brooks was on a first-name basis with Maddie. She was an attractive woman, and he was always on the prowl. Langdon also knew that the man would wait until the case was completed before acting on his impulse.

"We just want Annie back," Meg said.

"If you can tell us anything that would give us hope, we'd sure enough appreciate that," Harold said.

"I'm working closely with the police," Langdon said. "I believe we have a lead on who may've taken Annie, but I can't say anything else right now. For her safety."

"Why are we here if you can't say anything?"

Langdon had thought about calling and canceling the meeting, but he was still grasping at straws, trying to put the pieces together. Jackson Brooks had called last night to say that, as far as he could tell, nobody knew where Jasper Ansari was, and his cell phone was turned off. He'd vanished just like Annie. Leaving them back at square one.

"Tell me about the phone call again," Langdon said. "From Annie."

Maddie frowned. "I told you everything. She said that her anxieties had gotten the best of her, and she flipped out and took off. Came to rest in Chapel Hill. Was doing some painting and healing herself."

"And that's it?"

"And then the whole Falmouth thing."

"How'd that come about?"

"I asked her where she was, really. Said I didn't believe her. She replied, 'I told you. I'm in Falmouth.' And then there was a clunk, Annie gasped, and the phone went dead."

"A clunk?"

"Yeah, like a slap, a thump, you know."

Langdon steepled his fingers under his chin and pondered what Maddie said. If Annie was indeed in Falmouth when she called Maddie, he guessed there might have been enough time to move her from the shed before Langdon and Chabal arrived and searched the premises. Jasper could've packed her into the trunk of his car, cleaned out all traces of her, missing the shoe in his hurry, and gone elsewhere, especially if he had two helpers.

But, he thought, something didn't seem quite right. Forensics was currently in the shed searching for further clues. Langdon wasn't sure that she'd ever been there. In which case, who put the shoe there and why?

~ ~ ~ ~ ~

"I saw your name in the paper."

Chabal took the empty to-go coffee cup from the young woman at the counter of the coffee shop and turned to the voice. It was Jade. "Hello, you."

Jade laughed. "Sorry. I guess I could've said hi before accosting you like that."

"No worries." Chabal put some creamer in her cup and filled it with coffee, then added two packs of sugar.

"That was some messed up stuff," Jade said. "That guy who poisoned himself. And you were there. Did you know him?"

"Not really," Chabal said. "Just a case I'm working on."

"That thing we all talked about at your house? At the barbecue?" Jade shivered. "Don't tell me there really is some group of people running around Brunswick making sacrifices during supermoons?"

"I don't know about any of that," Chabal said. She thought of the images on the television in Popa's basement. Him talking about the Wendigo eating people. Sacrifices during the supermoon. "We're just looking for a missing woman."

"Annie Brown?"

Chabal looked at Jade over the rim of her cup as she took a sip. "What do you know about Annie Brown?"

Jade shrugged. "Just what I read in the paper. Scary. If I ever had considered using one of those dating sites, well, no more, that's for sure! I'll be meeting men the old-fashioned way. In a bar." She laughed, her giggles spilling forth like the sound of wind chimes.

Chabal snickered. "That'd probably be safer."

Jade stopped laughing. "Speaking of, that was your friend who got attacked down to the Bernard Hotel. I remembered his name because it was so odd. 4 by Four. John or Jim or something. Was that related to all this?"

"Maybe." Chabal looked at the door. "Look, I got to get going."

"I was on my way out," Jade said. "I'll walk with you. Where are you off to?"

"Across the street to my bookshop."

"Ah, great. I've been meaning to pop in and check things out, buy myself a couple of books, local-like."

Chabal and Jade left the Lenin Stop and went to the Coffee Dog Bookstore, chatting about things other than the case, a welcome change for Chabal, who got to hear about a student who Jade said had set her notebook on fire with a Bunsen burner.

As they came into the store through the propped open door, Langdon emerged from the back office with Maddie, Meg, and Harold. Jade shot them a questioning look, her brow furrowed in thought, but she didn't say anything. Chabal helped her pick out three books. She was particularly excited to find *A World of Deceit*, as she was a big fan of the Kate Flora series featuring Joe Burgess.

As Jade went to leave, she turned back to Chabal. "The Blood Moon is in just four days, isn't it?"

~ ~ ~ ~ ~

Langdon and Chabal were sitting silently in the office about noontime at a loss as to what to do next when Starling cracked the door and stuck his head in.

"Boss, there's a gent here who wants to see you."

Eddie Couture pushed his way past Starling and into the office. "Been three weeks, and you ain't found my brother yet. I guess that thousand bucks I gave you was so you could sit around here on your ass?"

"Eddie," Langdon said. "I've been meaning to give you a call, give you an update on what's happening. The truth is, I don't have much."

"What'd you call me for then?"

Langdon raised his eyebrows at the question, then shook his head. "Have a seat." He pointed to the chair across from him and Chabal. "This is my partner, Chabal."

Eddie grudgingly sat down. "Miss." He nodded at Chabal.

"What's this about me calling you?" Langdon asked.

"Woke up this morning and had me a voice message on my phone from you." Eddie tugged at his bristly white beard. "You said that you had a break in the case and to get down here by twelve o'clock. Said you'd tell me everything then. So spill it."

Langdon looked at Chabal. "I didn't call you."

"You sure enough did. I got it right here on voice mail." Eddie pulled his phone out of his pocket. It was a flip phone. He opened it and pecked away, then held it up for them to hear. "*Mr. Couture. This is Goff Langdon. I think I may have found your brother. Get down to my office in Brunswick by noon today and I'll fill you in.*" The voice was low and deep, as if it was somebody trying to disguise their true voice.

"That's not me, Eddie," Langdon said. "I think somebody is playing a game with us."

"What sort of game? This ain't no goddamn game. I just drove four hours to get down here because you told me you had news of Liam."

"That wasn't me," Langdon said patiently, his mind whirling with the implications. Why would somebody have Eddie Couture come down to Brunswick? It had to be Jasper Ansari. The Wendigo. Trying to throw him for a loop, confuse him. "But I do think that whoever called you is the person responsible for your brother going missing."

"What in heck for? Why would anyone kidnap Liam?"

"I don't know." And Langdon truly had little idea why. It had to be Jasper. But why? Was this some sort of smokescreen he was trying to create?

"What do you know?" Eddie asked angrily. "What the hell do you know?"

Langdon had told him some of it over the phone about a week back. That Graham, the homeless man who had seen Liam picking up another man, had now himself gone missing. That the *Cousin Freddie's* advertisement for the four-wheeler had been purchased with a credit card number stolen from a woman named Donna Reed. That Donna Reed's nephew was an accountant in Brunswick named Gregory Popa, and how Popa had admitted to being part of a strange cult of people who supposedly killed strangers before committing suicide himself.

He went on to tell Eddie that the police were currently searching for a suspect in connection to another disappearance that they thought was likely connected to the missing Liam.

"You think he's dead, then?" Eddie asked after the room had been silent for a whole minute. It'd been a lot to digest. "You think these people killed Liam?"

"The police have a video of people the cult has supposedly killed. I don't know yet if your brother was one of them. The images weren't very clear, and what I saw of it, the faces of the victims were often in shadows."

"So, he could still be alive?"

"It's possible."

"Who are these people?" Eddie put his face in his hands like he was going to cry. "*What* are they?"

"I think I may know who their leader is," Langdon said. "But we don't know where he's got to."

"Can you find him? Please? Before they kill Liam. *Please.*"

Langdon looked at the man. He was almost certain that Liam Couture was dead, but if there was even a shred of possibility that he might be alive, he couldn't take that hope away from Eddie. "I'll do my best."

There was a knock on the door, and then Starling opened it. "Boss? Sorry to bother you, but a package just came." He held out a box, showing him the writing on the side. **URGENT. OPEN IMMEDIATELY.** In black marker. "It's addressed to Edouard Couture, care of Goff Langdon, with the store address."

"To me?" Eddie asked.

"Who brought it?" Langdon asked.

Starling shook his head. "I signed for it. Some courier service. The paper's out front."

"That's why somebody tricked me into coming down here," Eddie said. "So as I'd get this package."

"Looks that way," Langdon said.

"Maybe we should call the police," Chabal said.

"You don't think it's a bomb, do you?" Starling asked. He walked over and gingerly set the package down on the desk.

"A bomb?" Eddie asked.

They all looked at Langdon.

Langdon shook his head. "We might as well open it up. I don't think it's a bomb."

"You don't *think* it's a bomb?" Chabal said incredulously. "And you *think* we should open it."

Langdon grinned. "It's not a bomb. Go ahead, Eddie."

"I paid you a thousand bucks. *You* open it."

Langdon chuckled. "Okay." He took a pair of scissors from his top desk drawer and pulled the box closer. Careful to disturb the packaging as little as possible, he cut the tape, slit the top, and pulled the box open.

"What is it?" Eddie asked, leaning forward.

Langdon pulled out several layers of bubble packing. Then he reached carefully into the box and pulled something out.

"What the…?" Eddie said.

"Is that a human head?" Chabal covered her mouth with her hand.

It was a human skull. White and gleaming like it'd been polished. The wide eye sockets stared soullessly at them.

Across the cranium in what appeared to be the same black marker as the writing on the box were words:

Hello. I am Liam.

Chapter 25

"Waiting on lab tests," Jackson said, "but I'm betting that the skull is Liam Couture's." He, Langdon, and Bart were sitting in a dive bar in Lewiston.

Bart snorted. "Yeah? What gave it away? The writing on his forehead that said, 'Hello. I am Liam'?"

"Could easily be somebody trying to throw us a red herring," Langdon said.

"Or a publicity seeker getting a rush," Jackson said. "Do you have any idea of how many calls we've had from people confessing to abducting Annie Brown?"

They were meeting in the relative obscurity of Lewiston to share notes as both Jackson and Bart would be in hot water for even being anywhere near Langdon. In fact, they'd both had recent job reassignments and demotions for having worked with the PI less than a year earlier. Both men, frustrated at the slow pace of bureaucracy with a young life in the balance, had gladly risked their careers to save a kidnapped boy. Again, they were already skating on thin ice.

"I'd say it's a bit late to throw us off the scent," Bart said. "Annie Brown's shoe is found in the shed behind Dr. Jasper Ansari's house, he disappears, and now facial recognition has confirmed that it is *his* picture on the Patience dating site." This report had come in just a few hours back, which was what had led to this impromptu get-together.

Langdon thought of having allowed Chabal to go down and flirt with Ansari and how close she may have come to being taken as well. He shuddered at the image, as Chabal had painted it, of the doctor walking her to her car in the parking lot. At the same time, he had his doubts. It was all a bit too pat for him. He wasn't quite ready to let Corbett have a free pass.

"Why would he do that?" Langdon asked.

"Do what?" Bart said.

"You're telling me that Jasper lifts Corbett's credit card number at some point, which could've happened. They're hanging out together at some medical conference, Corbett calls to order his mistress some lingerie, some self-flagellation tool, or whatever that sick doctor purchases online, and Jasper memorizes the number that Corbett reads into the phone. Easy-peasy. Got the number, expiration, and that code on the back."

"Easy enough," Bart said.

"So, my question is, why does Jasper use his own photo? Why not just lift a picture of Corbett from the internet and use that? Simple enough to do."

"Because he wants Annie to recognize him when they meet," Jackson said.

Langdon grimaced. "But the two men already look alike."

"Let's say they show up at Sugar Magnolia's and find it closed," Jackson said. "Jasper offers a suggestion of another place he knows, and they decide to ride over together. That'd certainly give her an opportunity to get a good look at him and realize that he was somebody different than she thought."

"Yeah, Jasper's got quite the beak on him," Bart said. "That's not something you can hide."

The bartender came over to their table with another pitcher of beer. The joint was the kind of place where your feet stuck to the floor and you wanted to avoid the food, but it was dark and off the grid. Even so, they'd probably been pegged for cops by the few patrons who weren't already half in the bag on this Sunday afternoon.

"The photo is about ten years old and is all shadowed," Jackson said. "I'm thinking he felt it unlikely that it would lead to him. And it wouldn't have if Corbett hadn't pointed us in that direction."

"How's the hunt for the good doctor going?" Langdon asked. "Any luck?"

Jackson shook his head. "Nothing so far. Jasper told his staff that he'd be out of cell phone range for the week and had another doctor covering any emergencies while he was gone. We've interviewed everyone in his office, but no one knows where he might've gone. We started pulling friends and acquaintances in. The man has a brother in Oregon who hasn't spoken to him in a year, and that's it."

"What about his girlfriend?"

Jackson pursed his lips and cocked his head. "Girlfriend?"

"He told me he'd been dating a woman he met on Patience. I think he said they'd been together for about four months now."

"First I've heard about a girlfriend," Jackson said. "I'll look into it. And he said he met her on the Patience website? That all ties together."

Langdon took a sip of beer. "He told me that he used Patience a while back but stopped when he met his present girlfriend and hasn't been back on since, under his name or any other name."

"Shouldn't be too hard to track down," Jackson said. "I'm headed back down to Gray once I leave here, and I'll get right on it."

"Find Jasper's girlfriend, and we find Jasper," Langdon said. "I'm betting on it."

"Oh, we'll find both of them," Jackson said.

"Still not sure it was him," Langdon said.

"Seems cut and dried to me," Bart said. "Jasper knew Popa, has Annie's shoe in his shed, and it's his picture on the Patience profile of Tom Corbett, who he knew well enough to possibly lift his card number."

"The shoe was found by a dog in the forest preserve behind

Jasper's house," Jackson said drily. "And even that might not stand up in a court of law."

"It was enough to get a warrant and search his house and shed," Langdon said. "Any signs of Annie turn up yet?"

Jackson shook his head. "Forensics has gone over the place with a fine-tooth comb with nothing like the shoe so far, but we're waiting for lab results. A slow process in the best of circumstances, like a snail on the weekend."

"This is a goddamn mass murderer case," Bart said.

"Everything is pretty thin," Jackson said.

"The fact that Jasper and Popa knew each other, along with a shoe, and his working relationship with Corbett paints a pretty good picture," Bart said, ignoring the state cop's comment.

"Yeah, that's quite a coincidence," Langdon said. And I don't believe in coincidences, he thought.

"I'm off to search for Jasper Ansari and his supposed girlfriend," Jackson said, standing up. "Where you two headed?"

"We're going to swing by 4 by Four's house and see if we can get anything more from him on the woman who attacked him the other night," Langdon said.

"We got to find that woman," Bart said. "We're running out of time."

Langdon figured he was talking about Annie Brown and not the woman who'd attacked 4 by Four. He looked at his phone. "Sixty-one hours until the partial lunar eclipse is visible here in Maine. That's our timetable."

~ ~ ~ ~ ~

Chabal needed a change of space, so she took her laptop to the Lenin Stop for an afternoon coffee while she used the LocateNOW software to search for any traces of Jasper Ansari. It obviously wouldn't tell them where he was, unless of course, his credit card was used or he got stopped by the police, but it was an excellent resource for finding out more about the man.

Purchases, debts, arrests—all were a matter of public record. But the truly interesting piece was to find people whom he'd interacted with and then follow their trail to see where it might lead. She'd yet to locate the supposed girlfriend. Maybe the police would have more luck in pressuring the dating platform. Still, she figured that if 4 by Four had already squeezed information out of that organization, then he might be the best one to do so again if he were up to it.

The Lenin Stop was sparse on this Sunday afternoon, giving her some privacy in the corner armchair she'd set up shop in. She called 4 by Four, but it went to voice mail. She texted, waited a moment, and when there was no reply, went back to her laptop screen.

When she next looked up, Eddie Couture was sitting down at a table toward the front of the café. She peeked at him over the top of her laptop, wondering what he was doing still in Brunswick. He was again tugging at his Brillo-pad beard, his fingers hooked through the straggly hair as he looked at his phone. There was a cup of coffee next to him and a Danish.

A woman with long blonde hair sat down opposite him, her back to Chabal. They chatted for a minute and then stood up and walked out the door. Chabal hurriedly slid her laptop into its case and stood up to follow, leaving her half-full coffee mug behind.

Eddie and the blonde had crossed Maine Street and were walking down the other side when Chabal came out the door.

There was something oddly familiar about the woman who was clearly much younger than Eddie, but Chabal couldn't place her. She'd not yet gotten a look at her face, but the way she moved was oddly familiar. Chabal followed from across the street until they turned right on Cumberland right before the Coffee Dog Bookstore. Chabal stepped into the crosswalk to cross and narrowly missed being hit by a UPS truck.

By the time Chabal managed to get to the other side, they were turning left into a parking lot, and when she reached the entrance, they were gone. Who was the mysterious blonde woman who Eddie seemed to know? Chabal wondered, staring at the cars in the lot as if they might hold some clue. Family? Friend? They certainly didn't fit together. She'd been well-dressed, athletic, and healthy-looking, the exact opposite of Eddie.

Chabal shook her head and went in the back door to the Senter Building, figuring she might as well stop in and check with Star at the bookshop. There'd been something about how the woman moved that her mind couldn't quite shake.

~ ~ ~ ~ ~

Jimmy 4 by Four lived in a log cabin in the woods of Bowdoinham. Langdon had tried to text and phone him that they were coming by, but the man hadn't replied to either. He figured the lawyer would most likely be home recuperating, so it wasn't much of a stretch to stop by on their way back from Lewiston as it was just off the highway exit. They could pass their visit off as checking in on him after his attack and, at the same time, grill him about the woman who had done the attacking.

Langdon knocked twice with no response. 4 by Four's sleek sports car was in the driveway next to a black Audi, suggesting the man was home and most likely had a visitor. It was only after Bart pounded on the door that 4 by Four opened it up, wearing nothing but shorts.

"You been working out?" Langdon asked. 4 by Four was well-toned and did work out six days a week.

"What do you two want?" 4 by Four asked.

"Come to check on you, see how your recovery is going," Langdon said.

"Move," Bart said, stepping forward and pushing the man out of the way.

A woman with blonde hair came down the stairs. She was short, had a no-nonsense look on her face, and only paused to kiss 4 by Four on the cheek before brushing past them to go through the door and get in the Audi.

"Who was that?" Langdon asked as she drove off.

"Doctor something or other," 4 by Four said. "I told you I gave some woman my number at the hospital." He had a smug, cat-who-ate-the-canary look on his face. "She came by to… check up on me."

"Put on some damn clothes," Bart said. "You got any beer?"

"Got some Dogfish Head in the fridge," 4 by Four said as he went back up the stairs.

"Dog piss, you mean," Bart grumbled as he went toward the kitchen. He was strictly a Bud Lite or Coors Lite kind of guy. But beggars couldn't be choosers, and a beer was a beer.

Langdon sat down in a leather armchair. The furniture was all leather, contrasting with the homey wood interior of the house.

"You want one?" Bart asked, coming out with two beer bottles, both opened.

"I'm good."

Bart shrugged and sat down on the couch, happy to have both beers.

"You should've called," 4 by Four said, coming back down the stairs with pants and a shirt on.

"Look at your damn phone," Bart growled.

4 by Four patted his pants, looked around, shrugged, and sat down in a second armchair.

"You seem to be bouncing back just fine," Langdon said drily.

"That's what she said," 4 by Four said with a straight face.

"You didn't have any concerns after what happened last time?" Langdon asked. "You know, when the lady tried to kill you?"

4 by Four chuckled. "She's a doctor, not a killer. A mighty fine doctor at that."

"Tell us something we don't know about the woman who tried

to kill you," Bart said. He was already on the second beer.

"Mm. Natasha." 4 by Four leaned back in the chair, staring at the second-floor railing as the living room was open air to the roof. "She was delicious."

"She tried to kill you," Bart said.

"Might've been worth it if she jumped in the sack with me first."

"You said she had blonde hair, blue eyes, was slender, and about forty," Langdon said. "Anything else?"

4 by Four closed his eyes. "Full lips, just right boobs, and dark skin, like she might've been Hispanic or Asian or something."

"I'm thinking Natasha was just an alias," Langdon said. "Certainly nobody named that living in Pownal, and only three in the whole state, all of whom don't fit the profile."

"It might've been a wig." 4 by Four opened his eyes and leaned forward. "There was something a bit off about her hair. Couldn't place it until right now. I think she was wearing a wig."

"A disguise," Langdon said. "Fake hair, fake name."

"Basically, we have nothing," Bart said.

"I'd recognize her lips and her boobs," 4 by Four said.

Bart snorted.

Chapter 26

Annie woke. She'd not dreamed. Not one whit. There were no evil remnants of the Overlord to banish. She was free of him. Free of them. She, Annie Brown, formerly Annie Nergal, had liberated herself from those monsters.

Now, with her eyes closed, instead of replacing the evil of her past life with the pleasantries of her adopted life, Annie began to plan how to escape her current imprisonment. The Wendigo had told her the other day that she had four days until her sacrifice, which would occur at 5:30 in the morning. The morning of May 26th, he'd said, when the partial eclipse would be visible in Maine, and the supermoon would turn to blood.

That meant that she had two days. Annie knew that the Wendigo would be in soon to bring her breakfast and then would take her for a walk, which would be just after sunrise. This was a time of first light, the beginning of a new day, and the hour of potential, when anything was possible. Annie figured that sunrise at the end of May was just about six o'clock.

That meant that instead of eating breakfast two days from now, she'd be hanging upside down, and a knife would slash her throat so that her life's blood would spill into a tub below. The Wendigo had explained exactly how she was going to die in great detail. Her death would be preceded by invocations pleading to the force of nature represented by Satan calling for a greater understanding of the power that writhed through the earth, filled the air all around, and drove the appetites of mankind.

These appeals to the power of nature would last for several hours with ritual chanting, dancing, and fornication. Then her throat would be cut. They'd watch carefully, silently, meditating, as she bled out. Then the Wendigo would butcher her, cutting pieces of flesh from her body as the others prepared the huge pot over the fire in which to stew her. Slabs of Annie would be tossed into the boiling meat broth, and she'd be slow-cooked through the day and that night until finally, the Wendigo would gorge on her flesh as the others watched silently. Then they'd be one. She'd be part of the Wendigo for all of eternity.

Annie didn't particularly want to be part of the Wendigo for perpetuity, hell, not even for ten minutes. That was the worst of it. Tawdrier then being eaten, stewed, butchered, having her throat slit, or being shackled to a tabletop naked for days. That this man would somehow have the gall to think that he possessed her. Therefore, she had to escape. And then avenge the wrong done to her. But first, she must get away.

She'd tested the bindings that stretched her body, a cuff around each wrist and ankle, chains that disappeared through a hole in the tabletop and attached to iron bars. There was no give. Annie had spent hours each night trying to pry herself free to no avail. Freeing herself from the restraints during the night was not an option.

When the Wendigo came in each morning, he put the collar around her neck and then freed her arms and legs. It seemed this would be the optimal time—when his stink was in her proximity. To bite into his neck, gouge his eyes, knee him in the balls. The problem was that her limbs fell asleep after being stretched taut for ten hours overnight. It always took several minutes of stretching and moving her arms and legs before she was even able to totter over to the breakfast table. The Wendigo held the end of the leash and took that time to share his personal philosophies or tell her the exultation they would both experience when they were one.

No, the moment to seek her freedom was not on first waking. The best time for her personal rebellion was as she was eating her breakfast. He was sometimes preoccupied then, staring at his phone, and became a bit lax at times while holding her leash. She plotted each move, knowing that waiting until tomorrow might not provide her the best opportunity, and that given the slightest opening, today had to be the day. Today, she'd be free.

"And there is your normal morning smile, Pumpkin Pie," the Wendigo said. "I was waiting for that moment with all of the patience of a mountain lion stalking his prey."

Annie opened her eyes. "Good morning."

"And what lie do you want to tell me this morning about what made your face light up like a full moon?"

Annie smiled wickedly. "I was thinking about cutting your heart out with a rusty can cut in half."

The Wendigo put his head back and roared in laughter. "You are so different from the others, Pumpkin Pie. By this time, they were begging, crying, and pleading to be let go. You, on the other hand, have never once asked for mercy. And now you speak of killing me, not just killing, but in a particularly nasty fashion. My hat is off to you, Annie Brown. I will very much enjoy eating you and merging our souls into one. You may be the one who makes me immortal. A god in the heavens, a spirit that lives forever, part of the life force surging throughout every single thing in the universe."

"What's for breakfast?" she asked as he put the collar around her neck.

"Flapjacks and sausage. Tomorrow will be your last meal, so you will choose it, whatever you want."

"It doesn't matter as long as my drink comes in a rusty can cut in half."

The Wendigo rumbled with mirth once again as he released her restraints and she slid to the floor. He put the cowl over her naked body, pulling the leash through the opening along with her head. He stepped away from her, out of reach, leash in hand. "The American Dream is one of capitalism and materialism," he said. "These two foundational blocks of our country are based upon the premise that there is never enough, there is always more. More money. More power. More respect. More things. More. More. More. This is the Wendigo Way as well, that the consumption of flesh can never sate the appetite, that the hunger grows deeper with every meal, every taste of human flesh. And I have never been so ravenous as I am now, my dear Pumpkin Pie, so hungry to eat you. To consume your body and soul. My time is not yet, but soon, oh so soon."

"Maybe your appetite would be filled if you ate yourself," Annie said. "Piece by piece."

"You are too precious." The Wendigo tugged at her leash. "Come. It's time for you to eat."

Annie struggled to her feet and allowed herself to be guided to the chair at the small table which held her breakfast. She sat and dutifully began to plow through the stack of pancakes as the Wendigo regaled her with Satanic doctrine. While she chewed, she watched for her opportunity. He was very attentive this morning, giving her no chance. Not until after she was done.

The Wendigo's phone vibrated. The buzzing noise was harsh in the silence of the barn. He looked at the screen, hit a button, and held it up to his ear. "What are you doing calling me at this time?"

Annie lunged across the table and drove the plastic plate into the Wendigo's throat. He gagged and she went for his eye with the spoon, but he turned his head, the metal sliding across his cheek instead. The Wendigo grabbed her by the neck with one huge hand, choking her, and Annie brought her knee up into his groin. It was as if a balloon burst, an explosion of air emitting from the man's mouth around his gagging, his face coming forward as she brought the spoon thrusting upward and into his eye with a squelching sound.

Annie ran for the door. There was a scream behind her as if she'd angered some large bird, a prehistoric pterodactyl squawking in pain and fury behind her. As she pushed through the door, Annie risked a look, half expecting the Wendigo to be transformed into a reptile with a twenty-foot wingspan and razor-sharp teeth. Instead, she saw a man struggling to his feet, blood streaming down his cheek from his eye, choking, cursing, coughing, and coming after her in a twisted gait.

Annie ran around the barn and into the woods. She'd thought about the road but didn't want to pass by the house in case the other Wiccans were there, watching, and she didn't know how far the next neighbor was or even if there was one. So she fled into the forest, a path she knew well from her walks. She'd scoped out her escape route painstakingly over the past week, and now her feet flew over the ground as if she were weightless.

The morning was gray, clouds hiding the rising sun, making visibility poor. She tripped and fell. Got up and ran into the branch of a tree, knocking her back to the ground. Bushes grasped at her, branches clawed at her, and rocks leaped in front of her. And then she heard the voice of the Wendigo.

"*Annie.*"

She ran from the sound with fear, panic dripping from her pores, driving her forward. Trip. Fall. Get up. Then her leash got tangled around some bushes and she had to pull it free, her hands shaking. She could hear her breathing, loud and harsh, then his hoarse bark getting closer.

"*Annie.*"

It was closer again. Musical. Threatening. Annie ran. Spittle flew from her mouth, blood dripped from a bloodied nose, and still, she clawed her way forward. She was not going to be a victim. She would not be sacrificed, throat cut, and left to bleed out. She'd not be butchered and cooked and eaten.

"*Annie.*"

It was right behind her. She could smell his stink. She could feel his sour breath on the back of her neck underneath the collar.

The stench of something dead. The reek of foulness filled her nose, seeping into her skin, pouring into her being. The fetor of rotten eggs and skunk and shit tickling the back of her neck, his hand reaching for the leash around her neck.

"*Annie.*"

It was time for plan B, she thought. The quarry. Maybe she wouldn't escape or live. But she wouldn't be sacrificed, stewed, and consumed. It was just up ahead.

"*Annie.*"

She tripped, righted herself, and ran for the edge of the quarry, looming out of the gloom, a gaping chasm in front of her. Death opened its welcoming arms, and Annie Brown reached the edge and flung herself off into space.

And then her head jerked back, twisting her neck with a snap, and she was suspended over the quarry, the leash holding fast.

"Annie." The Wendigo pulled her back up over the edge. "Don't you want to be with me?"

Chapter 27

Langdon was sitting at his desk at home in the living room. He was still in his pajamas, red plaid bottoms, and a T-shirt that had a Hostess Twinkie on it. He was on his second cup of coffee, and though at his computer, was staring into space over it.

Chabal sat next to him in sweatpants and a sweatshirt. "What's the plan?" she asked.

"If the plan is to sacrifice Annie Brown at the time of the lunar eclipse, 5:30 Wednesday morning, then we have forty-seven hours to save her."

"Yes. But that's not a plan."

Langdon sighed. "Interesting that Eddie Couture was still in town yesterday."

"Especially as he didn't mention to us that he was staying around for some reason."

"I guess there's one way to track down why he's here."

Langdon took his phone out, scrolled through, tapped on Eddie's name, and put it on speaker. It rang four times.

"Hello," Eddie said.

"Eddie. Langdon here. Wanted to check in with you."

"You find something about the bastards who did that to my brother?"

"We think we know who did it. The police are hunting for him now. It'll only be a matter of time."

"What'd you call for?" Eddie's voice was angry.

"You back up Machias way?"

"Yeah. Came home right after the police were done with me Saturday. Why?"

Why indeed, Langdon wondered? And why was the man lying? "I just thought it might be better to speak in person, but if you're not around, I can do it over the phone."

There was a pause. "What you want to talk about?"

"Do you know a woman down this way? Blonde hair. About forty?"

The pause was longer this time. "Don't know nobody in Brunswick."

"And you are home in Machias?"

"Is there a point to this bullshit?"

"You were seen in Brunswick yesterday, Eddie. What're you doing here?"

"What's the name of the man the police are searching for?"

"I can't tell you any more right now, sorry."

"Is it that doctor—what's his name?—Jasper Ansari that the police were asking me about? Is that who killed my brother?"

Langdon contemplated telling the man everything. But Couture's actions were suspicious, to say the least. "I don't know."

"Then what the feck good are you?" Eddie hung up.

"What do you suppose that was all about?" Langdon asked Chabal.

"He could be looking to avenge his brother's death," she said. "I can only imagine how upsetting it would be to get a package with the skull of my brother in it."

"Yeah, that could be it," Langdon said. But who was the mystery woman? "Might be nice to track Eddie down and confront him face to face."

"What other leads do we have to work on?"

"The police have committed a great deal of resources to track down Jasper Ansari. I don't think there's anything we can find there that they won't have already investigated."

"We find Annie Brown, then we find Jasper."

"I'm still not convinced that Jasper is the Wendigo," Langdon said.

"It's his face on the Patience site, Annie's shoe was found in his shed, and he's disappeared. Sounds pretty convincing to me."

Langdon nodded. "Yeah. Yeah, it does. Unless that's exactly what we're supposed to conclude."

"The original Wendigo Grotto was based in Durham, right?" Chabal asked. Langdon nodded, and she continued, "It seems to me that this group of freaky Wiccans are local. Jasper can't have gone far."

"I agree," Langdon said. "Annie is close by. I feel it in my bones."

"We know that Gregory Popa was a member of the group," Chabal said. "How about we have Star do some research on him? See what he can dig up."

"I don't want to involve anybody in this. It's my fault that Danny T. was killed."

"He can go on the computer in our office at the bookshop. No contact with anybody. No asking questions or phone calls. He'll be perfectly safe."

Langdon hesitated, then nodded. He called Star, again putting it on speaker.

"Morning, Sunshine," Star said by way of greeting.

"Morning to you."

"Hi, Star," Chabal said.

"Oh, conference call," Star said. "This must be serious when the brains of the outfit is on."

"Can you get Bill and Sally to work the shop today so you can do a bit of computer work?" Langdon asked.

"Already done," Star said. "Was planning on watching old movies and reading the new book by BJ Magnani, *The Power of Poison*. The back cover says that Lily Robinson is 'dressed to kill.'"

"You suppose you can put that busy day on hold and do some research for us?" Langdon asked. "You can use the office computer."

"Sure thing, boss. Whatcha need?"

"Can you do a deep dive on Gregory Popa, Jasper Ansari, Tom

Corbett, and Eddie Couture? Cross-check them against each other. Oh, and add Annie Brown in there."

"What am I looking for?"

"Do they know any of the same people, did they go to college together, are they members of Knights of Columbus, things like that? We're looking for any kind of connection, no matter how thin. Popa and Annie are the only ones we know for sure are involved. And Liam Couture. Do any of the others have a connection to them? That kind of thing."

"You got it, boss."

"Run them all through the LocateNOW software first and then expand to general internet searches. Let me know if you come up with anything. Anything at all. No detail is too small. We're grasping at straws here and running out of time."

"I'm on it. Anything else?"

"Keep your head down. These are dangerous people."

"Will do."

Langdon hung up the phone. "That leaves us with paying another visit to Dr. Corbett and searching for Eddie Couture and his mystery woman."

"Which one you want?" Chabal asked.

Langdon stared silently at her for a few long seconds. "I think we should stick together."

"Faster if we split up."

"We got some crazy-ass people-eating wendigo out there. I think it best if we stay together and watch each other's back."

"Is that like washing each other's backs?"

Langdon chuckled. "Not quite as much fun. But we can do that later."

Chabal snickered. "Where do we start?"

"With the backwashing?" Langdon said. "No, I suppose not. How about we pop in and see Corbett."

"Dr. Corbett called in sick this morning," the receptionist said. "I've had to cancel two surgeries."

"Oh, that's too bad," Langdon said. He and Chabal were standing in the austere waiting room across from a woman who looked like she may've enjoyed Dr. Corbett's services on her upper story. "Did he say what was wrong with him?"

"No. Just that he wasn't feeling well."

Langdon thought that perhaps they could swing by his house. "Did he say if he was at home?"

"No, but if he's sick, I imagine that's where he'd be," the receptionist said. "Although, he has taken the rest of the week off. I hope this doesn't mess up his plans."

"He took the rest of the week off? You mean because he's sick?" Langdon asked.

"No, that was preplanned. He said he was going to his house on Cape Cod." The receptionist put her hand over her mouth. "Don't tell him I said that. He'd be so angry. He likes to keep his personal life private. Can you blame him?"

"No, can't blame him at all. Thanks for your time."

Langdon and Chabal walked out the door and got into the Jeep. Dog had been left home, much to his chagrin.

"Hmm," Chabal said. "Sick? House on Cape Cod?"

"Let's swing by his house."

"Wait," Chabal grabbed his arm.

"What?"

"That's Jade," Chabal said, "going into Dr. Corbett's."

"Interesting," Langdon said. "Why don't you run into her when she comes out. I'll watch your back."

"You wash my back and I'll wash yours," Chabal said, stepping out of the Jeep.

Two minutes later, Jade came back out the door. "Jade? How are you?" Chabal asked. She'd been walking lazily back and forth in front of the doors to the practice.

"Chabal?" Jade's voice was restrained, perhaps a hint of color rising in her cheeks. "What are you doing here?"

Chabal nodded to the next building. "Picking up some chemicals for our hot tub. What about you?"

Jade looked over her shoulder at the sign above the door: Plastic Enhancement Surgery of MidCoast Maine. She didn't reply.

"Do you know Dr. Corbett?" Chabal asked.

"No."

"You want to get a cup of coffee? I'm meeting up with my husband at Dunkin' after I grab some chlorine."

"Another time," Jade said. "I have to get to work. I'm running late. Can't leave a pack of seventh graders without a teacher." She hurried away, got into her car, and drove off as Chabal watched.

Langdon pulled up in the Jeep and she climbed in. "What'd she have to say?" he asked.

"Nothing. Nothing at all."

"She mention why she was going into the good doctor's place of business?"

"Nope. Seemed a bit taken aback that I'd seen her, and then she rushed off."

Langdon typed out a text to 4 by Four. Remember the woman Jade from the barbecue? Is this the woman who almost killed you? He attached the picture he'd taken and hit send.

"4 by Four said he'd remember the lips and boobs of the woman who tried to kill him," Langdon said. "Doubt it would be Jade, as he met her and would've recognized her even with a wig and disguise. Just to be sure, though."

"Jade certainly doesn't need any enlarging in that area," Chabal said.

Langdon put the Jeep in gear and pulled out of the parking lot. "What do we know about this woman?"

"Only that she recently moved here and is a teacher at the junior high school," Chabal said. "She seems nice. Friendly. Engaging. She fit in well with our group at the barbecue."

"Hmm."

Corbett wasn't at home. Langdon considered breaking in but could see the alarm system from the front door. Probably not the best idea.

"Maybe he just decided to get an early start on his vacation," Chabal said.

"Maybe." Langdon took out his phone and texted Starling. See what you can find out about Tom Corbett owning a home on Cape Cod.

"What now?" Chabal asked.

Langdon called Corbett's cell phone. It went directly to voice mail. He called Jackson Brooks, which also went to voice mail. This time, he left a message regarding Corbett's sick leave and planned vacation time, as well as the house on the Cape.

Chabal's phone buzzed. She looked at the screen, wrinkled her nose, shrugged, and answered it.

"Hello?" Her eyes widened and she put the phone on speaker. "Thank you for getting back to me, MaryAnne," she said. "I was wondering if we could get together and chat for a few minutes."

"What is this about?" The voice was cautious.

"What can you tell me about your husband, Dr. Tom Corbett?"

"That we're separated."

"Can you tell me why?" Chabal asked.

"What is this about?"

Chabal looked at Langdon. Tilted her head. "I'm investigating a missing person and would like to rule him out as a suspect."

Silence filled the Jeep as they awaited the response.

"Tom is a lying, cheating, no-good bastard," MaryAnne said finally.

"Can we get together?"

"No."

"Do you think that Tom is capable of killing somebody?"

"Is this about that woman from Cape Elizabeth? Annie something or other?"

Chabal looked at Langdon who nodded. "Yes."

"And you think Tom has something to do with her disappearance?"

"Possibly."

"Tom had affairs during our entire marriage. He'd be gone all night, sometimes for a week at a time, always with some ready excuse, but then I started to catch on. He wasn't actually at a doctor's conference in Boston, was he? So where the fuck was he? When I confronted him about it, he told me I was being silly, treated me like a child. When I persisted, he got angry. He has quite the temper. He could do anything when his ire is up."

"Where are you, MaryAnne?"

"Somewhere safe."

"Safe from what?"

"I have to go."

And the phone went dead.

Chapter 28

Langdon's phone buzzed just as they got back home.

"Jackson," Langdon said.

"Mighty odd that two doctors who look identical and are both suspects in an abduction and murder case take the same week off," Jackson said by way of greeting.

"Mighty odd," Langdon said.

"It was easy enough to find his address on the Cape. Couple of Hyannis' finest are swinging by his house to say hello and ask him to give me a call."

Langdon sat in the Jeep as Chabal got out to go into the house. "He's supposed to be sick today," he said. "So, it seems strange that he'd go off to his vacation home on the Cape if he was too sick to go into work."

"Bart and some cop who doesn't like him much are keeping an eye on his Brunswick house."

"Just had a call from MaryAnne Corbett, the doctor's wife. She suggested that Tom's capable of anything."

"You know where she is?"

"She wouldn't say. Seemed scared."

"I'll see if we can track her down," Jackson said. "If I recall correctly, one of her friends said she went out to Colorado. We'll follow up."

"Sounds good."

"Anything else?"

"Eddie Couture is still in town," Langdon said.

"Interesting." There was a pause. "We found the woman who Doctor Ansari met on Patience and is dating. Grace Allen. I'm texting you her picture now."

Langdon looked at the picture that came through on a text. The woman was attractive, slender but athletic, and had striking features with high cheekbones and long black hair. "Doesn't look familiar to me. You know anything else about her?"

"She has a post office box in Pownal. Don't have a physical address for her as of yet."

"That's where the woman who attacked 4 by Four said she was from."

"Yep."

"I'll send him the picture and see if he recognizes her."

"Not that a woman can't change her hair color daily," Jackson said, "but he said the woman who kicked the shit out of him was a blonde."

"Talked to him yesterday after we got together with you, and he thinks that the woman might've been wearing a wig."

"Let me know what he says."

"Sure. Any luck on tracking down Dr. Ansari?"

"Not yet. What's your next move?"

"Trying to find connections between all the people involved. Why Annie? Liam? Was Popa friendly with Corbett or Ansari? There are too many moving pieces. We need to connect some of them, and we need to do it fast."

"Amen, brother. Time is waning." Jackson hung up the phone.

Langdon took another look at the picture, shook his head, and sent it on to 4 by Four. He was just walking into the house when his phone buzzed.

"4 by Four," Langdon said.

"That's her," 4 by Four said. "That's the woman who kicked me in the face and stuck a knife in my leg."

Interesting, Langdon thought. "You sure?"

"Her hair and eyes are a different color, but you know, the lips and the breasts are the same."

Langdon chuckled. "I guess you'd know."

"Who is she?"

"She's the girlfriend of Dr. Jasper Ansari. They met through the Patience site."

4 by Four whistled, the low keening noise vibrating through the phone. "Hot dog."

"Yeah, hot dog," Langdon said. "You at home all day?"

"Yeah, still mending."

"No doctor visits today?"

"Maybe later tonight."

"I imagine some Staties are going to be paying you a visit to get a formal identification of this woman and grill you about anything else you might know."

"That sounds like a grand time."

"You bet," Langdon said.

"I suppose her name isn't actually Natasha, is it?"

Langdon chuckled again. "Grace Allen. Jackson Brooks just called with that bit of info. Don't know much more about her at this point."

"I'll put some coffee on and get the donuts out for the State Police."

Langdon hung up the phone and opened the door to find dog dancing around, waiting for him. He scratched the pooch on the head and butt and went inside where he sat at his desk and texted Jackson Brooks. 4 by Four ID'd Grace Allen as the woman who attacked him. He's at home all day.

Chabal swiveled on her chair. "Found Eddie Couture," she said. "He's staying out to the Village Motel."

An image of a young Bowdoin College student lying dead on a bed in that motel flashed through Langdon's mind. Though it happened twenty-five years ago, it still haunted him every single day. "Jackson got the name of the woman Ansari is dating, and 4 by Four has identified her as the lady who attacked him."

"Whoa, interesting couple. Like Bonnie and Clyde."

Langdon's phone buzzed with a text from Jackson. Sending a couple of officers over to get a statement from 4 by Four. The plot thickens.

"Guess we should stop by and see if Eddie's in his motel room," Langdon said as he texted his reply to Jackson. Yes it does.

Langdon's phone buzzed with a call from Starling as they went out to the Jeep. He put it on speaker and climbed into the vehicle. "Star, what do you got?"

"Did you know that Annie Brown was adopted?" Star asked, the excitement bursting in is tone.

"Yeah, the Browns mentioned that. Her parents died when she was eight, I think it was, and they adopted her when she was ten." Langdon put the phone on speaker and into its holder, starting the Jeep and backing out of the garage.

"Yeah, well, her parents died in a meth lab explosion, but that's not what has me all lathered up."

Langdon chuckled. "Why don't you tell me what does have you all lathered up?" He backed out onto the road and started driving.

"Annie's father was Ralph Nergal. He moved to Maine in 1972 when he was eleven years old."

Langdon's thoughts churned with various scenarios. "Go on."

"Nergal seemed a strange name, so I looked that up. It's the name of the Babylon god of the underworld, Hades, or as we call it, Hell."

"Are you telling me that Annie's father was the devil?"

Star laughed. "Just about. Her grandfather legally had his name changed to Nergal in 1969, soon after he joined—"

"The Church of Satan," Langdon said. "And then he moved to Maine in 1972 to start a Grotto in Durham with his wife and son."

"You got it. I haven't been able to find out anything about what happened between the years 1972 and 1989 when Ralph Nergal and Annie's mother blew up in a meth lab, but Annie is definitely connected to the Wendigo Grotto, the fanatic offshoot of the Church of Satan."

"And it comes full circle," Langdon said.

"What comes full circle?"

"I have no idea." Langdon turned onto Church Road. "But something has come full circle. It seems that perhaps Annie was targeted because of her grandfather's involvement with the Wendigo Grotto."

"Maybe because Ralph Nergal left the Grotto," Star said.

"Or maybe he never did. Maybe it's because *she* left the Wendigo Grotto."

"This is some weird shit."

"Yes, it is," Langdon said. "See if you can come up with the names of any other members of the Wendigo Grotto. I'm sure they're long gone by now, but it might be their descendants who abducted Annie."

"Got it, boss."

"Let me know what you find." Langdon hung up the phone as he pulled into the Village Motel.

"Holy cow," Chabal said.

"Cow from Hell is more like it," Langdon said. "You want to go work your charms at the front desk and get Eddie's room number while I call and fill Jackson in?"

Chabal tossed her hair. "Sure thing, lover," she said coyly.

Langdon laughed and called Jackson as Chabal got out of the Jeep and went inside. He filled the state cop in on what Star had just told him and was hanging up as Chabal came back out.

"Room 29," she said.

Langdon got out of the Jeep and they walked across the parking lot to the other side of the U-shaped motel and up to the second floor. The past again came back to haunt Langdon. He'd been in that room before, talking with his brother, unaware that a young Bowdoin College girl was being brutally murdered in the room below.

Eddie opened the door on the second knock. He was barefoot and had no shirt on, just a ragged pair of jeans. "What are you doing here?" he asked.

"I thought I might ask you the same thing," Langdon said. He noticed that the man had a tattoo, 666, on his chest just above his heart.

"Somebody die and make you my goddamn keeper?" Eddie asked.

"I'm trying to help you, Eddie," Langdon said.

"Thought I'd stick around in case I could be of any use with… you know… my brother."

"Why don't you put a shirt on and we'll have a talk?" Langdon brushed past the man into the room with Chabal following. "Cover up that tattoo."

"Talk? About what?"

"The Wendigo Grotto of the Church of Satan," Langdon said.

Eddie jerked as if he'd been punched in the gut, and his face went white as goose feathers. He walked over to a canvas bag, pulled out a white T-shirt and put it on. He sat down on the bed as Langdon and Chabal sat in the two motel chairs.

"I don't know what you're talking about," Eddie said.

"What's with your tattoo?" Langdon asked.

Eddie shook his head. "We were young and stupid. It was just a phase."

"You and Liam?" Langdon prompted.

"Yeah," Eddie breathed the word. "He was twenty, and I was eighteen. Got running with some people and thought it'd be cool to follow old Beelzebub himself, you know? Just a stupid thing that kids do. It wasn't like we were doing anything bad, not at first, not until we came to Maine, that is."

"In 1972," Langdon said.

Eddie looked surprised. "Yeah, in 1972."

"With Nergal."

"You been doing your homework," Eddie said. "Yeah, me and Liam threw in with Pan Nergal and a few others and came to Maine to spread the word of Satan, but then Pan got real twisted and started to do some real weird shit."

"Like human sacrifices and eating people," Langdon said.

"Fucking *sick* shit," Eddie said and put his head down in his hands. Then, he looked back up with a dawning awareness spreading across his face like the incoming tide. "They're still out there, aren't they? It's those sick fucks who killed... Liam."

Langdon and Chabal said nothing, letting the man process things for himself.

"We split after they killed the first person, some homeless fellow they picked up down in Portland," Eddie said. "Slit his throat open and let him bleed out like he was a goddamn deer. We wasn't in for that shit. September 23, 1972, it was. We lit out that very night. Didn't tell anybody where we was going. Just drove north. Stopped when we got to Machias and haven't left since."

"Did they eat the homeless fellow?" Langdon asked.

"They talked about doing it, yeah. We kinda lit out of there, so I don't know if they actually did it."

"Who were the other members of the Wendigo Grotto?" Langdon asked.

"The leader was Pan Nergal. He had his wife, Helena, and son, Ralph, with him. There were nine others."

Langdon handed him a pad of paper and pen from the desk. "Write down all their names for me."

Eddie took the paper and pen in slow motion, the information barrage seemingly freezing his brain and body. "If they're still out there, and they targeted Liam, they must be after me, too, right?"

"Who was the blonde woman I saw you with yesterday?" Chabal asked.

"Just some broad I ran into out on that grassy place you got in town, what do you call it? You know, with the food vendors?"

"The Mall," Chabal said.

"Yeah, I was sitting on a bench eating a hot dog and she sat down next... you think she's one of them?"

"Do you often get approached by beautiful women thirty years younger than you?" Chabal asked.

"Said she was writing a story on fish hatcheries and when she heard that I work in one, she wanted to buy me a cup of joe and pick my brain. Then she showed up and invited me over to her house instead, said it'd be more comfortable there." Eddie shrugged. "Wasn't going to say no to that, now, was I?"

Langdon took out his phone and opened the picture of Grace Allen that Jackson had sent him. "Is this the woman?"

Eddie screwed his face up tight and then nodded. "That's the broad."

"So, you went to her house?" Langdon asked.

Eddie shook his head. "We got to my truck, and she got a phone call. Said she'd have to take a rain check but she'd call me. Got my number and took off in a hurry."

"I'm thinking that whatever that phone call was, it saved your life," Chabal said.

Chapter 29

Tuesday morning, Langdon and Chabal were back in the bookshop office with Starling going over what they knew so far when Maddie Campagna pushed open the door and came in. Her short black hair was askew, and her green eyes blazed.

"I've had about enough of being kept in the dark," she blurted by way of a greeting. "I want some answers, and I want them now!"

"Have a seat." Langdon pointed at the empty armchair next to Starling. "Good morning."

"There are things you're not telling me." Maddie stood defiantly in the center of the cramped office. "And I'm paying you to find Annie, and you're not doing anything about it."

"Sit and I'll tell you what I know," Langdon said.

Maddie sagged, took a step, and sat down. "It's just that if you're right about that Blood Supermoon thing, then they're going to kill her in less than twenty-four hours."

"I know," Langdon said. "We believe that Annie was targeted because of her father's association with a group called the Wendigo Grotto."

"Harold is part of this group?"

Langdon shook his head. "Not Harold Brown. Her biological father by the name of Ralph Nergal. He was a boy of just eleven when his father, Annie's grandfather, started up the Wendigo Grotto, a group of Wiccans who are trying to harness the power of the natural world. They worship the moon and sacrifice human beings during the times of the supermoons."

"That's not the worst part," Chabal said.

"What's the worst part?" Maddie had settled into the armchair like she'd melted there, all the anger and defiance gone.

Langdon cleared his throat and looked her in the eye. "We believe that the leader of the remainder of the Wendigo Grotto is practicing cannibalism in his effort to grow stronger and harness the power of the natural world. He's planning on eating Annie."

"Eating her?"

Langdon nodded. "Has Annie ever spoken about her biological father with you?"

"They're going to kill and eat her?"

"I know that it's a lot to take all at once, Maddie, but we don't have much time. Has Annie ever spoken about her biological father with you?"

Maddie shook her head no.

Langdon took out his phone with a picture he'd taken of the list of names that Eddie had written out for him. He held it out for Maddie to take. "Did she ever mention any of these names to you?"

Maddie took the phone and read through the nine names. "No." She looked up from the phone. "But you know who has her, right? That doctor. Jasper Ansari. It was his house you found her shoe at. Have the police arrested him yet?"

"They can't find him." Langdon took the phone from her hand and scrolled to the previous picture. "Do you know this woman?"

Maddie shook her head, looked again, and said, "no."

"Are you sure?"

"Yes, I'm sure," Maddie said. "Who is she?"

"I believe that she is the woman who Jasper Ansari is dating," Langdon said.

"They met on the Patience website," Chabal added.

"And she tried to kill a friend of mine who was helping me search for Annie," Langdon said.

"What is going on here?" Maddie asked.

"Believe me, we're doing everything we can do to find Annie before five-thirty Wednesday morning," Langdon said.

"Five-thirty?"

"That's when the moon will turn red," Langdon said.

"What can I do to help?"

"I'll let you know," Langdon said. "But right now, let us get back to searching for Annie."

Maddie stood up. "I'm going to get a room at the Village Motel out on Pleasant Street until this is settled. Call me if you think of anything."

The Village Motel. Again, Langdon thought. "I promise," he said.

After she left, Chabal went and closed the door behind her, watching her leave the bookshop before coming back to sit down. "Whew," she said. "Guess I can't blame her for being angry and anxious. Can't imagine how I'd be feeling if it was Jewell missing. Or you."

"Yeah," Langdon said. "If you were abducted by a freak who sacrifices and eats people, I'd pretty much be a basket case."

"What's the plan?" she asked.

"How about you call Jackson and see what he might've gotten out of Eddie, and I'll call the Browns," Langdon said. "Star can keep plugging away at how—or if—these people are even connected."

Star moved to the couch with his laptop as Langdon dialed the Browns. Meg Brown answered, and Langdon spoke with her for about twenty minutes. She said that, yes, Annie had been born Annie Nergal, and one of the first things they'd done was to have her name legally changed to Brown, especially once they learned of the name's satanic reference. She knew that Annie's parents had been killed in a meth lab explosion, not because the welfare agency told her, but because she'd seen it on the news and connected the names. That was all they knew but promised to dig out the old paperwork to see if there might be more information, details, about their daughter's family. Langdon asked her to check in with the adoption agency for anything else as they were required by law to keep any records from her childhood.

Chabal was still on the phone with Jackson, so Langdon looked up the information on the explosion that had killed Ralph Nergal and his wife, Christina. He had a subscription to newspapers.com, which had digitally archived almost every newspaper in the U.S. and so made searches for old news items incredibly easy. It took him only a few minutes to find the story from October of 1989. There was no indication of what had touched off the explosion, but it was widely believed that Ralph and Christina were some of the first to cook meth on the East Coast, skills possibly brought back from a trip to San Francisco they'd taken the year before.

"Jackson says that the police are looking for the people on the list that Eddie gave them, but the man wasn't able to help much more than that," Chabal said, interrupting his research train of thought. "The name Popa wasn't on the list, nor was Ansari, or Corbett for that matter."

"They could've changed their names as Annie did," Langdon said.

"Ansari is about the same age as Annie," Chabal said. "Meaning it might've been a grandfather of Ansari that was an original member. Then, if his mother marries a guy by the name of Ansari, well, you get the gist. They're still digging."

"They swing Eddie loose?"

"Not yet," Chabal said. "They're trying to figure out if they should charge him in connection with killing a homeless man that nobody knew was missing all the way back in 1972. Seems to be a stretch, even though he's confessed."

"I take it Jackson still has no leads on finding Ansari?"

"Nothing. Grace Allen and Jasper Ansari have both disappeared off the face of the earth." Chabal turned to her computer.

"I'm tracking the original group members of the Wendigo Grotto, trying to reconstruct family trees," Starling put in. "See if can locate anybody with ties back to the founding fathers, if you will. Maybe one of them will be one of the other two Wiccans."

"Oh, that reminds me," Chabal said. "Jackson did say that Eddie mentioned that the founder, Pan Nergal, had started some sort of trust for the group."

"Trust?" Starling said. He looked up and clattered away on the keyboard.

"Yes," Chabal said. "He was some rich kid, born with a silver spoon in his mouth out in San Francisco, and inherited a caboodle of money."

"The WG Trust owns a farmhouse in Durham," Starling said, looking back up with a triumphant look on his face. "I saw that yesterday, but it didn't sink in."

"The Wendigo Grotto Trust," Langdon said.

"Could be," Chabal said. "Anything more about it?"

"I'll see what I can find," Starling said.

"In the meantime, I might swing on over there and poke around a bit," Langdon said, standing up.

"I'm with you," Chabal said, rising to her feet. "Should we call Jackson or Bart?"

"Let's see if anything pans out," Langdon said.

"Ha, I see what you did there," Chabal said. "Pans. Pan. Nergal."

"Text me the address of the farmhouse," Langdon said to Starling. "If you don't hear from us in an hour, send the big guns out to the place."

"Got you, boss," Starling said.

Dog thought he'd go along as well, the three of them walking out through the bookstore with a purpose to their step.

"Looks like we're breaking and entering again," Langdon said. They'd parked a half-mile down the road and walked back to the woods across from the driveway.

"We don't know if there's anybody home this time," Chabal said. She pulled her pistol from the holster under her blouse. The driveway was about two-hundred yards long, leading straight back to a farmhouse, the kind of house that had originally been quite small, with, over the years, additions being built until it now stretched across a wide expanse.

Langdon took out his Glock. "Knocking on the front door doesn't seem to be a good idea," he said. "Excuse me, do you have an abducted woman in your barn who you're preparing for dinner?"

Chabal snickered. "There's smoke coming from the barn." A lazy tendril of smoke was rising from an opening in the roof.

"How about we start there," Langdon said. "Give me a twenty-foot lead and then follow along covering me. I'll loop around through the trees to the left, go around the back of the barn, and work my way to the front door, and we'll see what we find."

"Try not to get killed," Chabal said. "Or worse, captured. I hear they eat people around here."

"Looks pretty serene to me," Langdon said.

"You know what they say about the quiet ones," Chabal said.

Langdon chuckled. He went back down the tree line until they were out of sight of the house, crossed the desolate road, and back into the trees on the other side. Not a single car had gone by since they'd been there.

He worked his way through the woods, stealing a glance over his shoulder at Chabal, trailing along behind. Langdon took a moment to appreciate, thinking she looked pretty damn sexy with her SIG in hand, capris, and green blouse.

There were four windows along the side of the faded red barn that had been painted black. The front had a sliding door large enough to drive a tractor into. Langdon looked over at the house for signs of life. It was quiet. There was no car in front. No lights on. No movement.

Langdon motioned for Chabal to cover him from where he now

stood, and then worked his way further back so that the barn was between him and the house. With a deep breath, Langdon left the cover of the woods and walked toward the back of the barn, which had two windows, also painted black.

His heart beating strongly in his chest, Langdon put his back to the side of the barn, and worked his way sideways to the front, his Glock held overhead. When he got to the corner, he nodded at Chabal, and she nodded back. He stepped around the corner, went to the door, and tugged on the wooden handle.

It was then he noticed the heavy chain and padlock. He'd rushed out here without proper preparation, not bringing his binoculars or bolt cutters. The hairs on his neck prickled as he imagined eyes from the house on him, a gun pointing his way, perhaps a crossbow. With a curse under his breath, he slid back around the corner and out of sight of the house.

Langdon took his phone out and texted Chabal one-handed. Locked. I'm going to break in through window at the back. Keep watch on house. Fire a warning shot if anybody comes toward barn.

K.

Langdon moved to the back of the barn, found a rock, took his shirt off, wrapped the rock in it, and smashed the window. Quickly, he knocked out the jagged pieces, pulled his shirt back on, and clambered through the opening.

He was in the back of the barn that had not held animals in quite some time. There was a small fire smoldering in the corner, wisps of smoke drifting upward and out through a trap door in the ceiling. There was a small table with two chairs next to that and a four-wheeler on the other side.

A circular wooden table was in the middle of the room, tilted away from him, though Langdon caught a glimpse of brown hair. Outside, a gunshot rang out.

Langdon moved quickly around the table. Annie Brown, naked was attached to the front, restraints around her wrists and ankles and neck, a gag in her mouth, and a look in her eyes flittering between terror and hope.

A barrage of gunshots filled the air coming from the direction of the house, possibly some sort of semi-automatic weapon. Langdon removed the gag from Annie's mouth and set to releasing her restraints. "Hi, Annie," he said as he worked. "My name's Langdon, and I was hired to find you by your friend Maddie and your parents, Harold and Meg."

Her body was covered in scratches and bruises. "Hurry!" she said in a screechy voice. "The Wendigo is coming!"

A gunshot rang out from the woods. His wife was still alive, Langdon thought with relief. This was followed by another burst of shots from the house.

Langdon released the last restraint, and Annie crumpled to the ground. He took off his shirt again and put it over her battered body, the bottom hanging down to her knees. Langdon picked her up and carried her to the back and the broken window, tumbling her to the ground and diving outside next to her.

He picked her up again and broke into a run for the woods, careful to keep the barn between him and the house. As he reached the cover of the trees, an ATV roared to life.

Langdon worked his way back toward Chabal's position, carrying Annie in his arms. She was babbling hysterically about something, but he wasn't paying attention, wanting to ensure that his wife was okay.

Chabal was reloading her pistol with no signs of injury. "I think there was only one of them," she said. "Took off the other way on a four-wheeler."

"Who was it?"

"That bitch who stuck 4 by Four with a knife."

Chapter 30

"How is she?" Maddie asked as she got out of the car. "Oh, thank God you found her, please tell me she's okay."

Chabal embraced the woman. They were in the parking lot of the hospital.

"Is she okay? Can I see her?"

"Not yet," Chabal said. "She's drifting between hysterics and unconsciousness. The police are hoping to get an identification of who did this, but it doesn't look like she'll be much help for some time."

"Is she… injured?"

"She's pretty bruised up and is covered in scratches. That's as much as I know."

"Where's Langdon?"

"He's looking for the woman who ran off when we rescued Annie," Chabal said. "Along with half the cops in Maine. I rode in with her in the ambulance."

"It was a woman who took her? Not that Dr. Ansari?"

"We believe there are at least three in the group. This one was the woman who attacked our friend, Jimmy 4 by Four."

Maddie opened and closed her mouth like a gasping fish, then began sobbing, her knees wobbling under her.

Chabal took her arm. "Let's sit in your car and wait for the Browns to get here," she said.

Maddie allowed herself to be guided back into her car and Chabal went around and got in the passenger side.

"Will we be allowed in?" Maddie asked, sobs wracking her body.

"Only one visitor at a time, but not until she's stabilized, which could be quite some time." Chabal found tissues in the glove box. "We can wait at our house for any updates."

"Thank you. Thank you so much."

Chabal handed her a tissue, but Maddie's hand went past her outstretched offering and pressed a black object against her chest. It was the most excruciating pain Chabal had ever felt in her entire life, even worse than childbirth. Her brain rattled in her head like it was popping popcorn, and it felt like bees were crawling through her skin.

Then it stopped. Chabal tried to focus on Maddie.

"I'm sorry," Maddie said. She pressed a needle into her arm. "But the Wendigo is hungry."

Chabal felt a blackness swirling around her and encompassing her being.

The Wendigo was hungry.

Chapter 31

Langdon had called in the troops. Bart had been the first to the scene, followed by an ambulance, five more Brunswick cops, and finally Jackson Brooks and four other Staties. Chabal had hopped in the ambulance with Annie and gone off to the hospital.

Grace Allen had disappeared into the woods. Roads were closed. Dogs were brought in. Forensics arrived to look through the house. Langdon thought about commandeering the ATV in the barn, but that was now a crime scene, and besides, the mystery woman, Grace Allen, had too large of a head start.

He'd given his statement to three different people. Officers were dispatched to get Chabal's version, as well as Annie Brown's, if the women were up to speaking.

Langdon called Chabal. It went directly to voicemail. He texted her to call when she could. Let him know how Annie was doing. If she'd said anything on the ride.

There was no reply.

When his phone rang, he answered without looking at it. "Hey, Babe," he said.

"This is Meg Brown."

Langdon winced. "Sorry, Meg. Did Chabal share the good news with you?"

"Yes. Thank you so much. You're a true hero. We're here at the hospital trying to get answers about how she is but we're being given the runaround."

"What'd Chabal have to say? I didn't get a chance to speak with Annie before the ambulance took her away."

"She just called to tell us that you'd found and rescued Annie and that they were on the way to the hospital, MidCoast in Brunswick, and to meet her there. Then she called back when we were halfway there and told us she'd meet us on a bench just outside the front door." Meg was speaking fast and hard, her emotions raging across the phone line from joyful to fearful to tearful as she began sobbing.

"Meg, can you put Chabal on the phone?"

"What's that? This is Harold." Harold's deep voice rumbled over the phone. "Sorry about Meg, we just don't know what's going on and can't get any answers."

"What's Chabal have to say," Langdon said. "She probably knows more than anybody else what is going on."

"Chabal isn't here," Harold said. "We looked all around before we came inside, and there was no sign of her anywhere. The lady at the desk agreed that we could both be in the waiting room after a bit of persuading but she—"

"Mr. Brown, excuse me, but you said Chabal isn't there? Is it possible she's with Annie?"

"I guess that might be so, but the lady here says nobody can see her. Wait, hold on a second, I'll ask."

Langdon listened as the phone rustled and voices could be heard, but he couldn't distinguish the words. After a minute that seemed to be an hour, Harold came back on the phone. "Nope. The receptionist said that the lady who came in with Annie was waiting outside. We sure enough didn't see her anywhere, though."

"Can you take another look?"

"Hold on," Harold said. "There's a policeman coming over."

Again, muted voices that Langdon couldn't hear, and after an eternity, Harold's voice came back over the line. "I got to go."

Langdon looked at the disconnected phone in his hand with growing unease. Where could Chabal have gotten to, he wondered?

Had she just gone for a walk? No, he knew that, if she'd told the Browns she would wait, she would wait—unless something very important had come up. Had she followed up on a lead Annie had given her on the ride over? Langdon cursed silently and then aloud. Was Chabal tracking down the Wendigo on her own?

"What's up, partner?" Bart asked, walking over. "You look more shaken now than you did when I arrived."

"Chabal's not answering her phone."

"She's probably just busy."

"She was supposed to meet the Browns outside the hospital and isn't there." Langdon tapped on his phone to call her. Straight to voicemail. "Phone's off."

"Shit," Bart said. "That's not like her."

Langdon texted her. Give me a call, babe. You're starting to freak me out. "Look, I gotta go," he said to Bart. "Am I done here?"

"Yeah, sure. Just keep your phone on," Bart said and then grimaced. "I'm sure everything's fine. She'd probably just got the thing silenced and went to get a bite to eat and lost track of time."

Langdon was afraid. More afraid than he'd ever been in his life. He'd hoped that he'd pull up in front of Mid Coast Hospital on the circular drive, and Chabal would be sitting on the bench. She was not.

He tried calling her again. Left a message on her voicemail. He parked and went inside. Harold and Meg Brown were not there.

There were two ladies behind the reception desk. One was obviously in charge. She gave him a stern look. "Can I help you?" she asked.

"Yes. I'm looking for Chabal Langdon."

"I can't talk to you about patients."

"She's not a patient, and I'm her husband," Langdon said.

The woman looked at him disapprovingly.

"She was waiting outside but up and left," the other woman said.

"She arrived in an ambulance," Langdon said tightly. "And planned on meeting Meg and Harold Brown here. Where are they?"

"We are not at liberty to say," the stern woman said. The phone rang, and she picked it up.

"They're back there in a conference room speaking with the police," the other lady whispered. "Your wife said that she was supposed to meet with another woman, and that if she missed her, to tell her she was outside. Just in case the woman came in another door, or something like that."

"Who?"

The lady screwed up her face. "Maggie or something like that."

"Maddie? Maddie Campagna?"

Her face brightened into a smile. "Yes. That's it."

"Did she come in looking for my wife?"

"No. Haven't seen her at all."

Langdon's stomach churned and he could feel his heart tightening. "I need to speak with Annie Brown."

The stern lady hung up the phone and said, "Absolutely not."

"I need to speak with goddamn Annie Brown, and I need to do it now."

The stern lady blanched. "I'm sorry, sir, but I must ask you to leave."

"And I need to speak with Annie Brown. What room is she in?"

"I will be forced to call building security."

"Good. Call the police out from the conference room."

The stern lady suddenly smiled wickedly. "Excuse me, officer, could you escort this man out of here? Better yet, arrest him."

Langdon looked over his shoulder at Bart who came walking up. "What's going on?" he asked.

"This man is—"

"Not you." Bart held up a massive hand palm outward. "What's up, partner? You find her?"

"No," Langdon said. "She's just up and disappeared. No matter what, she'd have at least let me know where. If she could."

"Let's go outside and talk," Bart said.

"I need to speak with Annie Brown. See if she said something to Chabal. Like who the fuck kidnapped her? Don't you see?"

"As you said, she probably just went to follow up on a lead."

"You know that's bullshit," Langdon said. "Chabal wouldn't turn her phone off and go off chasing the fucking wendigo without contacting me."

"We're doing everything we can to find this wendigo and the two accomplices," Bart said. "Trust us. If they indeed took Chabal, we'll find her."

Langdon stared hard at his friend, his gall rising, his atavistic Viking temper rearing its ugly head. It was something that he feared. Once let loose, there was no putting his rage back in the bottle until it was spent.

"If the Wendigo took Chabal, she has less than eleven hours to live," Langdon said, checking his voice, his fury, and his fear. "The only person who can help to possibly track them down in that short of a time is Annie."

"Okay, partner. Let me see what I can do." Bart turned away and spoke into the two-way on his shoulder as he walked down the hall. He stopped, turned, and waved for Langdon to follow him.

The stern lady did not look happy.

"The doctor who treated her is available to speak with us," Bart said.

They went upstairs and down the hall to where a police officer whom Langdon knew as Max sat outside a door. Bart walked past him through the door with Langdon following without saying a word. Max had never liked Bart much and had tried to arrest Langdon on more than one occasion.

A doctor stood looking at a clipboard while a nurse was adjusting the IV that led to Annie Brown's arm. Her face was pale, bruised and scratched, and there were stitches across her cheek. A blanket was pulled up snugly under her chin. She was twitching in her sleep, a bit of drool running from the corner of her mouth.

"What can I do for you, officer?" the doctor asked.

"We need to speak with your patient," Bart said. "Can you wake her up?"

The doctor shook his head, looking down his nose at them. "I can't do that."

Langdon started to reach for the man's throat but was able to restrain himself. "This… this woman is the only one who might know of the identity of a group of Wiccans, serial killers, who murder and then eat their victims. They may currently be holding my wife for a ritual sacrifice tomorrow morning at the time of the Blood Moon. She might know where they are hiding."

The doctor looked like he wanted to ask what the hell Langdon was talking about, opened, shut his mouth, and shook his head again. "I'm sorry, sir, I truly am. It's not that I won't, but that I can't. She was hysterical, out of her head, and we had to give her a sedative. She won't wake up for ten or twelve hours, hopefully calmer, as she was on the verge of a complete mental breakdown."

"Can you give her something to counteract the sedative? An upper of some sort?" Langdon heard his voice rumbling across the room. A red rage was floating past his eyes. "I need to speak with her."

"I'm sorry, but that is completely impossible, as well as medically ill-advised."

Langdon wanted to hit something. Throw a chair through the window. Anything. The smug-faced bastard doctor. He wanted to shake Annie and tell her to wake up. He could feel his hands curling around the neck of the Wendigo and snapping it.

Some fucking wicked Wendigo was going to sacrifice and eat his wife, and there was nothing he could do about it.

Chapter 32

"Easy, brother," Bart said. "Breathe."

Langdon wasn't quite sure how they'd gotten outside. The burly Bart had one massive arm around his back and the other on his arm guiding him. "Chabal."

"We'll find her," Bart said. "We'll find her and rip the head off of that wendigo fellow, but you got to stay in control, or you're not going to do us any good."

Langdon shook his head and took a deep breath. Bart was right. The anger had to be kept at bay. Until the moment it was ready to be unleashed.

"I'll take you home, and we'll put our heads together and figure something out," Bart said.

"I need my own wheels," Langdon said.

"Okay. I'll ride with you and get somebody to pick up my cruiser."

"Aren't you supposed to be on duty?"

Bart laughed hollowly. "When you took off from that farmhouse worried about Chabal, I told the Commander I felt a stomach bug coming on and had to take the rest of the day off."

"And he bought that?"

Bart shrugged, easing his bulk into the passenger seat of the Jeep. "I've already been broken down to the lowest level I can go. His only recourse is to fire me, but I clear too much paper for him to do that, so I kinda got him over a barrel. Sometimes it's good to be on the bottom with no place to go but up."

"Thanks," Langdon said, pulling the Jeep out of the parking lot.

"I'd trade places with her in a minute if given the chance."

Langdon looked at his buddy, and his eyes teared slightly. "I know you would."

"There's still a chance that she's perfectly safe somewhere. She got a cab, lost her phone, got stuck with no money—I don't know, something," Bart said lamely.

"You know in your gut that's not true," Langdon said. "It's the Wendigo. I feel like he's been targeting me the whole time."

"Targeting you?"

Langdon sighed. "I don't know. I just can't shake the feeling that I'm being set up."

They rode the last few minutes in silence. Langdon thought about contacting Chabal's kids with the news that their mother had been abducted but couldn't see the point until the issue was resolved one way or another.

He wanted to hash it out with his own daughter, but knew that she'd be on the first bus, train, or plane from Brooklyn. The truth was, he didn't want her anywhere close to Maine. For once, Brooklyn felt like the safer place.

Langdon thought longingly of his younger brothers, the twins, Lord and Nicky. Two confirmed bachelors who'd bailed him out of a few scrapes before, but they were currently somewhere in Montana hunting big game. They'd also be on the first plane if he asked but there was just no time.

The clock in the Jeep said it was 6:00 p.m. Eleven and a half hours from the eclipse and the rising of the Blood Moon. Langdon didn't know where to start. So little time. So much at stake.

Parked alongside the street were several cars belonging to his best friends, and again, the tears welled up in the corners of his eye.

Jewell met him as he came through the door, throwing her arms around him and pulling him close. "We'll find her, baby. She's going to be okay," she whispered into his ear.

Langdon allowed himself to be led into the living room, followed by Bart. Richam, Star, and 4 by Four sat around the space, their eyes all on him.

"What' the deal?" Richam asked.

Jewell and Bart sat down while Langdon remained standing. He looked at the face and eyes of each of his friends, thanking them silently. "They took Chabal," he said simply.

"Who is they?" Jewell asked.

"First of all, we don't have much time," Langdon said. "I believe they plan on killing her at five-thirty tomorrow morning."

Jewell gasped, and Richam cursed.

"So, I'm going to make this short and sweet. A bit over three weeks ago, a man named Eddie Couture came into my office and hired me to find his brother, Liam, who'd come to Brunswick to buy a four-wheeler. A couple of days later, a woman named Maddie Campagna hired me to find her friend, Annie Brown. She went on a first date with a man named Tom Corbett who she met through a dating service called Patience. Only, he claims it wasn't him and that somebody else posed as him. Then, somebody tried to kill me in the woods out back here, a woman stabbed 4 by Four, and somebody succeeded in murdering Danny T." Langdon took out his phone and brought up a photo of Corbett and handed it to Jewell to pass around. "That's Doctor Tom Corbett."

"I know him," Richam said. "He comes into the restaurant once in a while."

"This all had something to do with that local accountant who killed himself, right?" Jewell asked.

"Gregory Popa was linked to the missing Liam Couture," Langdon continued. "Even if vaguely, but when I spoke with him, it was obvious the man was hiding something. After somebody tried to kill me with an arrow, we discovered that he's a champion archer. That, coupled with a few other things, led me to break into his house where I found a private room in his basement with videos of gruesome slayings, ritual sacrifices, if you like. I saw some of it, but Jackson Brooks is involved and tells me that it shows people being butchered and put into a large pot, presumably to be stewed. Popa said that the leader of the group—he simply called him the Wendigo—would sacrifice the victims at the time of the supermoon, and then stew and eat them."

"Fuck," Jewell said. "What the hell exactly is a wendigo?"

"A wendigo is a mythical Native American beast who feasts on human flesh," Langdon said. "It was you that pointed us at the group of missionaries from the Church of Satan, who, fifty years ago, came and opened a chapter in Durham that they called the Wendigo Grotto. They operated on the fringes for a few years and then just quietly disappeared. Sort of like the back to the land people that came to Maine at that time, one would think they just stepped back into society."

"What the...? Who was doing the killing, butchering, and stewing?" Richam asked. "Popa?"

Langdon shook his head. "The video never showed the person's face. They wore a monk's robe with a hood, what do you call that?"

"A cowl," Jewell said faintly.

"But whoever it was is tall," Langdon said. "Too tall to be Popa, who was most likely the one recording it."

"Tom Corbett," 4 by Four said. "He's easily five inches over six feet. And he was the profile person from Patience who had a date with Annie. It's gotta be him."

"Could be," Langdon said. "But he did provide the name of another doctor, down in Falmouth, guy by the name of Jasper Ansari, who may've had access to his personal information and credit card. Annie Brown called Maddie to let her know she was just off on a walkabout of sorts and perfectly fine, and at first said she was in North Carolina, but then slipped and said Falmouth, and there was a struggle, and the phone went dead. That, coupled with other things, led Chabal and me to search the shed behind his house where we found a woman's shoe, identified by Maddie as one of Annie's. One that she would've worn on a first date. And this Dr. Ansari is also very tall."

"Go figure," Richam said. "Two local doctors six and a half feet tall linked to ritual slayings. Freaky."

"The police pull them in?" Jewell asked. All eyes turned to Bart.

"They're both missing," Bart said grimly. "Supposedly both took vacation this week and are unreachable. Not at home. Not at the vacation home Corbett said he was going to."

"Don't doctors have to be *reachable*, even on vacation?" 4 by Four asked.

"They are supposed to be," Bart said. "By cell phone, but neither one is answering."

"It turns out that Eddie Couture, the guy who originally hired me, was a member of the Wendigo Grotto," Langdon said. "Did you find out anything about any of the others, Star?"

Starling shook his head. "Nothing helpful. The founder, that Nergal guy, died in a car accident in 1979. His son, Ralph, had one child who was Annie Brown and—"

"Annie Brown was the daughter of the dude who founded this offshoot of the Church of Satan?" 4 by Four interrupted.

"Granddaughter," Starling said. "There's nothing to suggest that Ralph Nergal continued on, but he *was* a drug dealer and died in a meth explosion. Then Annie was adopted by the Browns. Two of the others moved back to California and are still there, far as I can tell. Another couple, Sam and Sarah Wade, lived locally until they died in a house fire back in 2009. I'll keep digging, though."

"Star connected some dots to find that the WG Trust owned property out in Durham," Langdon said.

"The Wendigo Grotto Trust," Star said.

"Well, we weren't totally sure at that point that that was what the WG stood for," Langdon said. "So, me and Chabal took a spin out that way. I broke into the barn while Chabal stood watch and found Annie

Brown inside. A woman, who we believe to be named Grace Allen—"

"Grace Allen? I know a Grace Allen," Jewell said.

Langdon brought up the picture of Grace Allen on his phone and handed it to her. "That her?"

Jewell studied it for a second, enlarging the photo. "That's her. She does some work with CHERISH."

"Really? How so?" Langdon asked.

Jewell looked around the room, shrugged, and said, "She works with the illegals. Gives them food, finds them places to stay, things like that."

"She's also the bitch who stuck me with a knife," 4 by Four said.

Richam had taken the phone from Jewell and now looked up. "I've seen this woman having dinner at my joint with Tom Corbett."

"You sure?" Langdon asked. "Jasper Ansari supposedly met Grace Allen on the Patience dating site and the two have been seeing other for the past four months." He took the phone and flicked back to a photo of Ansari before giving it back to Richam.

"They do look a lot alike," Richam said slowly. "But I'm pretty sure it was Corbett. I'd of remembered this guy's schnozzer."

"Interesting," Langdon said. "We'll come back to that. Anyway, this Allen woman came out of the house. Chabal fired a warning shot, there was a brief exchange of gunfire, and then the woman fled the scene. An ambulance came to take Annie to MidCoast. Chabal went with her, and I stayed with the police."

Langdon rubbed his hand across his forehead and thought about the wildness of this latest case before continuing. The group remained silent, waiting. "Chabal called Maddie Campagna and Annie's parents, Meg and Harold, to let them know we'd rescued Annie. The Browns were supposed to meet up with Chabal, but she'd disappeared. Gone. Her and Maddie both appear to be missing. I can only guess that it has something to do with these crazy fucks who call themselves the Wendigo Grotto. And in a bit over nine hours, this wendigo is planning to kill, stew, and eat Chabal."

Chapter 33

At eight o'clock there was a knock at the door. The group had broken into pairs, each brainstorming ways to track down Chabal and the Wendigo. Langdon and Star at his desk trying to find leads on where Ansari might've disappeared to, and, at the dining room table, 4 by Four and Bart were digging through files on the WG Trust and looking for other property. Richam and Jewell were following up on the seeming connection between Corbett and Ansari, linked by the mystery woman, Grace Allen.

At the sound of knocking, Langdon's blood pressure spiked as raw emotion raged through him. It could be news that Chabal had been found and was fine. Or dead. Severely injured. In a stew pot. He strode to the door, shooing dog out of the way, to find the woman, Jade, on his doorstep.

"Hello," he said.

"I just heard Chabal has gone missing," Jade said. "And Madison Campagna."

It took Langdon a second to put Madison and Maddie back together. "Where'd you hear about that?"

Jade shrugged. "My cousin's a cop on Brunswick PD. She texted me about it because I'd told her about how much I liked your wife. But that's not the point. I might know something important about Madison. I saw her at your bookshop the other day but couldn't quite place who she was, not until I heard her name earlier, and then it came to me."

Langdon opened the door wide. "Come on in."

"I knew Madison when we were kids," Jade said, taking an offered seat on the couch as the group gathered to hear her news. "She was an odd duck. Home schooled. Except for math class. Her father would bring her and her brother in to take advanced classes. I think he just sat in his car in the parking lot waiting for the class to end. There was no dilly dally. When the bell rang, the two of them scooted out right quick."

"How was she an odd duck?" Langdon asked.

"Well, at first, she kinda freaked me out because she dressed all in black and had this real aloof personality. I thought she was stuck up but came to understand that she just didn't have any social skills. Coming to high school math class was the only time she ever left the house."

It didn't jive with the woman, Maddie, who Langdon had come to know, but what did he really know about her? "Where are you going with this?"

Jade frowned. "I'm not sure. Just, when I heard about Chabal missing, and that Madison was also missing, my first reaction was to think that Madison had finally blown her fuse. She always seemed to be on the edge of, well, crazy, if you want my opinion. Both her and her brother, Tom."

Langdon's mind churned, trying to pull pieces together that were swirling all around. "Madison and Tom both grew up in Brunswick?"

"No, I think it was Durham. You know how Durham kids used to come to Brunswick schools."

A piece snapped into place in Langdon's mind, the puzzle still largely undone, but a start had begun. He knew that Maddie had never married. "So, Maddie... Madison and Tom Campagna were homeschooled in Durham?"

Star turned to his laptop and started typing while the rest of the group listened silently.

Jade shook her head. "Tom had a different last name. I can't remember what it was. They were both adopted. Foster kids, you know?"

Snap went a piece of the puzzle. "Was Tom's last name Corbett?"

"Yes. That's it. I'm almost positive." Jade's eyes widened. "How'd you know that?"

"Weren't you at Tom Corbett's office the other day?" Langdon asked.

"What?" Jade said.

"Chabal ran into you coming out of his medical practice."

Jade looked confused. "Ah. Dr. Corbett. Dr. Tom Corbett. I never even realized."

"Can I ask what you were doing there?" Langdon said.

"I… well… I went to get some information. I've been recently diagnosed with breast cancer."

Langdon figured that was quite possible. The more important information seemed to be that Tom Corbett and Maddie Campagna were foster siblings, brother and sister, raised together. But why had Maddie hired him to investigate the missing Annie Brown if she had something to do with it? Was she a Wiccan and Tom the Wendigo? It had to be, but at the same time, made no sense.

"Holy mother of…" Starling said and swiveled his chair back around to face them. "Madison Campagna and Tom Corbett were adopted by Sam and Sarah Wade, two of the original members of the Wendigo Grotto."

That was it, then, Langdon thought. And now he had to figure out how this new connection might help them find Chabal.

"Is there anything else you can tell us about Maddie and Tom?" Langdon had stood up, towering over Jade. "Anything at all?"

Jade shook her head. "I never saw her outside of math class. She didn't do any extracurriculars. Never saw her around town. I can ask my parents if they know anything. Check in with a few others who I keep up with who might've known her."

"Please, do that," Langdon said. "No piece of information is too small." He stepped back and addressed the group. "That's it, then. Find out everything we can about Madison Campagna, Dr. Tom Corbett, Grace Allen, the WG Trust, and the Wades, Sam and Sarah. Where does Maddie live? Grace? Did the Wades leave any property to Maddie or Tom? Were there any other foster children? Go. I've gotta call Jackson and get the state police on this."

Everybody went to their computers, laptops, tablets, and phones while Langdon called Jackson Brooks. It went to voice mail. He texted him to answer the damn phone. He called back.

"What's going on?" Jackson asked.

Langdon told him about the connection between Maddie Campagna, Dr. Tom Corbett, and the Wades. How Sam and Sarah Wade were original members of the Wendigo Grotto and had adopted foster kids.

"There's a problem with the system when people too radical for the Church of Satan are allowed to adopt children," Jackson said.

"For sure," Langdon said. "Interesting that Maddie hired me to find Annie if she was one of the sick fuckers who took her."

"And that Corbett used his real information to sign up for Patience," Jackson said. "He had to know that he could be tracked as soon as Annie came up missing."

"Which happened so soon only because Maddie came and reported it and hired me." Langdon had walked down the hallway to his bedroom to get away from the buzz of his friends searching for the people who had abducted his wife. "And why use your own information for nefarious purposes on a dating site and then a picture of somebody else?"

"Ah, probably doesn't matter now," Jackson said. "But we got a record of Dr. Jasper Ansari's license plate going through the Augusta tollbooth heading north."

"The day he went missing?"

"Yep. Last Friday morning. About the same time you were... about the same time that dog found Annie's shoe in the woods at the back of his house."

"What do you think? Is Ansari involved?"

"I don't know. What do you think?"

Langdon stood looking out the front window of his bedroom with the phone to his ear and tried to impose some sort of order on his racing thoughts. But it was hard. He was in the bedroom he'd shared with Chabal for over twenty years now. Looking at their front yard, not yet recovered from the ravages of mud season, their yard. Their mailbox. Their street. His mind flitted to Chabal's laugh, like a brook flowing through rocks, starting as a ripple, and then burbling before bursting forth unchecked into a waterfall of merriment.

"Langdon?" Jackson said.

He shook his head, clearing the memories, banishing the fear, and putting the frustration at arm's length. "I think they're setting Ansari up."

"The fall guy?"

"Exactly," Langdon said. "Corbett thinks he's smarter than us. More than that, he wants to showcase his brilliance and play us like puppets on strings. He has Maddie point a finger at him and lure us in just so he can then subtly point us to Ansari, knowing that eventually facial recognition will match his picture on Patience. Then, when we get too close, he has Maddie tell me that she's heard from Annie who blurted out something about Falmouth—"

"Where they've planted one of Annie's shoes," Jackson said excitedly.

"Could be Annie's or could just be any shoe," Langdon said. "The only way we know it's hers is because Maddie told us. Forensics come up with anything?"

"Awaiting results, but there were hairs found consistent with the length and color of her hair. DNA testing will take a bit longer."

"Chances are the shoe and hair belong to Annie," Langdon said. "Be easy enough to plant those, especially seeing as Ansari's girlfriend seems to be one of the Wiccans."

Jackson snorted. "A carefully cultivated relationship months in the making to set up the poor bastard to take the fall for killing Annie Brown."

"Not just Annie Brown," Langdon said. "All of it. This is the crowning moment for the Wendigo, aka Tom Corbett, who's been killing and eating people for at least ten years at the supermoons. This is his exit strategy. He must've figured that his time was running out, and it was the right moment to get out and leave somebody else holding the bag."

"Meaning that Jasper Ansari is also in danger?"

"If he were around, he might be able to throw some doubt on Corbett's guilty ass," Langdon said. "I'm betting that they killed him. Dead men tell no tales."

"Open and shut case," Jackson agreed. "Plenty of evidence to convict him. We got no 24/24. We'd close that up right quick and move on to the next thing."

Langdon knew that 24/24 meant the last 24 hours of the victim's life and the first 24 hours after their death. Chances were, they'd have neither. Evidence would be scant. "If not for the stroke of luck that Jade knew Maddie and Tom back in high school, their smokescreen might've worked."

Jackson cursed. "Hate to say it, but Corbett was off our radar and Maddie was never on it. We were played like a fiddle."

"He doesn't know we're on to him," Langdon said. "I mean, we found Annie and rescued her, but unless we can link that farmhouse to Corbett, all evidence still points toward Ansari. The only person we saw there was Grace Allen, who is supposedly dating Ansari. You figure there's a way to use that to our advantage?"

"I don't know," Jackson said. "But the media is buzzing all over it. If I put an arrest warrant out for Corbett, it'll be on the eleven o'clock news, and then he'll go to ground."

Langdon appreciated that Jackson left unsaid that would also mean that Chabal was as good as dead and gone if that happened.

"How about you keep the info in a tight circle and just put out an ATL on Corbett."

"I can attach a tag of highest significance to the Attempt To Locate," Jackson said. "Once we get past the eleven o'clock news, we should be safe and not tip off Corbett until the morning news."

When it would be already too late for Chabal, Langdon thought. And if that happened, Corbett best be praying that the police got to him before Langdon did.

"I need to get into Corbett's house and see what I can find," Langdon said.

"It'll take me an hour at least to get a warrant," Jackson said.

"Thanks." The furor belched in the smoky regions of his guts and mind like the rumblings of a volcano before eruption.

Chapter 34

"Welcome back to the conscious world, Pumpkin Pie."

Chabal's eyes fluttered but the light was too bright, and she tried to flee back into the darkness.

"Join us, won't you, for the ritual celebration, Pumpkin Pie." The man cackled.

Where was she, Chabal wondered? She moaned slightly and could feel drool running from the corner of her mouth. Her head hurt something awful. Was she hung over? She couldn't move her arms or her legs and even her neck seemed stuck.

"My dear Pumpkin Pie, we are waiting for you so that we may begin the ceremony."

Her lips were so dry. Chabal creased her eyes open just a fraction. Blurry figures loomed in the glare. There was some sort of spotlight aimed at her, and she averted her eyes down and saw naked breasts below. Her naked breasts. She gasped.

"Ah, would you like a drink of water?" Dr. Tom Corbett stepped in front of the spotlight, providing some relief from the harsh light, but no comfort for her addled mind. He undid the strap at her neck and tipped a cup of water to her lips.

"You're the Wendigo," Chabal gasped.

Corbett cackled loudly like the screeching of some prehistoric beast. "Bingo, my dear Pumpkin Pie. You're a winner. Do you want to know what your prize is?"

Her neck wouldn't move but as far as her eyes could tell, she was completely naked. Her arms were out perpendicular to her body, and her legs were bound straight below her with some sort of restraint around her neck. Where was she?

"Maddie, do you want to tell our contestant what is behind door number two?"

The name jarred Chabal's memory. Maddie. The parking lot. Getting jolted with a stun gun and then having a needle stuck into her. "I don't understand." But she did understand.

Maddie Campagna stepped from the confines of the shadows. She reached up and tilted the spotlight, cutting the glare, and bathing the cabin in soft glow. "I told you. The Wendigo is hungry."

"I am famished," Corbett said grandly.

Chabal could see a third figure, still lurking in the murkiness, lost in the corner of her peripheral vision and the darkness. "You don't have to do this," she said, trying to control the terror shaking her being to its core.

Corbett cackled his piercing screech. "Oh, but I do. My hunger is ravenous. You will be my final feast before immortality. Fast and die or eat and live forever? It is no choice. I… we… will live together for eternity."

Images from the television screen in Popa's basement flashed through Chabal's brain. People having their throats slit, twisting and bleeding, hung upside down like animals, thrashing as their life drained away to the ground below. Butchered. Cut into pieces of meat and thrown into a large pot to be stewed.

"Why?" she screamed at the images in her mind.

"I told you," Corbett said. "To become one with the natural world and take my place in the never-ending universe, I must feast upon flesh and grow stronger."

Chabal shoved the thoughts and horror and panic from her mind. She had to think. There had to be a way out of this. "Why did you hire Langdon? Us? If you are the one who took Annie?"

"Oh, you have been a great help to me," Corbett said. "In fact,

Maddie retained your services to allow us to abscond freely into the night, and not, as you say, to find little Annie Brown." His face darkened. "You took my final supper from my table when you found and freed her, but Maddie, my dear Maddie, has found me a suitable replacement. A feast worth devouring, I might say." He looked with appreciation at Chabal's naked body. "Annie may have been slightly more succulent, but I believe you will taste most scrumptious, my fine Pumpkin Pie."

Chabal's body quivered in revulsion within the restraints. She tried to move her arms and legs to no avail. She was bound fast. "Why Annie?"

"Because within her flowed the blood of the greatest wendigo to ever exist before me," Corbett said.

"The granddaughter of Pan Nergal," Chabal said. "The man who created the Wendigo Grotto and began this twisted game."

Corbett stepped forward, and Chabal realized he had a knife in his hand, a long glimmering blade slightly curved and about eight inches long. He pressed it lightly against her neck and she felt the prick and then a thin rivulet of blood trickling down her body. She gasped. Her eyes watched as the dribble of blood came into her sight, a thin stream that coursed down between her breasts, moving slowly like mud, like lava, thick and dense, her life's blood. It reached the tiny bulge of her stomach, paused, and then continued before pooling into her belly button.

"Pan Nergal was a god who now walks with the immortals, my dear Pumpkin Pie," Corbett said.

Chabal tore her eyes from the line of blood that looked to be an upside-down exclamation point. Her blood. "Pan Nergal died in a car crash along with his wife and is now nothing more than a bit of revolting smarm, a sideshow in the history of humanity."

Corbett bared his teeth. "You have spirit, Pumpkin Pie, and will make a suitable replacement feast for the granddaughter of Pan Nergal." He brought the blade up so that she could again see it. "This is a butcher's knife. I will use this to cut your throat and then I will skin you with it." He raised his left hand, and Chabal saw that he held another gleaming blade, this one shorter and sleeker. "This is a boning knife. I will use it to cut through your ligaments and connective tissue to remove the meat from your bones. For some of the finer work, I'll use my surgeon's scalpel."

Was he planning on killing her now, Chabal wondered? The videos had shown the victims upside down, bleeding out on the ground below. She had to keep him talking. "You said that we'd been helpful." Chabal fought the quaver in her voice. "How so?"

Corbett laid his butcher's knife on a table at the side. He reached out his pointer finger and touched her lips before trailing it down her chin, neck, following the trail of blood to her belly button, scooping out her vital fluid as if dipping into cake batter, and brought his finger to his own mouth and sucked it dry, his lips smacking in appreciation.

"You used us as a misdirection," Chabal said desperately. "To make the police believe that the Wendigo was Jasper Ansari."

"And you did that mighty well," Corbett said. "Unfortunately for you, somehow you found our farmhouse in Durham and freed the flesh of my upcoming feast."

"I still don't understand. Why Annie? Just because she's descended from Pan Nergal?"

"Because she turned her back on the Wendigo Way," Corbett said. "She would've been the third traitor sacrificed to Pan Nergal and the forces of nature paving my way into immortality. I'm trusting that you will be a suitable replacement."

"Why three?"

"One for each six that represents the beast," Corbett said. "Here is wisdom. Let him that hath understanding count the number of the beast: for it is the number of a man; and his number is Six hundred threescore and six."

"Liam Couture was another traitor," Chabal said, "so you sacrificed and ate him?"

"That I did. He was a stringy old goat, that one was, but I managed to soften him up enough to chew up his tired flesh."

Corbett and the Wendigo appeared to be changing places in front of her eyes, Chabal thought, first the polished speech of an educated doctor, and then the guttural rant of some savage beast. Hold it together, she commanded her inner being, sanity and whatever darkness that threatened to engulf her fighting for the upper hand. "Who was the first?"

Corbett smiled. "Mm. In March, in honor of the Chaste Moon, the smallest supermoon of the year, I enjoyed the flesh of my sister. Samael. The only true blood of Sarah and Samuel Wade, she turned her back on the Wendigo Way. She came here, to this cottage, and tried to leave society behind, hide here in plain sight. We tried to bring her back into the fold. We even brought a ceremony to her a few years back, an immigrant woman who didn't speak English and was absolutely delicious. She threatened to turn us in. To the police. To the authorities. To have *me* arrested. So, we kept her here, in this cottage that she inherited from our parents. It was easy, because as far as the world knew, she never existed. So when she disappeared, there was nobody missing. No birth records. Never went to school or to the doctor. We saved her for almost two years waiting for the right time. This past March. It has been a good year."

The plates in Chabal's brain shifted with a wrenching thud, and her breathing grew ragged. Breathe in. Breathe out. Her eyes widened, and with all her might she brought them to focus on Maddie. "Why are you here? Why did you do this to me?"

"The Wendigo is hungry," Maddie said. "I brought him food."

"But why?" Chabal asked. "Why do you bring him… food?"

"Tell her," the Wendigo commanded.

"I was adopted when I was seven years old," Maddie began, her voice a monotone. "Father and Mother Wade. Tom was already there, having been chosen some years earlier, even though we're the same age. Grace came later. We were brought up to hate the system.

To scoff at religion. Jesus Christ was a creation meant to keep the innate nature of man in check. Governments were established to punish the poor and support the rich. Schools were tools used to brainwash children. On and on. Drilled into our heads." Maddie's voice had grown increasingly angry, her words guttural, grating.

"We went our separate directions when we became adults," Corbett said. "I went to medical school to save people during the day while I killed and tortured at night. Maddie fell into alcohol and drug abuse. When Father and Mother Wade died in a house fire, I went to find her, to tell her that we were free, that she was free. I found her with her wrists cut in the bathtub of a cheap motel in Portland. I treated her wounds and nursed her back to health and revealed to Maddie her true nature. The Wendigo Way."

"It turned my life around," Maddie said. "I got a law degree. Began practicing. Now that I truly understood who I was. The Wendigo Way."

"The Wendigo Way?" Chabal gasped, straining against the restraints to no avail.

Corbett placed the back of the boning knife under her breast. "Tell me, Pumpkin Pie, when you eat a roast chicken—do you like the breast or the thigh better?" He trailed the blade down to her thigh, and then circled it around her hip and under her buttocks. Then the voice of the Wendigo rasped forth. "I'm an ass man myself." He roared in laughter.

"What is the Wendigo Way?" Chabal spit the words out, suddenly panic-stricken that if he stopped talking, that he'd start cutting. Langdon would come for her, she thought. It was up to her to stay alive until he arrived.

"We don't have much time, so I'll give you the abbreviated version," Corbett said. "Man, by his very nature, is a consumer. He consumes everything that he touches. Food. Ideas. Thoughts. Land. Earth. There is nothing that man does not consume. It only goes to stand that sooner or later man must consume himself. That is the Wendigo Way. Now, we must begin."

"Wait," Chabal screamed. "Is that you in the shadows, Grace Allen? What part did you play in this?"

Corbet smiled nastily. "You have done your homework, Pumpkin Pie. For that, you shall have your reward. Tell her quickly, my lovely Grace."

The woman who'd met Jasper Ansari on the Patience site, the same one who'd kicked and stuck 4 by Four, the lady who'd met Eddie Couture at the Lenin Stop and walked off with him, his life only spared by a phone call—Grace Allen—stepped forward out of the shadows.

"I wanted to change who I was," she said. "I was naïve enough to believe that possible. I became a missionary. Went to Africa. There, I witnessed what I at the time thought was the true depravity of human nature. People forced to live in squalor. Men who raped women with indifference. Children starving to death. Villages chopped to pieces to send a message. And nobody cared."

"After I reconnected with Maddie, I decided to try and find Grace," Corbett said. "I tracked her down and found her living on the streets of New York City, broken and alone."

"The Wendigo revealed to me that our parents, Sam and Sarah, were the only true human nature," Grace said. "That what I'd witnessed in Africa was but the essence of humankind, unleashed, unfettered, and loosed in a world that tries too hard to cloak the pure nature of their being with a shield. The Wendigo lifted that obstruction and let me grasp who I was. And I became whole again. My true and highest self for the first time in my life."

A drum began beating. Chabal jerked her eyes from Grace and found a figure squatting on the floor beating upon a worn drum with their hands. She thought it might be Maddie, but it was hard to tell, as they wore the head of a deer. A doe, Chabal thought, the flickering tendrils of insanity seeping through the cracks. It must be Maddie. Chabal snickered. Blanched. Felt sick to her stomach.

Around the drummer, the tall and gaunt figure of Corbett, the

Wendigo, began a slow and convulsive backward dance. His head was that of a majestic buck, twelve points, Chabal thought, blood dripping from its mouth, eyeballs gouged out, while it cast eerie shadows flittering through the cabin.

Boom. The Wendigo bowed its head. *Boom.* The Wendigo reached for the ground. *Boom.* The Wendigo spasmed upward. *Boom.* The Wendigo cast its arms high. *Boom... Boom... Boom...* The Wendigo began to chant words that Chabal didn't understand. With horror, she realized that the ritual had begun, the ritual that would culminate in her sacrifice. And then she'd be butchered, stewed, and eaten.

Chapter 35

Langdon sat in his Jeep looking at Tom Corbett's house. It was a Cape with additions. In the wealthy area of Brunswick known as Mere Point. A mixture of locals, summer residents from away, and those with money who chose to live in Brunswick year-round. Or almost year-round. The back of the house looked out on Maquoit Bay and what were most likely beautiful sunsets.

It was long past sunset. Langdon looked up at the cloud-covered sky, and at that moment, the moon broke through, shining hard and bright. It looked as if it might pop right out of the sky and engulf the Earth, it was so large and white. And then it was gone again. He was parked on the road and got out and began walking down the driveway.

Two weeks ago, Langdon had visited this house to question its owner, Dr. Tom Corbett, the morning after Danny T. had been killed. At the time, he'd been convinced that the man had nothing to do with the death of his friend. Now, he knew, he'd been wrong. Corbett had been responsible, and most likely the person who murdered Danny T. If Langdon had been more astute at that time, better at his job, Corbett would be behind bars now, and his wife wouldn't be in the clutches of this monster.

There was no time for subtleties. Jackson had given Langdon an hour head start before the police showed up at the crime scene. A dim piece of Langdon's brain realized that the man was taking a chance in allowing him to potentially taint a crime scene. But they both knew that the protocols and procedures of the machine of the law would not move fast enough to save Chabal. He pulled on a pair of leather gloves.

The door was locked, of course, but the living room window broke easily enough, and Langdon tumbled his way into the house. The alarm began to blare. It didn't matter. Jackson would slow the police arriving until he had a warrant. An uncomfortable set of leather furniture adorned the room with expensive looking artwork on the walls. One particular print caught Langdon's attention, and he pulled up the app on his phone that identified artwork. It was of a naked figure standing high above on a rock with flames in the background while writhing figures rose from below. "Satan calling up his Legions" by William Blake. No surprise there.

The room was austere. A flat-screen on the wall. Recessed lighting in the ceiling. Hardwood floors with a rug. No photographs. No papers. No books. No magazines.

The dining room and kitchen were much the same way. No junk drawers with bits and bobs to search through. Everything was pristine, as if it were about to go up for sale, every bit of personality stripped, other than the solitary print in the living room.

There were four bedrooms upstairs. Langdon quickly tossed the bureau in the master bedroom. Nothing. Other than the fact that Corbett wore banana hammocks, tight micro-brief underwear that made Langdon grimace to just think about wearing. He was using his phone as a flashlight and glanced at the time. 10:17 p.m. He had twenty minutes at the most until the police arrived, and he most certainly didn't want to get caught up in that mess. Even Jackson wouldn't be able to keep him from being detained if he was found in the house of a serial killer in the dead of the night rifling through the man's stuff.

There was nothing under the bed. There was a bookshelf against the wall filled with medical books. Langdon scanned the titles. A few books of fiction were on the top shelf, and these he homed in on. He pulled one free, *The Shadow of the Wendigo* by Dale T. Phillips.

There was a photograph inside. Four children. Three girls and one boy. Langdon thought that the boy could most certainly be a young Corbett. He was about twelve, gangly even then, with eyes that were distant, empty.

Sirens split the air in the distance.

The three girls and one boy were on a dock with a lake in the background. A canoe was tied to the side.

Langdon shoved the photograph in his pocket and went out the door and down the stairs as the sirens grew louder and turned into the driveway. He crossed over to the back and went through a door onto a patio overlooking the bay, the moon now puncturing the sky and lighting up the salt water like a bed of diamonds. Langdon could feel the closeness of the moon, the power emanating from it, the power to move the tides, and shift the natural world around him.

~ ~ ~ ~ ~

"That is Madison for sure," Jade said, studying the photograph.

Langdon had returned to his Jeep as police cars continued to squeal into Corbett's driveway. Once they'd gone by, he'd driven back to his house.

"And I'd say that the one to the left is most definitely Grace Allen," Jewell said.

"Who is the fourth?" Bart asked. "One of the victims?"

Langdon shook his head. "Couldn't tell you. The only one I was pretty sure of was Corbett."

"Where are they?" 4 by Four asked.

"A lake." Langdon shrugged. "I can't pick up anything else."

"Looks like an island over their right shoulders," Bart said. "Else the lake is pretty damn narrow."

"Son of a bitch," Jewell said.

Langdon had never heard her use that particular curse before. "What?"

Jewell closed her eyes and tilted her head back. "Grace Allen mentioned a cottage. A couple years back she found temporary housing for a young immigrant woman I was working with, and she said she had a place on a lake."

"Where?"

Jewell pulled her tablet onto her lap and began tapping away. "The address has to be listed. Astur was her name. Astur Elmi-Dihoud."

"Is that a public boat access?" 4 by Four asked, holding the photograph close to his face. "There on the left?"

Langdon took it from him, peered intensely at it, and then used his phone to take a picture, which he expanded to the spot 4 by Four indicated. "Pretty darn blurry, but you could be right."

"What does it matter?" Richam asked. "You found a photograph of Tom Corbett with his sisters and a fourth stranger on a dock on a lake when they were kids. It could be anywhere."

"Wikipedia says there are 2,677 lakes in Maine," Starling said. "And another thousand too small to be listed, whatever that means."

"They could be in New Hampshire or Vermont for all we know," Richam said.

"Readfield," Jewell said triumphantly. Then, "Shit. A P.O. Box."

"There's a lake in Readfield, right?" Bart asked.

"Maranacook Lake," 4 by Four said.

"Jackson said that Jasper Ansari's license plate was tagged at the Augusta toll booth," Langdon said. "Perhaps on the way to what he thought was a lake vacation with his girlfriend."

Langdon's phone buzzed. Text from Jackson. Annie B. is awake.

"Okay, see what you can find," Langdon said as he stood up. "I'm going back over to the hospital. Seems Annie is awake."

~ ~ ~ ~ ~

"What did she say?" Langdon asked.

Jackson shrugged. "Nothing much. She was pretty hysterical,

crying, screaming 'wendigo,' something about Pumpkin Pie, and not wanting to be fucking one with the universe. The doctor doped her back up and out she went. I spoke to her for less than a minute, or rather, listened to her rant."

"You find anything at Corbett's house?"

"It looks as if somebody had broken a window," Jackson said drily. "There were some interesting things. Vials of medicine under the bathroom sink that I'd guess could be used to put somebody out. The lab is examining them now. More sharp knives than a regular joe. Nothing suggesting where he might be, though. Anything turns up I'll be notified immediately. How about you?"

They hadn't gotten a chance to compare notes on Corbett's house yet. Jackson had gotten the call that Annie was awake and come straight to the hospital, letting Langdon know on the way.

"Found a photo of Corbett, Maddie, and Grace at a lake when they were kids." Langdon handed the picture over to Jackson. "I don't know who the fourth one is. Jewell knew Grace from her work at CHERISH and remembered her housing an immigrant up to Readfield. Which is on a lake. Could be something. Could be nothing."

"I'll have the computer geeks give it a go, see what they can find."

"You talk to Annie's parents yet?" Langdon asked.

Jackson shook his head. "Was about to when you told me about Corbett being the perp. Had to go bother a judge at home and get a warrant. That's what bought you some time. Straight to the house and then back here when my guy called to say Annie was awake."

"What say we go have a word with them." Langdon looked at the time on his phone. 12:01 a.m. They had officially started the day his wife was to be sacrificed, butchered, stewed, and eaten. He shuddered. The fear and anger were simmering within.

They walked out into the lobby where Meg and Harold Brown sat huddled together. They'd grown old in the days since Langdon had first met them. Gaunt figures with lined faces and black circles ringing their eyes. Harold went to stand as they came over, but

Langdon motioned him back with his hand and sat across from them and alongside Jackson.

"Is there word on Annie?" Meg asked in a quavering voice.

"She's fast asleep," Jackson said, omitting that she'd woken for a brief spat in hysterics before being put back under. "She has no real physical injuries. Bumps and bruises. It appears she was well fed."

Langdon choked back a grunt and covered it with a cough. "Is there anything that you can tell us about Maddie Campagna?"

"Where is she? Is she okay?" Meg asked.

"I'm not sure," Langdon said. It wasn't clear if he was answering the first or the second question. "We'd love to ask her some questions but don't know where she's gotten to. Do you have any idea where she might be?"

"Home, I suppose," Meg said. "But I don't know quite what would keep her from coming to check on Annie."

"She's not home," Jackson said.

"Do you know who her friends were?" Langdon asked.

Meg shook her head. "Just Annie. I only met her a couple of times before… before this whole thing came about. She came by the house one day with Annie for lunch, and another time we all went to the Portland Museum together."

"She never mentioned any names of people?" Langdon asked.

"Not that I can remember," Meg said. "Why?"

"You think this monster may've taken her?" Harold asked.

"I don't know," Langdon said. "But I'd sure feel better knowing where she is. She didn't happen to mention a lake where she might've visited?"

"No, not that I…" Meg pursed her lips and half-closed her eyes. "Annie told us that she went to a lake with Maddie once, to a cottage. It was up by Augusta, it was. Maranacook Lake, I think."

Langdon felt his insides freeze up solid. "Was it Maddie's home?"

"She said it was a quaint little cottage. Right on the water. They went swimming and kayaking."

"Who owned the cottage?" Langdon was unable to keep the intensity from bursting out of the cracks in his voice. "Do you know whose cottage it was? Or have an address?"

Meg leaned back, away from his seething ferocity. "No, no, she never said, I don't think."

Harold snapped his fingers. "Samael Wade Freeman."

"Samael Wade Freeman," Langdon said. "Are you sure?"

"Pretty sure," Harold said, rocking back and forth slightly in his chair. "I remember, because when Annie told us the name of the girl they were visiting, I thought it interesting that that her initials were SWF, you know, like how people used to look for dates in the newspaper, you know, single white female, looking for a man who likes long walks on the beaches and—"

"Did she give you an address?"

"No."

Jackson stood up and moved away, speaking into his two-way.

Langdon stood up and went towards the door. "Call me when you have the address," he said to Jackson as he walked past.

Chapter 36

The phone rang just as Langdon reached the toll booth in Augusta. "What do you got?" he asked as he zipped through the E-ZPass lane.

"S.W. Freeman owns a cottage on Lake Narrows Road. Number 51."

"And who is this person? Samael Wade. Sam Wade. But he died in a house fire twelve years ago."

"We're working on that. His full name was Samuel. Not Samael. I can find no record of a Samael Wade Freeman. But I got you an address."

Langdon looked at the Jeep clock and subtracted the eleven minutes it was currently off. It was now 3:33 a.m. "You send the bubble tops in with sirens blaring, they're going to cut Chabal's throat and abscond into the night."

"That's why I'm calling you first," Jackson said. "I'm getting on the highway now."

"Give me until five. Then bring in the cavalry."

"We'll be parked just down the street. I'll say that we're waiting for a confirmation phone call. At five, we'll light it up."

"Thanks."

"Langdon?"

"Yeah?"

"First, save Chabal, but if you get the chance?" Jackson paused. "Rip this fucking wendigo a new asshole and shove him back up from where he came."

Langdon almost chuckled but it didn't quite make it to his lips. He hung up the phone and plugged the address into the GPS as the Jeep rocked along at eighty MPH. How many times had he spoken to Corbett? He should've known it was him. His instinct should've told him. He'd had every opportunity to knock his block off, drag him down to the police station, bust his nose. If he had, Chabal would be home in bed with him right now instead of tied up somewhere awaiting execution. If she hadn't already been killed.

Langdon saw in his mind's eye the naked body of Annie Brown bound to the top of a table tilted at a forty-five-degree angle. Her body scratched and bruised. Her eyes like that of a terrified bird. Spit dribbling down her chin. And then Chabal's face transposed onto Annie's body. Her eyes were pleading with him. Begging him. Blaming him.

He managed to tear his gaze from her disapproving and disappointed eyes, realizing that it was now her body bound to the table. Her naked body. His wife's naked body restrained on a tabletop as if some buffet dish ready to be served.

Like a nightmare he couldn't wake up from, his mind's eye jumped to the Wendigo and the three Wiccans, Maddie, Grace, and the mystery child, who may or may not be Samael Wade Freeman. His brain pictured them as the children in the photograph, young rosy faces, cheeks kissed by the sunshine, eyes bright and inquisitive. In his nightmarish vision, each of them had a bib on. They held a knife in their right hand and a fork in their left, pointed upward, expectant eyes trained on the Wendigo, waiting for the OK to dig in.

He looked from them to the nakedness of his wife and his eyes trailed up to her face, and she was screaming but no sound was coming out.

"I'm coming," Langdon said into the still air of the Jeep as he rocketed off the highway onto Route 202. "I'm coming, babe. Just wait for me."

In the darkness, Chabal's voice came from the passenger seat. "I love you. I forgive you."

Langdon went through downtown Readfield at seventy miles an hour. There was not a soul to be seen or a light on at this early morning hour. He passed a police car parked in an empty lot just before he was to turn on to Lake Narrows Drive. Langdon figured it was the local cops waiting for the arrival of Jackson Brooks and the state police. Else, they would've pulled him over for going forty miles over the speed limit, but tonight, they had bigger fish to fry. What they didn't know was that their serene small town was about to spring into the national news.

When the GPS said the destination was on the right in 400 feet, Langdon pulled off to the side and parked. The time was 4:03 a.m. If he was right, if the sacrifice was to take place during the eclipse, the time of the Blood Supermoon, he had time. Not much, but enough. He was already out of the Jeep, jogging down the road, pulling his Glock out and checking the rounds.

When he reached the drive to the house, Langdon steeled himself for what was to come. He hoped with every fiber of his being that Chabal was still alive, that she hadn't had her throat slit and was currently bleeding out, upside down, like a deer in a garage. The possibility existed that he could burst into the cottage and find the Wendigo cutting strips of his wife from her body and dropping them into a pot to stew. That was the worst-case scenario.

The best-case scenario was that Chabal would be naked and restrained and terrified. Both possibilities filled Langdon with a rage that was pulsing under his skin and threatening to burst forth. This anger had consumed him a few times before in life, and he knew that he'd have no memory of what transpired when he was within the grip of the fury.

There was a single light on in the cottage. It was a one-story affair maybe thirty by twenty, with no garage. There were two vehicles in the driveway, a small pickup truck, and a Toyota Prius. It was quiet.

Too quiet. Langdon crept to the window with the light. It was the kitchen, the sole light over the sink, faintly illuminating the room. No corpse of his wife. No Wiccans dancing around chanting. No wendigo presiding over the ritual sacrifice. He moved from window to window. Living room. A bedroom. Another room with the shades drawn. He stepped back, assessing the cottage. It looked like it had a basement.

It was possible that Chabal was being held captive in the dungeon of the cottage. Langdon supposed that if you were going to sacrifice humans and hold rituals in the process, a space, perhaps soundproofed, would be the way to go. But it didn't have that feel. Two nondescript cars in the drive. Neither one Corbett's BMW. Nor Maddie's Subaru. He wasn't sure what Grace drove, but he had a sneaking suspicion that this, his last card played, was not enough to take the pot.

He had to know. The door leading into the kitchen was flimsy, a simple knob and lock that rattled when pressed. Langdon kicked it open. He stepped into the room with his Glock leveled. He went to the room that had the shades pulled and kicked that door open, stepping into the entrance with pistol sweeping the inside. There was a night lite illuminating the room in a soft glow. By it, he could see an elderly man, frail and wiry, huddled on the floor with a woman who was as plump as he was thin.

In his arms, he held a rifle. "This 12-gauge will blow you all over the hallway if you move an inch," the man said.

"Where is she?" Langdon asked, the Glock pointed at the man. "Where the hell is my wife?"

"Your wife?"

Langdon lowered the pistol. "I think I've made a mistake." He put his back to the corner of the door jamb and slid down to a sitting position, dropping the Glock, and putting his face in his hands. "Fuck. Fuck. Fuck."

The old man stood up and walked around the bed, the woman trailing a step behind him. "What's the problem, youngster?"

It'd been some time since Langdon had been called youngster. "They took my wife and are going to kill her. I thought she was here. I'm obviously wrong."

"Who took your wife?"

Langdon shook his head, trying to bring clarity, sense, a strategy back into play. He had nothing. "The Wendigo."

"What in tarnation is a wendigo?"

Langdon again shook his head, this time in defeat. "It doesn't matter. They're going to kill her at 5:30. During the Blood Moon."

"Does this wendigo have a name?"

"Dr. Tom Corbett. He and his Wiccans are going to kill, butcher, and eat my wife."

"Holy cow, m'boy, that's something wicked, that is."

Langdon pulled his phone out to call Jackson and let him know they had the wrong place. "You're not related to Samael Wade Freeman, are you?"

"That's the girl who has the cabin on the island," the woman said. "Haven't seen her for some time, though."

"On the island?" Langdon asked.

"Little island right across the narrows here," the old man said. "They got themselves a right of way just past our house with a mailbox at the end of the road. Number 51, they is."

"Number 51?" Langdon grabbed his pistol and stood up. "On an island, you say."

"Yessir. There's some people out there now. Three to four cars parked down on their right of way. Arrived late afternoon, they did."

"Can you show me?" Langdon asked, grabbing the man's arm.

"I can point you right to their cabin," the old man said. "C'mon. It's right across the way." He led Langdon out the back door onto a rickety deck overlooking the lake. The moon was low on the horizon, so close it was touching, bathing the lake in a shimmering white, soon to turn to a blood red. "They even got a few lights on over there for you to see 'em."

Langdon followed the man's gnarled finger. About two hundred yards across the water was the shadowy outline of land, an island, illuminated in the moonlight. Tucked into the pine trees, light blossomed like a mushroom cap, and Langdon could make out the faint outline of a cabin. He looked at his phone. 4:59 a.m.

"Do you have a boat?"

"Got a canoe." The old man went down the crumbling steps to the backyard to a canoe lying upside down on the grass. "Welcome to use it." He flipped it over. The oar was inside.

Langdon grabbed the front and began dragging it across the lawn to the water. "Listen. Any second now, the police are going to come streaming in here with sirens blazing and guns drawn. The man in charge is Jackson Brooks. Send him to the island. Tell him the Wendigo is there. And Chabal. Tell him Chabal is there."

He walked into the water up to his knees, clambered into the canoe, and struck out for the island of the Wendigo. Behind him, sirens suddenly split the serenity of the night, but he didn't turn to look, focused on the illuminated cabin across the narrows on the island.

Chapter 37

The Wendigo had left the strap holding her neck undone so that she might swallow her food. He'd shoved pieces of deer meat into her mouth, covering her mouth so that she'd chew and swallow. *I am the deer,* he'd said. *You eat me, and then I eat you. The world comes full circle.*

Maddie, her head covered by that of a doe, steadily beat upon a drum. Chabal had realized after a bit that the skull of the animal rested atop her head, and that there were eyeholes slit into the skin of the neck, the same for the Wendigo. His already tall figure was now massive, the twelve points of the rack on his head soaring to make him look to be an eight-foot monster, which in effect, he was.

After he'd fed her, the Wendigo and Grace resumed their spasmodic dancing, jerking this way and that, arms flailing, uttering their incomprehensible chants. At one point, the Wendigo bent Grace over a table, and took her from behind, his thrusts just as choppy and convulsive as his dancing.

Chabal couldn't turn her eyes away from them. *Boom.* He thrust and grunted. Grace moaned. *Boom.* Torches flickered around the room, casting fluttering shadows on them. *Boom.* Chabal's eyes were drawn to the tattoo on Grace's back, a long figure with the head of a deer, winged, holding a pitchfork in hand. She could just make out the words at above the horned figure—Baphomet. Underneath, Wendigo.

Boom. Thrust. *Boom.* Grunt. *Boom.* The Wendigo leaned his head, the head of a buck, backward and caterwauled, the howling screech of animals rutting. Grace screamed. *Boom. Boom. Boom.* The Wendigo let out a primordial roar. The drumming stopped.

The Wendigo turned and faced Chabal, his manhood dangling free in front of him, his pants gone, his shirt off, buck naked. Grace stood next to him just as bare as he.

"Lucifer. Satan. Leviathan. Prince of Darkness. Wicked One. Baphomet." The Wendigo raised his long arms toward the ceiling of the cabin. "Hear me, oh great one. I swear henceforth to be your loyal servant and son. I will give my full allegiance to you and will despise all false religions on earth. I am one with you, my Lord."

Maddie rose to her feet, and the Wendigo handed her a knife, the boning blade, Chabal thought, her mind fighting not to slip into hysteria.

Maddie stepped forward, between Chabal and the Wendigo, and raised the gleaming steel. "Maddie," Chabal whispered, her voice barely audible in the silent cabin. "Don't."

Maddie grinned wickedly. She raised the knife and cut a slice into her own upper arm. She handed the blade over her shoulder to the Wendigo and stepped forward to Chabal, dabbing the forefinger of her right hand into the flowing blood from her left arm. She ran her finger around Chabal's breasts, first the left and then the right.

The Wendigo resumed his chanting prayer. "We offer to you this woman of the enemy who denies your existence. Her life will become my own as I consume her and make her one with me and with you, oh great Baphomet."

Chabal couldn't see what Maddie was drawing or writing on her naked body in blood. The woman continued to dab into the blood upon her arm and trace upon the body of Chabal, from neck to toes, and then her foul breath was in her face as she stepped up on a footstool to smudge her face with blood, her lips brushing Chabal's, her sightless eyes devoid of any emotion, as if in a trance, rubbing blood on Chabal's face.

"Stop. Don't do this. Help me. Let me go. Maddie."

The Wendigo continued to chant but now in some foreign tongue again.

"You are fucking crazy," Chabal said. "You are all fucking loony tunes."

Maddie stepped back to survey her work as the Wendigo stopped his chanting.

"Let it begin," the Wendigo said.

Maddie and Grace retreated into the shadows. Chabal could hear them rustling around, and then they returned with a figure attached to a cross, it being on some sort of pulley attached to ropes or wires above. Chabal realized that she was also fastened to a cross, her arms stretched out to each side, and her legs together on the bottom.

The figure was a man. It was Jasper Ansari. Not only were his limbs and neck secured to the cross, but his mouth was covered by what looked to be duct tape. His eyes were bulging from his face as if they were about to pop out of his skull.

Grace ripped the duct tape off and took a pink rubber ball from his mouth. Ansari gasped, choked, coughed, and began to inhale huge breaths of air.

"Your time has arrived," the Wendigo said. "Will you consent to the teachings of Baphomet? This is your last chance to step into the paradise of being true to your nature. You will drink when you want to. Eat what you want to. Fuck when you have the urge. You will no longer be bound by the dictates of a false god who merely wants to enslave you and make you obedient to His will. To do so, you must consent to the way of Baphomet."

Ansari looked at Chabal, seemingly taking in whatever designs in blood adorned her body. His eyes were desperate. Beaten. Forlorn. "Go to hell," he said, his eyes going back to the Wendigo. "Burn in hell."

The Wendigo screeched in laughter. "You have been misled about hell. It is the one true place in all of nature. Hell, as you call it, is merely truth. Truth of emotion, thought, and action. I will gladly step into hell and leave this godless planet behind. Don't you see? You are a slave to an idea that is not real. The Romans came up with the whole tale of Jesus Christ over 400 years after his death just to keep people like you in line. It was brilliant. The best job of branding that has ever been done. Walk on water and turn that same water into wine? What nonsense. But you believe because you want to believe. You and billions of others believe because you can't accept that the one true god lives within each and every one of us. That god is called many things. We've chosen Baphomet, but it could be as simple as Joe. Unleash yourself Dr. Jasper Ansari. Open your arms and heart to the true you. Free yourself!"

"Verily we belong to Allah, and truly to Him shall we return," Ansari said. "Verily we belong to Allah, and truly to Him shall we return."

The Wendigo screeched. "Ah, of course, you believe in another false prophet, another slaveholder devised to keep you in place." He nodded to Grace, who took the knife from Maddie, and approached Ansari.

"Grace, why are you doing this?" Ansari was talking in gasping gulps of air. "Don't do this. Please. I thought we had something special. *Please. Don't.*"

Grace stopped in front of Ansari, her face even with his midsection, her eyes level with his penis as he hung suspended from the cross.

"What are you doing? Allah, save me!"

"As we begin our journey to the place you call hell and I call paradise," the Wendigo said. "We would rather not be enslaved by false authorities interfering in the very baseness of our human nature. This, then, is your role, Dr. Ansari. You will take the fall, as they say in the crime movies. You will be vilified for countless deaths and what this misguided society of ours believes to be perverted actions of sacrificial killing, butchering, stewing, and cannibalism. I now give you a choice."

"A choice?" Ansari asked. "What choice?"

"If you were to cut your own throat, it would look more natural. I ask you now to slit your throat. To commit suicide. Traumatized by your villainy, unable to cope with the burden, you will have killed yourself."

Grace reached up on tiptoes and pressed the knife into his hand. With the same movement, she undid the strap restraining his arm and stepped back out of reach. Ansari swung the knife around in front of him, a wild and crazed look on his face. A sly smile manically crossed his face, and he moved the knife to the restraint on his left arm.

"If you try to free yourself, Grace will tase you, we will take the knife back, and we will torture you, Dr. Ansari," the Wendigo said.

Grace held up the taser, a small black box in the palm of her hand. Ansari paused, the knife clenched in his hand, his eyes on Grace, his ears listening to the Wendigo.

"If you force us to kill you, we will butcher you piece by piece while you are still alive. You will watch as we stew and eat parts of you. And then we will kill you."

"Why?" Ansari asked.

"I told you. We must prepare for our journey, and you are but one vehicle in our escape."

"If you butchered me, it'd be obvious that I didn't kill myself."

"Right you are."

"You could easily slice my throat and make it look like I'd done it," Ansari said. "You're a doctor. You know you could. So, why?"

The Wendigo screeched, a harsh chuckle. "I forget that you are a doctor and an intelligent man. Of course, you are right. And that is what I'll most likely do. But I will do it so that it takes hours for you to bleed out. The authorities will also be surprised to discover that you like to shove things up your ass, as they take item after item from your rectum. Or, you can do it quickly." He looked out the window. "Quickly, for our time of sacrifice is near. Choose. Quick, painless death or slow and agonizing."

"You are a sick fuck," Ansari said.

"I am going to count to three, and then Grace will stun you and the choice will be made. The blood moon approaches. One. Two."

Ansari brought his hand back across his throat, and it sprouted a geyser of blood onto Grace. He dropped the knife, his arm flailing, as Grace stood unmoving.

They watched until Ansari's arm stopped thrashing about.

"Bring the oblation," the Wendigo said and strode out the door of the cabin.

Maddie and Grace approached Chabal, tipping the cross upon which she was hung so it could be unhooked. They picked her up, one at each arm, a hand on each leg, and carried her out into the night air.

What now, Chabal thought? What perversions awaited? "Why do you serve that monster?" she asked, her voice cracking and dry.

"The Wendigo saved us and offers us truth and immortality," Maddie said.

"The Wendigo Way is the one and only true way," Grace said.

Flames burst forth from a clearing behind the cabin, and it was there that they went. A rope was thrown over the limb of a tree, and Chabal was raised up, feet first, her head dangling about five feet off the ground. She was able to turn her head and look desperately around. She could feel the warmth of the fire on her bare skin.

Maddie, at least Chabal thought it was her with the head of a doe, returned with the drum and began beating it again. It was a slow beat. *Boom... Boom... Boom...* Grace, also with the head of a doe, lay on the ground underneath Chabal, writhing in the dirt. Shadows from the fire flickered wildly in the bright moonlit morning in Maine. The Wendigo began a slow strut around her, circling out of her vision, reappearing, his steps miming the beat of the drum, his arms gesticulating in time with the beat, a gleaming blade in his right hand.

The drumbeat increased in tempo. Grace twisted in seeming ecstasy below. The Wendigo increased his pace. Shadows danced in time with the drumming.

Chabal found herself screaming for help, cursing the Wendigo and the Wiccans, her convulsions causing the cross upon which she was attached to sway on the rope suspended from the tree limb.

The Wendigo took the head of the buck off, lay it on the ground, and stepped up to her. He grabbed her hair, leaned down, and thrust his face into hers, the foul stench of his breath rolling over her in waves, her revulsion mixing with terror, but slowly succumbing to the anger she felt. Who the fuck was he to mess with her?

"Quiet, my Pumpkin Pie," the Wendigo whispered in her ear. "It will be over soon now, and we will be one, together for all of eternity."

Chabal felt the knife caress her neck, the blade sliding over her skin. "Fuck you," she said, her mouth opening and her teeth clamping down on his nose.

He screeched in pain and tried to pull back. Chabal clenched her teeth firmly, shaking her head from side to side, sawing at his snout, trying to rip the appendage right from his face. The cross was pulled as he tried to escape her teeth, and she refused to let go, the rope straining, the hooks creaking, the limb groaning, the Wendigo screeching—and then something gave way, and Chabal found herself crashing to the ground.

She landed on her shoulders and back as she'd been pulled forward by the Wendigo, but she was still bound to the cross, even though there appeared to be more give in the rope. Chabal spat the Wendigo's nose out onto the ground next to her.

Chapter 38

Langdon had just started out when his eyes caught a new glow emanating from behind the shadowed outlines of the cabin. A fire, he thought.

Almost halfway across to the island, he heard the faint sound of a drum beating slowly and some sort of chanting.

He wasn't very versed in paddling a canoe, especially by himself, and cut a zig-zag course across the lake.

Almost to shore, he heard screaming. Cursing. The words were unintelligible. High pitched. It was Chabal.

She was still alive. Langdon took a quick glance at the moon on the horizon. It was humongous, perched on the lake, white, oh so white, except for a sliver of redness starting to crease one side.

The canoe ran aground, and Langdon leaped out into the shallow water and stumbled ashore through the rocks and muck.

The drumming stopped. A screeching replaced it. The sound of some prehistoric creature, harsh, in pain and anger.

Langdon ran toward the cabin, set back about a hundred feet from the water. Light glowed from within, but he was intent upon the bonfire in back where Chabal's screams and the caterwauling of another beast were coming from.

"*Fuck you, you pig-monster!*"

It was the voice of his wife. Langdon came around the side of the cabin, and a macabre scene came into view. A fire, flames ten feet high, illuminated the stage. His eyes were drawn to the figure of a naked man astride a woman, who was also naked. Langdon couldn't make her out, but he knew in his heart that it was Chabal.

The man struck her in the side of the head with his left hand and then raised his right arm over his head. The glint of steel reflected the light of the flames.

Langdon had his Glock in his hand. The arm holding the knife began to descend. He pointed and pulled the trigger. The Wendigo screeched and toppled face-down onto Chabal.

Something sharp plunged into Langdon's back just below his shoulder blade and he lost the grip on his pistol, the weapon falling to the ground as he turned.

A creature with the head of a deer stood there. It was a woman deer, Langdon thought, catching sight of her naked breasts, the curves of her body, her arm coming forward again with the blade. Langdon deflected it with his forearm, sending the thrust wide, following it with a blow with his right to her head, his fist crashing into the skull of a doe and knocking it toppling off the woman's head. It was Maddie Campagna, he thought through the pain, his punch having set the gash in his back into agony.

Maddie snarled, her lips curling ferociously, animal-like, and slashed again with the knife, the steel slicing across his side, not a direct cut, but taking skin off to match the pain in his back. Langdon roared, the guttural bellow of his Viking ancestors, his left hand cupping the back of Maddie's head as his skull crashed down into her face. He felt the obliteration of the cartilage all the way down to his toes as she dropped to the ground as if poleaxed.

Langdon turned back toward his wife. The Wendigo had risen to straddle Chabal, one hand grasping her neck, pinning her to the ground, the other searching for the knife that he'd dropped. Langdon realized that Chabal was attached to a cross on the ground, twisting and writhing, trying to get loose from her restraints, even as the Wendigo choked her.

There was no time to look for his lost pistol. Langdon took two steps toward Chabal when, out of the shadows, came a demon, another creature with the head of a doe and the breasts of a woman, shrieking, the sound piercing the night air, rising above the bawling of Maddie behind, the gurgles of Chabal in front, the screeching of the Wendigo.

This slender figure attacked Langdon from the front, her nails scratching at his face. He put one hand in her crotch, the other around her neck, and threw her against a tree, her body crumpling, the head of the doe flying free. A fleeting recognition passed through Langdon's mind that it was Grace Allen as he turned back toward Chabal and the Wendigo.

The Wendigo had found the blade in the dirt and was sweeping it toward Chabal's throat as Maddie suddenly wrapped her arms around Langdon's ankles.

"No!" he screamed, pulling one leg free and stomping down on her face, knowing in his heart that it was too late, that the knife had already done its nasty work, that Chabal's jugular had been severed, and that her lifeblood was now spewing into the dirt of earth at this zenith moment of the blood moon. "NO!"

Langdon jerked his other leg free from Maddie, his eyes again going to his wife, expecting to see the Wendigo rising triumphantly to face him, Chabal dying at his feet.

Instead, he saw the Wendigo sitting rigidly astride Chabal, his arms at his side, his screeching having risen an octave or ten.

"Fuck you!" Chabal yelled.

Langdon realized that she'd freed a hand and had a firm grip on the Wendigo's penis, twisting and turning and jerking his member like she was conducting an orchestra.

From behind, Grace jumped upon his back, her breath fetid and foul as she bit his cheek, her nails raking his eye, her feet clamped around his waist, even as Maddie, face bloodied and broken, again grasped his legs.

Langdon inserted his thumb into Grace's mouth with one hand, his other around her neck, and pried her from his body like a leech. He grabbed her by the crotch and raised her high above his head, driving her downward, headfirst, into Maddie's upturned face. Both bodies lay inert as he stumbled forward.

The Wendigo lay on his side, his hands at his midsection. Chabal was sawing away at the restraints on her legs. As he staggered toward her, she rose shakily to her feet, the gleaming blade in one hand and the Wendigo's penis in the other.

"Fuck you," she said again, her eyes on the Wendigo. She spat on him and threw the dismembered member in his noseless face. "Fuck you."

Chapter 39

Jackson Brooks was the first to disembark from the police boat, jumping into the waist-high water and staggering to shore. He'd thought to get the boat in place for the raid, but too late, and it hadn't shown up for ten minutes after they'd stormed the cottage and been told that Langdon was going across the channel to the island. Ten minutes is a short amount of time, but the scene that met his eyes seemed to have played itself out over hours.

Pistol drawn, he ran toward the flickering light behind the cabin from which a prehistoric screeching of pain and anguish was emanating. As he rounded the structure, his eyes first saw the fire, leaping and dancing like some devilish incarnation.

Two figures clung together in front of an upside-down and cockeyed cross attached to a broken tree branch. Jackson recognized the red hair and height of Langdon with his back to, blood straining his white shirt—a lot of blood.

"Langdon," Jackson called. "Are you okay?"

Langdon turned, revealing Chabal at his side, totally naked, her body painted in red, possibly blood, her eyes crazed, a knife clutched loosely in her right hand. The two of them merely stared at him.

Jackson realized that off to their side was the figure of a person, twisting and turning, writhing in the dirt. The source of the screeching. It was Tom Corbett, no longer the suave doctor nor the fierce Wendigo, but a human being. Where his nose had been was a red patch of goo and gristle. Jackson realized the man was naked as well, and Jackson cringed involuntarily as he became aware that where Corbett's penis should be was also a stub of blood and gristle.

Something was crawling between Jackson and where Langdon, Chabal, and Corbett were. "Freeze," he yelled.

The thing paused, and then the shattered face of Grace Allen looked back over her bare-blood-streaked back, one eye dangling from the socket, broken teeth bared, bone sticking from her cheek. She moaned, low in her throat, and continued to edge forward an inch at a time.

Jackson took a step forward and almost stepped on Maddie Campagna—at least, he thought it was her, her face smashed inward to form a concave, hollowed-out bowl. Her neck was contorted at an impossible angle. He didn't need to check her pulse. She was obviously dead.

That was everything. As other members of the state and local police came around the corner of the cabin and froze in horror, Jackson held up his hand for them to halt.

"Langdon. Chabal." He stepped carefully around the broken Maddie Campagna, holstering his gun, hands up, palms out. "It's okay. It's over."

"They're... not... human," Langdon said. "Like banshees from Hell."

"It's all over." Jackson stepped past the naked figure of Grace Allen inching her way toward the Wendigo. "You can go home now."

"He was going to kill me and eat me," Chabal said, her voice hollow.

"He got what was coming to him." Jackson stopped a few feet from the bloodstained Langdon and the blood-illustrated nudity of Chabal. He took off his jacket and held it out. "It's over."

Langdon took the jacket and wrapped it around Chabal. "What now?" he asked.

Jackson looked at his two friends and then over at the screeching and writhing figure in the dirt. "I suppose we should check and see if he's an organ donor."

It took several long moments, but it was Chabal who broke the silence with a snicker and then a chortle. Langdon chuckled. And then the three of them stood in the macabre arena on an island on a lake in Maine and burst into uncontrollable laughter, skirting the edge of insanity.

Two Weeks Later

Langdon took a sip of the rum punch out of the coconut cup. He stole a glance at his wife, his love, Chabal, out of the corner of his eye. She was beautiful. This, their fourth day in Barbados, her skin glowed a healthy bronze. The tension had finally begun to seep from her body, and her eyes had lost their haunted look. He knew it would take some time yet, but a rum punch, a beach, and not a care in the world seemed to be the best cure he could think of.

Chabal had expressed a certain satisfaction and healing in her actions, first biting off the Wendigo's nose and then cutting off his weenie—her word, not his—and throwing it in Corbett's face. It helped to know that Tom Corbett and Grace Allen were still hospitalized prior to being tried, convicted, and sent away to prison for the rest of their lives. Langdon had to live with the fact that he'd killed Maddie Campagna when he drove Grace Allen down into her upturned face, caving her skull in like a piñata.

When Langdon and Chabal had been boarding the plane at Boston's Logan Airport, divers were still collecting bones from the quarry behind the farmhouse in Durham. The videos of Gregory Popa were particularly damning, as was Chabal's account of the threats used to force Ansari to cut his own throat.

Annie Brown had recovered sufficiently to share what she knew, and that was quite a bit, as Corbett had bragged profusely to her about the people he'd killed, butchered, and eaten. A whole mess of missing persons cases from all over New England had been reopened, and even some from further away.

From what Langdon had gleaned from the character of Annie Brown, he was betting that she'd recover from the ordeal with the help of her adoptive parents. She was a survivor who'd experienced the worst possible in life, both as a child and an adult, but she seemed to have the tools necessary to overcome such adversity.

It turned out that the cabin on the island on Maranacook Lake in Readfield had been owned by Sam and Sarah Wade and willed to their offspring, Samael Wade Freeman. Grace had broken down and told all, beginning with their childhood, and how Samael was the blood offspring of Sam and Sarah, even though she never left the farmhouse for any reason, with, hence, no record of her existence.

The authorities were still working out the details, as there was no record of her birth or life before she suddenly burst into existence after she married in 2011. Nobody quite knew how she'd done that without any birth certificate or social security number, but it was being investigated. Grace claimed that Samael had tried to turn her back on the Wendigo Way, to escape the life destined for her, and lived off the grid with her husband in this cabin. Much still had to be sorted out.

Langdon's friend Danny T. had been killed. This was never far from his thoughts. In the days since, Langdon had toiled in his mind over every interaction he'd had with Corbett, and Maddie, trying to decipher how he'd missed what was right before his eyes. If he'd only caught on that Corbett was the Wendigo and Maddie his loyal minion Wiccan, well then, maybe Danny T. would be alive, and that storm cloud of suffering and pain would be erased from Chabal's eyes.

For now, his concern was mainly for his wife after the ordeal she'd been through. Even if she bore fewer physical wounds than he— stitches like a zipper on his back from the knife wound and ragged scratches on his face from the women's savage clawing on that night of the Super Flower Blood Moon—Chabal's wounds were on the inside, deeper, and harder to recover from. Time will tell.

Beach. Rum punch. Waves. Steel drums. Love. Repeat.

About the Author

MATT COST (aka Matthew Langdon Cost) is the highly acclaimed, award-winning author of the Mainely Mystery series. The first book, *Mainely Power*, was selected as the Maine Humanities Council Read ME Fiction Book of 2020. This was followed by *Mainely Fear*, *Mainely Money*, *Mainely Angst*, and now, *Mainely Wicked*.

I Am Cuba: Fidel Castro and the Cuban Revolution was his first traditionally published novel. His other historical novels are *Love in a Time of Hate* (August 2021), and *At Every Hazard: Joshua Chamberlain and the Civil War* (August 2022). Cost is also the author of the Clay Wolfe / Port Essex Mysteries, *Wolfe Trap*, *Mind Trap*, *Mouse Trap*, and the latest, *Cosmic Trap*, which was published by Encircle in December 2022. Cost's love of histories and mysteries is combined in the novel, *Velma Gone Awry*, book one in his new series featuring private eye, 8 Ballo, set in 1920's Brooklyn.

Cost was a history major at Trinity College. He owned a mystery bookstore, a video store, and a gym, before serving a ten-year sentence as a junior high school teacher. In 2014, he was released and he began writing. And that's what he does: he writes histories and mysteries. Cost now lives in Brunswick, Maine, with his wife, Harper. There are four grown children: Brittany, Pearson, Miranda, and Ryan. A chocolate Lab and a basset hound round out the mix. He now spends his days at the computer, writing.

If you enjoyed reading this book,
please consider writing your honest review
and sharing it with other readers.

Many of our Authors are happy to participate in
Book Club and Reader Group discussions.
For more information, contact us at info@encirclepub.com.

Thank you,
Encircle Publications

For news about more exciting new fiction, join us at:

Facebook: www.facebook.com/encirclepub

Instagram: www.instagram.com/encirclepublications

Sign up for the Encircle Publications newsletter:
eepurl.com/cs8taP

www.ingramcontent.com/pod-product-compliance
Lightning Source LLC
Chambersburg PA
CBHW050143120726
47903CB00002B/474